A Simple Tale of Water and Weeping

Kami King Larsen

Copyright © 2021 Kami King Larsen

All rights reserved.

ISBN: 978-1-7377973-1-9
Lily Fern Books
Cover Design: Brian Larsen
Cover Photo: Kami Larsen

For my girls. Find the thing you love as much as I love you.

Weaving olden dances
Mingling hands and mingling glances
Till the moon has taken flight;
To and fro we leap
And chase the frothy bubbles,
While the world is full of troubles
And anxious in its sleep.

-W. B. Yeats

A SIMPLE TALE OF WATER AND WEEPING

PROLOGUE

Gentle swells made their way toward the sand and pebble shore. The dark water broke on the shallow shelf of rocks, creating a hypnotic lullaby for those who chose to sleep with windows cracked. The mist rising from the salty water mixed in the crisp evening air, a low blanket of fog blurring the atmosphere. As the tendrils reached above the sea, a dreamy veil blurred the full moon's light. Occasionally, a nesting sea bird would call into the gloom.

It was a typical coastal night. Briny and cool. Nothing out of the ordinary to those who lived along the edge of the sea. Perfectly beautiful and perfectly regular.

Some who lived by the sea would argue it was just as it should be; others might notice the sleek bodies swimming near the shore and think perhaps things were not so ordinary at all. Smooth grey and spotted white shadows spun and swirled, gliding through the murky water in a whimsical ballet. To the casual eye they were just seals. Seals were common enough in these waters. To a more gifted eye, they might be something more. And with the full harvest moon shining down? Well, just a touch out of the ordinary for certain.

Black eyes shimmered just above the surface, inky and wet. Long lashes blinked out the salt water. One set. Then three. Eight. Thirteen. An unlucky number on a night slightly out of the ordinary.

The waves continued the gentle assault on the shore, breaking and running over the coarse pebble-strewn sand. The thirteen sets of eyes peered at the land, waiting and watching for movement. The stillness stretched out, and the waves rocked the sleek bodies slightly—the ballet at an end. Floating in the tide, they waited—and waited some more.

When all was deemed quiet and abandoned, the oldest and most knowing eyes blinked once more. The moon broke free momentarily from the fog, and silver light flashed in the obsidian eyes. Slowly, the face of a harbor seal rose from the water—tilted back as if to observe the stars. It barked and ducked beneath the waves. Water rippled as its head broke the surface mere seconds later. Where spotted fur and whiskers had been, a head of wavy hair and pale smooth skin emerged.

One by one, the other dozen seals did the same. Locks of grey and silver, brown and gold covered the human faces where only moments before the pinnipeds had been. Eyes no longer black—but a myriad of blues, greens, hazels, and browns—peered out of the beautiful faces of men and women. And in those eyes, mischief danced. The exquisite creatures walked rather than swam up the beach to the shore.

Silently they stepped from the frigid water onto the slightly less frigid land. Each body naked and lovely. They seemed not to notice the cold but to bask in the glory of an unseen sun. Behind each one, dangling from a hand with elegant long fingers and comely shaped nails, trailed a flowing skein of seal hide.

Across the beach and down the road, in the upper level

of a building, in a small cozy room, a girl slept. She dreamed of fantastic things. All was perfectly beautiful and perfectly unordinary.

ONE

When Aylee woke from her slumber to begin the day's work in the small town without a name, the sun had not yet risen. The vague remnants of a dream floated around in her head—a rainstorm, a dish of cream, and a stray cat.

Her legs were pinned to one side of the bed courtesy of her dog, Pepper. She nudged the lazy beast over, grumbling about personal space. Pepper merely looked at her with mismatched blue and brown eyes but made no effort to leave the warmth of the blankets.

Pushing her mess of copper and strawberry hair from her face, Aylee swung her feet from the warmth of the quilt and shivered as her bare soles made contact with the chill of the floor. Sounds of movement and the clatter of kitchen tools rose from below, indicating her parents were already busy in the shop downstairs.

Washing her face and cleaning her teeth took only a few minutes. Then she donned a simple blouse and wool skirt along with her thick socks and boots. She left her small room after turning out the lamp and walked down the wooden steps, Pepper racing ahead of her, to the back of her family's mercantile. Using her hip, she pushed the door open and entered the warm space, inhaling the goodness of fresh-baked bread and strong hot tea.

Aylee's father was busy stocking cartons of dry goods

on the shelves, and her mother was placing warm sweet rolls into a glass case by the register. She looked up as her younger daughter entered the store.

"Morning, Love. You still fine with running the beach this morning? There's a bit of a chill in the air. We could pay one of the Cormack boys to do it if you rather," her mother said.

Aylee loved going to the shore to gather clams in the early morning dawn. It gave her a chance to really listen to the waves and feel the salty kiss of the air on her cheeks. Not to mention, she wasn't sure she could stomach the sight of one particular Cormack boy this early in the morning.

"Of course I don't mind, Momma. I'll be back in a tick. And don't worry, I'll have Pepper with me."

She grabbed a sticky hot bun in one hand and her clamming bucket and shovel in the other, kissed her da on the cheek, and was out the back door before any other discussion could take place.

The short walk from the main street of town took her past the stone walls of the church and small school grounds to reach the rocky inlet that separated the coastline from the bulk of the town. At high tide, the sea water would flow up the ravine, only to rush back out twice a day. It was low tide now, perfect for clamming. By the time Aylee and Pepper crossed over the small stone footbridge to the sand and pebble shore, she was licking the hot bun's icing from her fingers.

Many of the folks from town disliked and mistrusted the ocean. Aside from a few hardy souls and most of the reckless adolescents, they tended to stay away from the beach and the water's edge. Funny for a village built along the coast, but it was as it had always been. Aylee's mother had never feared the sea and, consequently, neither had either of her daughters.

Something about the way the light diffused in the early morning fog had always brought a kind of stillness and peace to Aylee—not just grey and not precisely golden but more of a tarnished silver, warm and cool mingled together to just the right shade of perfect. It was simply her favorite time of day and one of her favorite places to be.

She tossed a stick along the sand, and the shaggy black and brown dog raced to fetch it and return. Aylee grabbed the stick again and laughed as Pepper tore off when she made to throw the stick but did not. The dog gave its owner a baleful look, and Aylee chucked the stick as far as she could. A few more throws and the shepherd lay down on the damp ground near her feet—the sand a cinnamon and sugar coating on her fur.

Inhaling the briny air deep into her lungs, Aylee wiped her hand down her work apron, set her gear on the taupe packed sand, and pulled her unruly locks into a loose tie. The humid air made the strands heavy against her back. She took one long look out at the breakers and set to work.

When the bucket was over half full, a flicker of movement out in the surf caught her eye. Someone was out there, swimming in the frothy waters. Aylee smiled and shook her head. The chill in the air was bad enough, but to be in the water? That was altogether absurd. She walked toward the waves, hoping to catch a glimpse of who would be fool enough to swim this time of year. Some local kid, unafraid in the way only youth can be, most likely. She could just make out sandy blond hair, long enough to brush the tops of bare shoulders, but in this light it was difficult to be sure.

The bare shoulders disappeared to be replaced by a bare backside. She turned away from the sea quickly. She did *not* want to know whom she had glimpsed. She prayed it wasn't one of the local boys who couldn't keep their tongue in check. It would be all over town and would take days for the stories to stop.

"Apologies. I didn't mean to be nosy. I'll just be on my

way," she stammered over her shoulder.

When no answer came, she peeked around to the waves once more. No one was visible. Worried the swimmer might be in peril, she turned full around. Still no sign of anyone. After a long minute, Aylee was convinced she'd need to run into town and raise the alarm. Then, above the next swell, a head did emerge. Her eyes must have played tricks on her earlier, for it was not a nude man or woman in the shallows, but a large grey seal. It seemed to regard her directly for a moment, and she had the unnerving sense it would open its muzzle and speak. She blinked and broke the connection. As quickly as it had appeared, the beautiful animal ducked its head back beneath the surface and was gone. Pepper barked at the waves and rolled onto her back, looking for a few belly scratches.

"Apparently I need to get more sleep," she remarked to the dog and began again to fill her bucket with clams.

When it was full to the brim and a fine sheen of moisture coated her brow and neck, she stomped her way back up the beach toward the footbridge. The sun was making its way above the shops and homes of town. The rays caught the downslope off the beautiful copper roof of the largest residence in town, belonging to the owner of the local whiskey distillery. The orange-gold metal set a pleasing contrast to the green shingled exterior, and Aylee wondered what it might be like to live in such a home. Would she have a maid and butler or would she tend to it herself, holding warm receptions for the townsfolk each holiday season? The idea made her slightly nauseous.

Lost as she was in thought, she almost missed the bit of scarlet amid the brown and tan of the beach. She paused to retrieve a length of wool and was surprised to see a sturdy shawl unfold. Why would someone leave such a nice item on the rocks? Surely they would be missing it. She bundled the fabric under her arm and continued on her way, determined to track down its owner when she had

A SIMPLE TALE OF WATER AND WEEPING

an opportunity.

The air around her grew quiet, and Aylee had the strange feeling eyes were on her. The seal perhaps? What a fanciful daydream. She scanned the beach again, now alight with early morning sun as the fog was eaten away in spots by its rays. Both sand and sea were devoid of spies.

Satisfied, she walked on. Had she taken the time to look beneath the bridge however, she surely would have had a shock. Bright blue-green eyes stared out from the recess of shadows. After she'd passed and left the beauty of the beach behind, someone slipped out from under the bridge. The cerulean eyes, and the man they belonged to, followed her progress toward the warmth of the mercantile where a steamy mug of tea awaited her.

TWO

It was a busy morning in the little shop. Devon Garrow, shop proprietor and Aylee's father, had received a large shipment of dry goods and sundries the day prior. The town's residents were in and out picking up orders and placing new ones—taking the opportunity to purchase fresh clams, baked goods, and jarred jams as well. Aylee and her mother Una wrapped the purchases in crisp brown paper and tied them with sturdy knots or delicate bows depending on the patron and the package. When Mrs. Matlock requested her fabric and thread to be bound with matching ribbon, they obliged. When Mr. Bryan stated he could use some extra twine on his salted cod, they graciously double bound it. When young Ruby Larking asked for a sweet while her mother shopped, Aylee smiled, winked, and handed her not one, but two lemon drop sweets. It never hurt to do a bit extra to make people happy and to be kind. It felt natural to Aylee—like breathing. For her parents it was natural and also good business.

Una Garrow had just finished packing up a berry pie for Mrs. Larking when the bell above the door tinkled, announcing another customer.

Una smiled warmly and turned toward Aylee.

"Now, Love. Why don't you help Mr. Camden? I believe he's here to collect the order he placed last week."

The slight sinking feeling Aylee always had in response to the presence of Rupert Camden did not show on her face.

"Of course, Momma." Stepping over the prone form of her dog asleep behind the counter, she turned to the owner of both the town's distillery and the beautiful home with the copper roof she'd admired just that morning. "How can I help you, Mr. Camden?"

"Ach, Aylee. You know I prefer you call me Rupert," he responded, not unkindly.

Mr. Camden was perhaps a year or two older than Aylee's father but carried himself like a much younger man. He was always cleanly shaven save for a thick handlebar mustache. His hair was trimmed short and thinning on the top. He had the strong hands of a workman, but his nails were always clean and trimmed and his clothes clean and pressed.

"In the shop it's Mr. Camden," Aylee's father called over his shoulder.

"Of course, Devon. Understood."

Turning back to the counter, Mr. Camden smiled at Aylee. "Your mother's correct. I'm here to pick up my order. You should have a dozen glass jars and six sacks of yeast for me. I also wouldn't mind taking a few meat pies home if your mother has any extra."

"I believe she does. Cooked up quite a batch last evening. We've got both—lamb and beef."

"I'd be happy to take one beef and two of the lamb." He handed her a small stack of coins.

"I'll get those right together for you. It'll only be a minute."

Glad for a task to keep her busy and away from further conversation with Rupert Camden, Aylee gathered the sacks of yeast and wrapped the small savory pies in a tin. The jars, however, were nowhere to be found.

"Da, do you know about Mr. Camden's glassware?" She had to raise her voice to a near yell to be heard over the din and clatter.

"So I do. Those will be out in the storage. Do you mind running to fetch them?" Her father wiped his hand on his apron.

At the moment, nothing would bring her more joy. She

yearned for the crisp air to settle her. She needed to be away from Rupert Camden's gaze even more. Every second spent in his presence was uncomfortable, and she feared the rosy blush on her cheeks from the strain would be interpreted as a blush of innocence and admiration. Her words and manner might be pleasant and sweet, but her inner turmoil gave outward signs which might be misconstrued.

She excused herself and stepped from the back of the shop into the alleyway. Pressing her back and shoulders against the oak door, she drew a cleansing breath from the air and closed her eyes. Once she was stilled, she crossed the cobbled ground to a small, separate brick and stone structure. Taking a key from her apron pocket and placing her hand on the small brass knob, she felt the give of the unlocked door. Da must have left it open—unlike him to be sure, but not so much out of the ordinary it brought any alarm to her mind.

The smell of wood and damp earth mixed with touches of salty sea and spicy cinnamon welcomed her into the dim space. Stacks of crates, cartons, and tins sat neatly organized along the slate and wood shelves. Paper tags with her father's neat penmanship labeled each container with the contents and date received. In an effort to avoid accidents, the storeroom had no lamps, only two large windows to provide light during the daytime. The windows were in need of a good washing. The resulting effect was a dim, weak sort of watery light, making it less than easy to identify the tan and brown packages.

Aylee's eyes adjusted to the gloomy space rather slowly. She skimmed her fingers along the tags, looking for a recent date and "mason jars" inked together. Moving up one wall and then across the back of the shed, she found nothing. Preparing to scan the opposite wall, her eyes caught on a dingy tarp in the corner, heaped atop a lumpy pile of goods. Perhaps the jars were stacked there, waiting with other items yet to be sorted and tagged. Aylee lifted the top edge to peek beneath and shrieked when she saw not bolts of fabric and jars of pickling spice but a man looking up at her.

She stumbled back, hands searching blindly for any weapon she might use in her defense. They fell upon the handle of a broom. The pine was smooth and cool in her hands but likely not sturdy enough to do more than keep dust at bay.

"Da!" she called out, knowing it was likely of little use. The mercantile was busy, and the noise of the patrons would drown out even the loudest of screams. Hers was barely more than a croak.

The man raised his hands in a gesture which implied *she* was more of a threat to him than the other way around.

"Please." The stranger's voice was raspy as if from disuse. He cleared his throat and spoke again. "Please. I seek only the way to get home."

"I see nothing stopping you," she stammered.

He stood, wrapping the tarp around his waist. This time, the rosy flush on Aylee's face was more than discomfort. This man was bare save the tarp—no clothing in sight.

"Da!" she yelped again. The hammering of her heart did little to help her. She had to remove herself from the closed space and close proximity to this unwanted intruder immediately.

Aylee stepped back another foot, inching her way toward the door. She thought to turn and run, but the idea of having her back to him made her shudder. She squared her shoulders and kept her eyes on his face.

"Please. I should not be here. I dram . . . Not dram? Dream?" He shook his head. "I wish or desire or some word I can't place. I need nothing but to return home."

"Whatever word you choose, you are correct. You *need not* be here. I believe *I am* correct in stating nothing is stopping you from going." The tremor in her voice was equal measure fear and anger.

He glanced down at his chest—one hand holding the tarp and the other grasping at the notch above his breastbone. Searching for something, which evidently was not there. "But . . . my coat. . ."

Even in the weak watery light, she could see the pain of confusion and sadness etched on the planes of his face. While he did not appear embarrassed by the lack of modesty, he did seem conflicted—almost as if unsure how to proceed.

"I know nothing of your coat, I'm afraid." Only then did Aylee wonder where his clothing was and how he came to be in their storage shed without a stitch on. Surely parading naked through town would have garnered notice by at least one or two of the nosy residents.

"At the sea. At the shore," he stated as if she should already know this. "It was there where I left it and then it was gone."

His talking nonsense was doing little to ease Aylee's confusion. "I still don't understand."

As if not hearing her, he asked, "When is this place?"

She frowned at him.

"Not right." More to himself than to her. "When? Not when. Where is this place?"

"My family's storage shed."

He shook his head. "The town. What is this town?"

"Well, it's just . . . *town*." The gloom hid most of his expression from her, but she could sense his growing frustration.

"Just town? No town is just town." This seemed to agitate him more for some reason, the gravel in his voice grinding in the muffled confines of the shed.

"Right." The fear, while still present in her mind and voice, was being crowded out by something like sympathy. Surely this must be some sort of ploy, an act to have her let down her guard, flimsy though it was. He did seem genuinely innocent and confused. Perhaps he had suffered some sort of trauma to his head? Or belonged in an asylum? Neither were happy choices; however, something in his manner sparked that bit of herself which always longed to do the right thing. To help the sad creature was a small task, and she at least owed him for taking her mind off Rupert Camden for the space of a few moments.

The jars! She still needed them and didn't fancy sending her father in here to look for them. That would raise all sorts of questions about her time spent alone with a naked man.

"If you'll wait here, I can fetch you some things and you can be on your way."

Stepping into the light cast by the open door, broom still in hand, she saw the carton labeled "jars" set along the opposite wall. She grabbed the clanking glasses to her chest and returned to the shop.

Having gotten Mr. Camden on his way with a halfhearted promise to see him at the town jubilee later that week, along with his goods packed neatly into his wagon, Aylee ducked back out of the shop and up the stairs to their rooms above. She ran though the apartment, easily finding what she needed: a pair of drab trousers, a well-worn wool sweater softened with time and a hundred washings, a newish pair of thick socks, and an extra pair of not-so-newish boots. Her mother had recently taken up a charity position with the town and had been gathering used items from the neighbors to be distributed by the church to the less fortunate. Aylee had not gotten a good look at the stranger's build. She did recall her eyes, in preserving his modesty, had rested above the shelving at the back of the shed, making him a good head taller than her father, and Devon Garrow was not a short man.

Creeping back into the storage shelter like a thief, Aylee made certain no one was watching. The alleyway was blessedly deserted. Could her luck hold out? Would she find the shed equally empty?

She closed the door securely behind her. Her wariness

had less to do with concern for the stranger and more with self-preservation. Being caught with a naked man would do nothing for her reputation or that of her family. Her luck did not stretch, and she found the man standing quietly just as she'd left him—looking dejected, slightly confused, and just as naked.

Taking a deep breath, she took a moment to look at him. Shadows slatted across his face, making it difficult to see. His pale alabaster skin contrasted against the shock of dark hair crowning his head. In the dim light, she couldn't quite make out the color of his eyes, but he didn't appear to be much older than she was.

"I've brought you some things. You can get dressed and be on your way." She reached into her apron pocket and pulled out a small handful of coins. "I don't have much in the way of money, but this should be enough to get a room for a night or two on the road."

He opened his mouth, but she interrupted him. "No need to thank me. It's not exactly summer weather, and I wouldn't want to be in the cold if it were me."

He frowned.

"There'll be a bit of cheese and some fresh bread for you by the back shop door across the alley. I can grab you a flask of cider as well. That should get you on your way to home." She paused a moment. "Where exactly is home? Not town. I know that much."

Silence. It stretched out, the expectation of a response from Aylee and the lack of one from the stranger weighing the space between them.

"Well, then. Good luck." She sighed. "There's an inn at the edge of town—across from the dairy. The Bryans are good people and keep clean rooms. They're fair, and the coins should be plenty for a night or two."

Aylee thought he might speak, but once more he seemed at a loss. She was torn between incredible frustration and feeling overwhelmingly sorry for this man. Perhaps she should fetch her father and involve him in the cause. Fear won out and she elected to keep his peculiar arrival and interaction to herself for the time being. He had not threatened her and did not seem inclined to violence. She vowed silently to keep wary and mention his presence in the future if it seemed prudent.

She nodded once, smiled with a kindness that radiated from her eyes to his, and said simply, "Safe travels."

She returned to helping her mother in the shop but found her focus drifting the remainder of the day.

THREE

Dinner that night was . . . odd. Aylee was not sure how else to describe it. Maeve and her husband Graham Ruthven were at the table with the Garrows, just as they were every Monday evening. It was important to start the week with the ones we love, Una Garrow would say. Originally, Aylee's grandparents had hosted the weekly meal, but since they had passed, Una and Devon carried on the tradition, insisting Aylee's older sister Maeve and her husband attend.

Maeve generally seemed to enjoy these evenings together with her family. Tonight, she seemed on edge and subdued, almost as if her physical presence could not drag her mind along with it to the table.

What Graham thought of this evening, or any of the previous dozens of similar ones, was anyone's guess. Generally civil enough, he kept his own counsel about many things, dinner with his in-laws being one.

Two years after they had married, Aylee still could not make out what Maeve saw in him. He was handsome enough, but his eyes lacked a certain warmth Aylee generally looked for. His teeth were straight, and his straw-colored hair neatly trimmed. She could not find fault with anything individually, but in combination, his features just sat there—each part fine in its own right but together somehow less than fine.

Maeve was a different matter. When anyone spoke the word beauty, Maeve's face was the first in Aylee's mind.

She didn't envy her sister exactly, but she also couldn't help but see where she lacked in comparison. Where Aylee had copper hair, Maeve's was the deepest, richest auburn. Where freckles smattered Aylee's cheeks, Maeve's skin was as smooth as unchurned cream. Where Aylee's eyes were a mossy hazel, Maeve's were the clearest green of spring meadows. Folks in town compared Maeve's beauty to that of their mother, whereas Aylee took after their father's people. Truly, Aylee thought most people would call her pretty as well, but she knew she would never compare to Maeve.

Appearance was not the only reason for Aylee to question Maeve's choice of husband. He was cordial but not friendly. He was employed but not passionate about his work. He was knowledgeable but condescending and dull. Graham seemed forever reaching for some lofty goal but never managed to improve the state of his position and, by all accounts, did not actually do anything aside from talk of his dreams. Aylee wanted to like Graham for her sister's sake but fell short of her goal. What bothered her most was he never showed any sign of real affection for Maeve, at least not in public. Aylee had never found the courage to inquire about what happened when the two of them were alone. All the same, Maeve deserved better.

When they began dinner that evening, Maeve was not herself and Graham was somehow worse. Maeve complimented her mother's cooking, one of Una's most beloved dishes, and when she looked to Graham to do the same, he simply sat there, stone faced and aloof. Una smiled at her elder daughter and did her best to ignore the implied insult.

"So, Maeve, tell me. How is the quilt coming along? We can order some new fabric from the catalog tomorrow if you like," Una said.

"Thank you, Momma. I don't believe that'll be needed. I got some lovely scraps from Silvie last week. They match up fine. I should have it completed in time for the winter snap."

"Oh, I'm sure it's going to be a beauty. I can't wait to see it." She turned her attention to her son-in-law. "And now how about you, Graham? How are things at the distillery?"

"Fine, thank you." Graham went back to dunking chunks of brown bread in his fish stew and said no more.

Ever the charmer. Aylee rolled her eyes.

Devon Garrow, who doted on his wife and stood for no insult toward her, raised a single eyebrow in the young man's direction. Even for Graham, the level of discourteousness was unusual.

Quick to prevent harsh words, Maeve apologized. "You'll have to forgive him, Momma. Graham has had a bit of a rough day. His fatigue has gotten the better of him."

She was clearly embarrassed.

Graham just looked at her, a flush coloring his cheeks.

"My apologies indeed. My dear, I believe I need some fresh air. I'll meet you at home." He stood, shook Devon's hand, and strode out the door.

After the door to the back steps banged shut, Devon turned to Maeve. "Would you care to explain, or shall we chalk that up to your husband's lack of social graces?"

"Oh, Da. I'm so sorry. I don't know what's gotten into him." For the first time that evening, she looked more miserable than distracted.

Maeve explained how in recent weeks Graham had seemed closed off and preoccupied. He wasn't particularly unkind but was more brooding and quiet than was his norm. The more she inquired about the cause of his distress, the worse his mood became. Some days he was closer to his old self, and while she could not say he was overly joyful, on these days he was at least attentive and caring toward her. She was trying to pay him extra attention and do small kindnesses for him, but often to no avail.

"Well, this is complete foolishness!" Aylee was indignant on her sister's behalf. "Any man, and I do mean *any* man, should be over the moon to call you his wife. And here you are trying to coddle his ego."

"Don't be unkind, Love," her mother gently scolded. "We have no idea what he may be going through."

"Have things been tough down at the distillery? Rupert's been in and seems content, but it could be he's working his men too hard." Devon valued hard work but knew not every man was capable of putting in back-breaking hours for the sake of someone else's profit.

"Same as always," Maeve said. "It's a good job, and we are lucky he has it."

"Well, that's true enough, but it doesn't change the fact he might not be satisfied with it. Sometimes folks want more. It may be he yearns to make his own decisions and be the master of his own fortune," Devon added.

For all of Graham's shortcomings, Aylee could relate to that. She wanted to be independent as well. Unlike Maeve, she knew it would bring her no joy to sit at home making quilts. She would rather work for something herself, not be reliant on a husband to earn wages enough to keep them clothed and fed. Until roughly six months ago, she had thought she might have a partner who understood this about her. Ian Cormack hadn't cared if she wanted to work and had told her he fancied her independent streak. Apparently he had either lied or it hadn't been enough. Or worse yet, she'd been wrong about his feelings altogether.

She planned to take over the shop when her parents got too old to manage. There at least she could support herself, with or without a husband.

"I'm not sure, Da. I've not gotten a sense of discord like this from him before, but who knows?" Maeve wiped her mouth daintily and placed her napkin on the table. "At any rate, I should be heading home before it gets too late."

"I'll walk with you as long as Momma doesn't mind." Aylee looked at the dishes on the table.

"Go ahead then, Love. Your da can help me clean up."

Graham and Maeve lived up the road to the north of town, heading away from the main street and its shops. They rented a small cottage with a tidy garden and a well out back. The locals knew the small home as Hydrangea Place, owing to the wild patches of blue and green flowers covering the front face. Maeve had space to sew and a kitchen big enough for the two of them.

The sisters spoke little on the stroll to the cottage. Pepper raced along in front of them and trotted back to check they were still coming. Aylee could make out a thin wisp of smoke from the chimney as they neared the front gate.

Maeve stopped a few feet short of the break in the low stone wall which led up a squat path to the door.

"You're getting old enough to make some decisions about your future, Aylee. Talk has it you have at least one new suitor Momma and Da will think a good match for you." She paused and grabbed Aylee's shoulder to turn her and look her in the eye. "My advice, for whatever it's worth, is this: be choosey. Don't rush into anything. Love. Money. Happiness. They are all important and not important at the same time. Take your time and make a sound decision."

"Right...?" Aylee was at a loss for how to respond, but Maeve continued anyway.

"I love you, Aylee, and you deserve all the best things in this life." She gave her sister a brief hug and headed up the path to the cottage door. "You had better be getting home before the wind picks up. It's going to be cold tonight. I can feel it. There might be will-o-wisps or worse about."

Aylee smiled at her sister's reference to the tiny mischievous sprites. Maeve loved the superstitions and stories of the fey. The minor fact that none of it was real didn't stop her from acting as if it were. Aylee added it to the list of enchanting things about her sister, kissed her on the cheek, and headed home.

The wind had only begun to stir a bit, and the night air was still fragrant with freshly cut grass and clean ocean air. It was brisk, not yet cold, but still Aylee shivered as she made her way back into town. The stars were bright in the sky, and the moon cast a silver glow, fracturing the path with shadows. She passed several folks on the road home and smiled at each of them, stopping once or twice to exchange words with friends or customers of the shop. For all the well wishes and friendly conversation, she could not escape the off-kilter feel of the day. First the strange man in the shed, then Graham's unusual behavior and Maeve's equally unusual response to it—her odd distraction and the cryptic advice. Aylee was torn between wanting more mundane days to come and secretly wishing for another interesting day tomorrow.

FOUR

The next morning saw Aylee once again heading to the beach to collect the clams the townspeople enjoyed. Her mind was drifting as Pepper ran next to her, barking at the sea birds and sticking her nose in every bush as if she hadn't sniffed them all hundreds of times before.

Aylee was setting her things on the wet taupe sand when her sleep-addled brain caught on a figure down the beach. Sitting on the rock outcropping a few hundred paces up, a lone figure bent toward the surf, head in hands. While she couldn't see his face, the attitude suggested a depth of sorrow which made her chest clench in sympathy. The dark hair ruffled in the breeze, and Aylee knew it must be the stranger.

She prepared to leave the shore but stilled and observed a moment longer, pulling her shoulders back and gripping her shovel. She worked an area of the sand that typically yielded good-sized clams, and her bucket was full in no time. Dusting the grit from her damp fingers, she glanced once more at the lone figure. He hadn't moved as far as she could tell—just sat there—despair lining the curve of his broad shoulders. Even from this distance she could feel the weight of his anguish.

The *proper* thing to do would have been to fetch the man some help. The *right* thing to do would be to approach him and offer kindness. For reasons she didn't understand, she didn't do either. It made her feel like a monster, but she sensed it wasn't what he needed.

The next morning was the same. And the next. He

always sat in the same spot, in the same posture. He didn't look up at the sound of her shovel or the yipping of her dog. She didn't dare speak to him either.

When she returned for her morning chore on the fourth day, she was not only surprised to note he wasn't there but a smidge sad as well. She couldn't say why his absence should affect her. Perhaps he had finally made his way to the home he seemed desperate to find.

During those days, aside from the mysterious visitor on the sand, the time passed much the same as it always did. Aylee gathered clams at the shore in the mornings, collected apples from the autumn orchards in the afternoons, fetched eggs and cream from the dairy down the road, and helped in the shop and the kitchen. The apples were made into compotes to be jarred and pies to be baked. The clams sold quickly, and the cream sweetened their meals. Each morning she woke curious if something new or exciting would happen, and each night she went to bed pleasantly tired but perhaps just a touch disappointed.

Maeve had been by the shop once or twice to say hello to her parents. She never lingered long and did not bring up their previous conversation. Aylee was both too busy and too polite to broach the topic herself. They did not see Graham as he was working long shifts at the distillery, starting the fall harvest mash and bottling the aged amber whiskey as the old casks were opened to finally share their amber treasure with the world. Mr. Camden dropped in more frequently than Aylee would prefer; however, she was busy enough to politely avoid most conversation with him. He never lingered long—always anxious to get back to work and check on his staff and his product. It gave Aylee a small glimmer of hope that she was wrong and had misjudged the whole situation.

The annual town jubilee was approaching quickly. The yearly celebration brought people together for food and merrymaking before the cold of winter settled its frigid claws on the coast. Most families expected to attend and would contribute something for the festivities. The Garrows planned to bring small ceramic pots of apple and berry compote soaked in whiskey. When a candle was touched to the top, bright flames burned off the alcohol in a vibrant show. Jugs of cream accompanied the dish, balancing the warm fruit with cool creaminess.

Una Garrow was peeling and chopping the apples Aylee had gathered. It was taking her the better part of the morning, so she relied on her husband and daughter to mind the shop. The cream would be fetched from the dairy the morning of the jubilee, and Rupert Camden was due to deliver two large bottles of young whiskey later in the day. All that remained was to gather a few buckets of wild blackberries from the thickets, which grew like weeds along the outskirts of town.

Aylee planned to meet Deirdre Sommerson that afternoon to pick the ripe fruit. Deirdre was the youngest Sommerson sister of four. Silvie, the next eldest, was Maeve's closest friend. The four girls had grown up together, and now that Silvie and Maeve were married and settled, both families were expecting the same for their youngest daughters.

"I'm to meet Dee soon," Aylee informed her mother when she entered from the back of the shop. The space behind the counter was separated from the bulk of the store and served as the kitchen for both domestic and business purposes.

"I'm leaving Pepper here." She scratched the dog behind the ears. "I can't have you eating all of the berries now, can I?"

She waved a quick goodbye and headed out, bucket in hand.

The brambles ran out past the town in all directions, but Deirdre and Aylee had agreed to meet along the southern edge of town, the opposite way from Hydrangea Place. She had plenty of time to get there and could have stayed and helped her father a bit longer. Doing so, however, put her at risk of being in the shop when Mr. Camden arrived with his delivery of whiskey. It was a risk she preferred not to take.

Enjoying the extra time, she strolled slowly along the stretch of road between the main street and Mr. Bryan's inn. The dairy pasture stretched out on the other side of the lane, and the faint melody of lowing cows filled the air.

A speckled cat walked silently toward her from the back of the inn. It stopped to stretch in the sun and brushed its back along a wooden lamppost. She believed it belonged to Penny Bryan—a gift from her father in theory, but a tool for keeping mice at bay in practice. Aylee bent down and scratched the scruffy creature between its ears.

Straightening, she heard the bang of a door closing. Thinking it might be Penny in search of her wayward feline, Aylee turned to say hello. She was more than a little surprised to find not Penny emerging from the inn's small yard, but the stranger from her shed. Color flooded her cheeks.

How do you address a man you have met under peculiar circumstances? Unsure, she said nothing and considered turning on her heel and leaving. Sadly, she had nowhere to hide.

"I'm afraid I've startled you again." He stopped several feet from the place she stood.

His voice was low and rich, tinged with a bit of gravel and still with an edge of hoarseness, but not nearly so raspy as the first time she had heard it. She wouldn't say he had an accent, but rather he spoke with a note of formality.

The days since their previous meeting seemed to have erased most of the confusion and uncertainty from his manner.

"Clearly I've unsettled you," he continued. "I mean you no dagger."

Aylee felt the shock flash across her face.

A SIMPLE TALE OF WATER AND WEEPING

"Not dagger. *Not* dagger. I mean you no *danger*." His mind was still a bit addled then. "I would like to thank you for showing me kindness when last we met."

Now he was fully clothed, she felt more comfortable looking at him. He wore a clean white shirt in place of the sweater, but the boots and trousers were the same items she'd left him. He was indeed quite tall, with strong wide shoulders. The rest of his form was not slender per se but sleek in its build. Despite the youthfulness of his face, his dark jet hair was shot through with scattered silver strands. All of this was pleasing enough, but his most striking feature was his eyes. Thick, dark lashes framed bright cobalt blue irises surrounded by aquamarine. She had not appreciated their beauty in the dimness of the shed. In the full day sun they were brilliant, and their cool hue held a warmth that could not be imitated. She took an immediate liking to them.

Despite her wariness, his eyes put her at ease, and she found herself smiling at him.

"Forgive me," she sputtered. "I'm surprised to see you still in town. From our previous conversation, I had the impression you were meaning to leave our little village."

As she spoke, Aylee watched his shoulders slump and the light leach from his eyes.

Sensing his discomfort, she flustered. "I don't mean to be rude, only you mentioned going home."

She didn't mention seeing him on the shore, not wanting to give the impression she was either unkind by not speaking to him or in some way following him each morning.

"Please don't apologize. It was, or is still, my intention, yes. Unfortunately, there have been"—he looked skyward as if the word was floating above his head and he could snatch it and bring it to his lips—"*complications* with my journey."

"Oh? I am sorry to hear that. Have you traveled far?"

"In a way, yes. I suppose I have."

"Can I be of any assistance in making your arrangements? I know most of the folks in town, and I'm sure I can help sort a ticket on the next ferry or train." Aylee wasn't sure she could afford to purchase a ticket for him, but she might be able to borrow some coins from her father.

"Again your kindness is not lost on me. But no, I don't think that will be necessary." He raised one corner of his mouth in a half smile.

Not sure where else to go with the conversation, Aylee looked around grasping for something. "Are you at least finding town to your liking?"

He paused. "As much as I can, I suppose. Some are more welcoming than others. . ." This he drug out almost as if he were trying to solve a riddle in his own mind before he continued. "The inn is comfortable as well. The Bryans are a most graceful family."

She presumed he meant gracious but didn't correct the small slip.

"You aren't wrong there. I don't believe I know of a more cheerful and welcoming clan." She smiled. "I'm happy you've found some comfort with them. As I mentioned previously, the nights can get quite chilly this time of year."

A thought struck her then, and she bit back some dread. "You didn't mention to them that we'd met, did you?"

"No. I felt that would be. . ." Again he searched for a word. "Unwise."

Aylee released the breath she'd been holding and smiled. "Thank you for your discretion. Perhaps you will be staying with them for a few nights more? I'm sorry. I didn't get your name."

"Cailean." He stated his name in the same formal tone. Key-lan. She liked the sound of it. "My name is Cailean. And you are?"

"Aylee Garrow." She extended her hand in the

customary way when a young lady and man were introduced.

He stood gazing at her hand, a slightly confused look on his face. He must have been from very far away indeed. Instead of grasping her outstretched fingers, he absently rubbed at his neck. Not wanting to embarrass herself or him any further, she returned her hand to the handle of the berry bucket.

"It is delightful to make your acquaintance, Aylee Garrow. A lovely name in a nameless town," he mused almost to himself before his attention returned to her.

"And yours as well." She wasn't sure if she meant it was nice to make his acquaintance or if she too thought his name was lovely. Maybe both. "As I was saying, if you'll be here for a few days more, perhaps you might join us for the Autumn Jubilee tomorrow evening. The entire town is sure to be there, and it is always quite an experience."

"I don't know that word. Jubilee." His brow furrowed, and he smiled sheepishly.

"Oh, well, it's a sort of town party. A celebration. For the end of the harvest season and before the winter sinks its teeth into us," she explained.

"It sounds quite enchanting, and I thank you for the invasion. I mean invitation." He looked up at her apologetically. "Thank you for the invitation. I am not at all sure I will be in attendance as I still hope to be on my way as soon as I am able. I fear I have played on the hospitality of too many already."

Despite having just met, Aylee was disappointed. She tried hard not to let it show on her face, but perhaps her smile was too forced as he immediately responded.

"However, should I be able to make it, I am certain to look for your smiling eyes."

"I do hope to see you there," she replied truthfully. "I'll save you a dance. I've got to run now sadly. I am expected to meet a friend up the road. Goodbye, Cailean."

Aylee spent the entire afternoon with Deirdre picking blackberries. Almost half made it into the buckets. Fingers and lips stained a dark damson from the sweet juice, they laughed and joked in the way only young women who have been friends since toddlerhood could. Deirdre was witty and smart, a bit foolish and very flirty. She also took great pleasure in mercilessly teasing Aylee.

"Have you saved all of your jubilee dances for Rupert Camden?" she asked sweetly.

Aylee groaned. "Dee, why must you be so wicked? You've gone and ruined a perfectly glorious afternoon!"

"If he has his way, it will be you who is ruined!" Deirdre smirked and raised her eyebrows, breaking into fits of giggles.

"You are so vulgar sometimes!" Aylee smacked her friend lightly on the arm.

"He is a bit of mutton going after lamb now, isn't he? But really, Aylee, it could be worse I suppose."

"In what way? Being courted by Old Man Claver, the town drunk?" Aylee knew this was unkind and was sure she was going to walk into being the butt of another joke but couldn't help herself from asking all the same.

"He could be old *and* poor." Deirdre smiled and jabbed her with an elbow. "And who am I to talk? I've got none but Robbie Cormack looking in my direction."

She looked sorry the moment the words left her lips.

"Oh, Aylee. I'm sorry. I didn't mean . . . I just didn't think."

Aylee waved a hand at her friend. "Don't be. It's not your fault, or Robbie's for that matter, that his brother. . ."

His brother what? What exactly had Ian done? Made her think he loved her? Made her think she could love him? Played her for a fool?

For a time, Aylee had thought she and Deirdre would be sisters via marriage.

It had been almost six months, and she still wasn't certain what exactly had happened between her and Ian.

Like most others in town, they had known each other their entire lives. They had always been friends, and when they were older, she thought they had become more than friends. He walked her home in the evenings after school, and they met on the beach on the weekends. Last year, the night of the jubilee, they'd gone outside for some fresh air, and he'd kissed her softly in the moonlight. After that, they'd snuck off when they could, the kissing becoming more heated on several occasions. She'd allowed his hands to roam her body over her clothes, but it had never gone further. He had never pressed her, but she had imagined he wanted her in the same way she wanted him.

Ian had gone so far as to discuss what life could be like when they married. He stopped at the mercantile day after day when his shift ended at the distillery to help unpack cartons and boxes. They would work side by side, getting things done but also teasing each other and stealing secret glances when they thought no one would notice. He did the work for free and insisted to Devon and Una the occasional berry pie was payment enough.

Despite the fact that no one, Deirdre included, seemed to think Ian was worthy of her attention, Aylee enjoyed spending time with him. He was handsome, clever, and hardworking. At times he seemed to enjoy a mean joke or say the wrong thing, but it wasn't often and he always apologized quickly. He seemed to understand she wanted to run her family's shop and had no interest in being a kept wife. She had been happy those months and was content to know she might lead a simple life in the future next to a man she could rely on and love.

Then one evening he didn't show after work. She didn't think on it overmuch, but one day turned into two, two turned into a week, the week into two weeks, and still she didn't see him. When she finally tracked him down at his parents' home, he simply told her things had changed. He wasn't interested in her in the way she supposed. He wouldn't look her in the eye and seemed to be in pain when he asked her to leave and not come back.

She'd cried all the way back to the shop and for the better part of the following week. Then she told herself he wasn't worth the tears and got back to working in the store nonstop. Deirdre, Maeve, and her parents all told her he didn't deserve her, but she would occasionally catch them sharing knowing glances.

At least he had the good grace to avoid her as much as possible. He never picked up orders for his family and didn't join in the evenings out with his brother and those who had once been their mutual friends. He was careful to avoid events when he thought she might be there. She'd only seen him a handful of times since that dreadful evening—not an easy task in a community this small.

On more than one occasion since then, she'd been simultaneously thankful and frustrated they hadn't done more than kiss.

With Ian out of the picture, it seemed everyone assumed Rupert Camden was her only prospect. She tried to imagine Rupert kissing her the way Ian had. The thought alone was enough to turn him down should he actually ask for her hand.

"Robbie is a sweet lad, Dee." Ian had been a sweet lad too. Sweet, up until the day he wasn't.

"I suppose he is, even if he isn't much to look at." Deirdre sighed.

"Well, at least he isn't ancient enough to be your da. Every time I think about Rupert Camden, I cannot imagine marrying him. He means well enough, I suppose, but I don't truly believe a man of his position is going to want a young wife running her family's shop." Aylee stopped and let the berry bucket dangle from her hands—a far-off look in her eye.

How could people who knew her, her parents included, expect she would marry and not have *anything* just for herself? She *could* run the shop on her own. Yes, it might be nice to have someone with her, like her da and momma had each other, but was it really necessary? She came back to herself and looked at Deirdre. "Plus Robbie has kind eyes."

This thought brought the intense ocean color of Cailean's eyes to mind. She hadn't said anything about either the meeting in the shed or the one on the road when she had found Deirdre already at the brambles earlier in the afternoon. It had seemed like a small personal gem she wanted to keep only to herself. Perhaps it was the memories of Ian or the depressing thoughts about Rupert Camden, but she felt the need to spill each and every detail of the two conversations. She began speaking and became almost breathless with wanting to get it all out.

When she finished her tale, Deirdre, for once, was wide-eyed and nearly speechless. Nearly.

"Naked? He was naked, and you just now thought to tell me about this? What kind of a friend are you anyway?" She feigned mock indignation.

"There was just something about him, Dee, an innocence maybe? I don't know. I can't explain it."

"Innocence! Oh for the love of saints! Innocence she says! I can explain it for you! By your account he's a real looker, and you, my friend, are smitten. I suppose he could be a murderous cad, but at least you would die with that dreamy smile on your face!" Her round face crinkled in mirth.

"Happy my life's secrets are here for your amusement."

"Call it amusement if you like, Aylee. I'm just thrilled to see you smile for once. You've got a bit of lightness to you that's been missing these past months. I was worried maybe he'd broken you for good." Deirdre was uncharacteristically serious.

Aylee hugged her friend and blinked back a tear.

"Naked and innocent!" Deirdre cackled.

With that, Aylee hauled up her bucket and headed for home.

FIVE

The day of the jubilee dawned grey and damp, but not bitterly cold—what Devon Garrow referred to as a wet blanket day. The bright and cheerful mood in town was at odds with the weather. Joyful bubbling lay beneath the surface of each conversation, a happy sparkle in the corner of each and every eye. Mothers were harried but not snappish with their children. Lovers who had quarreled the day before kissed and made up. Shopkeepers forgot last week's losses in favor of today's profits.

The day was exciting for all of the town residents, but perhaps even more so for those young and free souls who yearned for multiple dance partners and warm cups of spirited cider. Aylee was one such young soul.

Deirdre had been right to be worried before, but no longer. Ian *had* broken Aylee a bit. Now, however, she was well on her way to being mended. Her biggest worry for the evening was in seeing Ian and being reminded of the wonderful night they'd had the year before. She chided herself and resolved not to fall into memory's trap.

The Garrow family closed the shop early, and Aylee changed out of her drab skirt and sweater and into her best dress. The bodice fit snuggly, accentuating her bust and trim waist. The soft cornflower blue fabric fell flaring into a full skirt, which ended just above her knees. She gathered her coppery waves into a knot at the crown of her head but allowed a few loose strands to fall around her face and down the back of her neck, touching the delicate pearl ornamentation along the scoop neckline. She applied a smidge of rose pigment to her cheeks and lips, and satisfied she had done the best she could, she hurried out into the humid night.

Because of the predictable chill in the air, the Autumn Jubilee was generally held in the town hall. This year was no exception. Benches, which normally resided straight and orderly inside the hall, were cleared out into the surrounding road and small central square. This allowed the bulk of the festivities to take place in the relative warmth of the hall but also provided the additional benefit of outdoor seating for those looking for a reprieve from the hectic noise and crush of bodies. Both the cacophony and the crowd would grow throughout the evening. Couples, friends, and neighbors could spill out into the cool air and carry the merriment with them.

Aylee entered the hall arm in arm with Deirdre, who looked lovely with her deep eggplant dress hugging her curves. Her round face was framed by thick brunette curls and her chocolate eyes held their usual sparkle of mischief.

All along one side of the hall, tables had been arranged with an assortment of dishes piled high with tasty treats, warm food, and refreshing beverages. Families had contributed everything from stuffed crabs, roast chickens, and sugar glazed hams to fine craft breads, plates of goat-cheese stuffed apples, and savory meat pies. A separate table displayed small bite-sized tarts and candies, and a third larger table held several varieties of spiced wine, hard ciders, fresh juice, and strong teas. The Garrows' small crocks of fruit waiting to be set ablaze garnered their own space in one far corner.

The jubilee drew almost everyone from town and often many others from neighboring villages. The Bryans' inn would be full to bursting that night with travelers staying over. The organizers had arranged for a small band of musicians to play, and they could be heard just outside the back entrance tuning up their instruments.

"If I don't have a mug of spiced wine in one hand and a berry and cheese tart in the other in the next minute, I am sure to faint," Deirdre exclaimed as they joined a small group of people inside.

Aylee looked overly serious. "The situation appears truly dire."

"Care to join me on my quest?" Deirdre asked.

"I was hoping she would join me for a dance first."

Aylee turned to see Rupert Camden standing just behind her. His face looked hopeful, and his hands were clasped firmly behind his back as if to still them. It was the look of a bashful schoolboy, not a man well into his years.

"Mr. Camden, I didn't see you there." Not an answer, just something to say to give her a moment.

A muscle ticked in his jaw. "Rupert. Please. We aren't in the shop tonight, are we?"

"Of course. Rupert. It certainly is a very kind offer. However, I don't believe the musicians are set to start just yet. Perhaps in a few moments? After I've had a chance to eat something?" She knew this was a poor strategy, but she needed to give herself a little time to enjoy the evening. "I haven't had much to eat all day, and I wouldn't want to swoon during the first waltz."

It wasn't a lie exactly; she had eaten quite a bit for breakfast but had skipped lunch, and she did *not* want to pass out, giving him the wrong idea regarding the *cause* of the swoon.

He had the good grace to cover his embarrassment at his eagerness with a firm nod. "Of course, of course. But please do plan for more than one dance with me this evening."

Aylee mumbled something in reply and scooted away with Deirdre in tow. They made it to the center of the hall before the giggles came bubbling forth from her best friend's chest.

"Not a peep from you." The warning in Aylee's voice was all empty malice.

Truth be told, Aylee *had* been hungry, but her appetite had evaporated right along with her good mood. Dancing all evening with the middle-aged distiller promised to be as much fun as wading in eel-infested waters. She would need to do her best not to let it ruin her evening. If she could overcome seeing Ian, dealing with Rupert Camden should be a snap. She plastered a smile on her face and headed toward the food.

Her quest was briefly interrupted when she caught sight of Shelby and Violet Abbott among several other friends and acquaintances. Violet chatted merrily with Mrs. Matlock as Shelby stood at her side, eyes wide, taking in everything around her. Her bright smile widened as Aylee approached. The two met with a warm hug and Aylee's instructions to stay out of trouble for the night. Shelby giggled and blushed as Aylee moved on.

She joined Deirdre in the simple ecstasy which accompanied the cheese and berry tarts and helped herself to a small bowl of mushroom and beef stew. The most appealing component of the meal was undoubtedly the large mug of spiced wine. It was warm and sweet—laced with hints of cinnamon, clove, and nutmeg. With each small sip, the tension in her muscles loosened.

"Careful with that, Aylee. It will go straight to your head, and my guess is you need to be on your toes tonight." Maeve had appeared out of the crowd looking every bit as beautiful as always. She'd chosen to wear the same emerald gown she'd worn last year. The color set off her hair and eyes wonderfully.

Aylee smiled at the protective tone in her sister's voice. "On the contrary, I believe I need it to fortify me."

"Well, at least take it slow, or you'll likely end up slumped on a bench out in the cold with none but the winter banshees to keep you company."

Deirdre chimed in with a comment about wise words and always wanting to meet a banshee and then left to chat with a group of young men who worked at the dairy.

"Have you managed to leave Graham at home?" Aylee asked hopefully.

Glancing around as if she was sure her husband had

been right beside her only moments before, Maeve answered, "Of course not. He's here somewhere. Probably trying to track down a game of cards or some other sport."

"There certainly is plenty to keep him entertained."

"Did you arrive with Momma and Da by chance?" Maeve inquired.

"No, I came after. Just as they finished setting up. Why?"

"I was wondering if maybe you noticed someone I was keeping an eye out for. A tall young man with broad shoulders and sandy colored hair?" Maeve scanned the surrounding crowd as she spoke.

Aylee eyed her suspiciously, and Maeve quickly added, "A cousin of Graham's. He was supposed to be visiting town, and I thought I might look out for him."

"Oh, well, no. I hadn't heard he had more family coming in, but I'll let you know if I see anyone as you describe," Aylee assured her.

Graham came from a large family—six uncles and one aunt on his mother's side. Many of the older ones had left up or down the coast to find jobs at the other dairies, distilleries, or farms. It seemed as though dozens of cousins were in and around town and even more out in the surrounding countryside. It was not unusual for a handful of them to show up for the jubilee.

"Any idea how I can avoid dancing with someone I'd prefer not to?" Aylee asked her sister. "You've been fending boys off your entire life."

Maeve smiled. "That isn't entirely true, despite what you might think. You could feign illness or injury. Neither of those is much fun. Stay outside the entire evening or volunteer to serve drinks. My best advice, however, is to be busy dancing with someone else. Someone you *do* want to be dancing with."

Easier said than done unfortunately. Deliberately not heeding her sister's advice, Aylee went to refill her cup of wine.

The musicians entered from the back of the hall and started a lively jig which had Aylee tapping her toes and smiling in spite of herself. One of the boys from the dairy approached—a good-hearted soul who had been a year or two ahead of her in school—and asked her for a spin. She accepted willingly and let him twirl her about the open room. Laughing and a bit breathless, they switched partners at the end of the song, and Aylee found herself enjoying the second dance with Deirdre's would-be suitor and Ian's brother, Robbie Cormack.

When the music faded, the dancers clapped and cheered, red cheeked and perspiring with both exertion and excitement. Aylee borrowed a small square of fabric and wiped the sweat from the back of her neck. She was thoroughly enjoying herself and planned to find another partner immediately. Looking through the crowd, she caught a glimpse of pale skin beneath a thick head of dark hair. Her mind immediately conjured the image of bright ocean-colored eyes. She blinked, and the dark hair vanished into the crowd. Likely she'd had too much wine and was imagining things. Cailean had, after all, told her he likely would not make it to the festivities.

She placed her cup on a small table and shook her head to clear it. Closing her eyes, she felt light tapping on her shoulder.

"Are your refreshed enough for our waltz?" Mr. Camden inquired.

Crestfallen but not impolite enough to decline a second invitation, Aylee let herself be led back to the center of the floor once more.

The music was a more somber tone and the pace slower. She would have preferred something more lively, if only to use the movements as an excuse not to have another awkward conversation with the older man. As it was, she owed him some kindness and reminded herself if she kept things superficial and light, the dance would be over and she could spend the remainder of the evening laughing, eating, and dancing with her friends.

"Are you enjoying the evening?" she asked politely.

"Very much, and you?" His voice was a bit high pitched, but he spoke with the self-assurance of one comfortable giving orders and having his directions followed.

"I am, thank you. I always love the Autumn Jubilee. But then again, I suppose everyone does."

He smelled faintly of wood smoke and had the distinct odor of whiskey on his breath. Not unusual given his profession, but she found it unpleasant when this close to him. His hands were firm, and a slight dampness formed where he held her waist on one side.

"It is certainly quite an event," he agreed. "I recall one jubilee, several years ago, when a pony got out of its stable and ate all of the stuffed apples. Made quite a mess, but folks just laughed and danced around the smashed remains."

"It sounds like quite an evening."

"Oh yes, it was. I was just about your age then."

He got quiet as if realizing the mistake he'd made, pointing attention to the considerable age gap between them. In all the years he'd attended these parties, why had he never married? Why look for a bride now? Why her?

That was if he in fact *was* looking for a bride. She still wasn't convinced she hadn't contrived the entire thing.

They danced on in silence for several more bars, Aylee trying to think of a topic of conversation to fit the silence. Nothing came to her.

Rupert was an easy partner to dance with. He knew the steps and led her through several graceful turns. He was only an inch or two taller than she was, with a sturdy build that might have been athletic ten years ago. His eyes were surrounded by crinkles of lines, feathering out to his hairline. His hair and mustache the nondescript brown of turned earth was shot through not with silver as Cailean's was, but a nothing shade of grey.

As he led her through the final spins and sways of the waltz, she could only imagine what her friends were thinking.

They made one last turn around the floor, and as she spun to the outside, she caught sight of Ian standing against the wall with Robbie. Without thinking, she smiled at him. He turned away without returning the smile, anger and shame both written on his face. Aylee's smile disappeared as quickly as it had come, a flush of embarrassment rushing up her neck to color her cheeks.

The song was nearing its close, and while the previous moments had devolved into a tense discomfort, Aylee was happy she would not have to fake her way through additional dialogue. The music faded, and she turned toward the band of musicians, clapping politely.

"Do you suppose we could go outside for a spell and talk?" Rupert asked, releasing his hand from her waist.

She did not want to go outside and talk with Rupert Camden. She wanted to stay in the hall and dance with her friends and be young. She couldn't very well tell him those things though, and her face became blank as her mind scrambled for some suitable excuse to *not* go outside.

"I'm afraid Miss Garrow has promised me the next dance." The deep hoarseness of the voice was music to Aylee's ears.

She turned and accepted Cailean's outstretched hand, grasping it like a lifeline in a turbulent sea.

"I suppose I did," she managed.

Not giving Rupert a chance to interject, they slipped back among the crowd of revelers to join in the next careen around the floor.

"Thank you," she breathed and truly meant it. Cailean had rescued her without even knowing it.

He responded with something as they took their places, but in the noise of the crowd his words were lost before reaching her ears.

She shook her head. "I'm sorry. I didn't catch that."

"I said *don't*." His voice was loud enough this time that several couples looked at them. "Don't thank me I mean. I owe you a much greater debt than a simple dance can repay."

"I don't believe that could be true. If you knew what you just rescued me from, you would surely agree with me."

"Indeed? Well *that* is a story I'd like to hear." With a twinkle in his beautiful eyes and a small lopsided smile on his face, he added, "You should know, I have not the slightest idea how to dance."

Aylee chuckled at his joke. Everyone on this part of the coast had, at minimum, the very basic dances taught to them from the earliest primary school years. It soon became apparent, however, his statement was told in truth and he clearly had missed every dance lesson. He had none of the simple steps at his disposal, yet he moved with a lovely grace. He went left when he was meant to go right, turned when he should be straight, and dipped whenever the fancy struck him. Before long, many eyes were on their flowing haphazard forms, most filled with mirth, but a few, Rupert Camden's among them, held something closer to outrage.

Cailean either did not notice the attention they garnered or simply did not care about it. With a fluidity Aylee had not seen before, he continued to move her in a gentle swirling pattern around the other dancers. She could not help but smile and enjoy each second of the wondrous dance. The steps held no pattern, just a smooth floating like kelp in the waves. She closed her eyes briefly. He smelled of the sea, a salty sandy scent. She opened them as the music ended. It left her nearly bereft.

"That was. . ." the right word eluded her.

"Amazing? Unusual? Ghastly?" he supplied. "I'm generally the one who can't catch the right word."

The flickering candles and lamps sent shimmers through the silver streaks in his hair. She watched his strong hand run along his collarbone, fingers seeming to search for an object they didn't find.

"Lovely," she concluded.

"Lovely. A compliment, I believe." He smiled again. "Perhaps you might promise me a second dance before the night comes to a close. For now, might I interest you in a glass of punch?"

"The punch is quite good generally, but I am partial to the spiced wine," Aylee informed him with a conspirator's smile.

"Spicy wine it is then."

She placed her arm in the crook of his as he led her toward the serving station.

SIX

Word travels fast in small towns, and as they walked, the whispers caught like wildfire. The townsfolk who witnessed the dance tried to describe it to friends and neighbors, but none captured the feel of the motions correctly. Some thought him simple, others magical. Was he someone to be pitied or something to be feared? Those who had been enjoying the cool humid air returned to the stuffy town hall to catch a glimpse of the outsider who danced like a faerie court king. The girls eyed him and the young men eyed him more, but for two very different reasons. Only a handful of folks from town had spoken to him in the past days, and they would say he was certainly welcome, but again, they were only a few.

Unaware of the murmurings, Aylee accepted a cup of wine and took a small sip, the lush berry and cinnamon flavors warming her cheeks and stomach.

"Once again you have surprised me. No luck yet in your plight?" she inquired.

"Sadly no. Fortunately this evening has gone a good way in making up for my disappointment."

A small group of partygoers approached them. Deirdre was accompanied by Silvie and Angus Freeman, as well a large bald man with a thick chestnut mustache.

"Mr. Bryan." Cailean smiled and shook hands with the tall, broad-shouldered innkeeper. *So he's learned to shake hands.* Ned Bryan seemed to make even Cailean look slight by comparison.

"Cailean. I'm happy to see you in such fine spirits and

enjoying the town's festivities. May I introduce Angus and Silvie Freeman and Silvie's sister Deirdre?" the innkeeper said.

"Happy to meet you all." Cailean inclined his head to each in the group.

"And I see you've already met young Aylee Garrow."

"I have in fact, Mr. Bryan."

The two men chatted on about the new shirt and trousers Mr. Bryan had so graciously placed in Cailean's room at the inn and how wonderful the music and food were. Deirdre caught Aylee's eye and made an exaggerated swooning face behind Silvie's back. Aylee tried to stifle a laugh but merely accomplished choking on her wine. This caused Deirdre to pull another face, resulting in more giggles and the need to excuse herself for some fresh air. Deirdre joined her, and the two exited the warm hall into the gloriously chilled evening air.

Braziers made from the used husks of old whiskey barrels lined the walkway out to the dim alley. The bindings were worn and crusted with rust, but the wood burning inside provided heat, light, and a glorious smokey perfume to the cool air.

"I am disappointed in you, Aylee Garrow!" Deirdre admonished her friend once they were far enough away to talk.

"Why?" Aylee asked, sincerely confused.

"You certainly failed to fully convey just how amazingly handsome your new acquaintance is. And to think, you saw him without all those clothes covering him." Deirdre's voice held genuine awe.

"Ssshhhh," Aylee scolded. "You can't let anyone hear you say such a thing. My parents would be mad enough to know I'd spoken to him and not told them. To add the remainder of the details. . . Well, it would be bad for them and worse for me."

"Calm down. I won't say another bit about it. I promise." The firelight twinkled in Deirdre's eyes and off her curls. "But honestly, I don't think I could have kept that secret if it were me. I would be shouting it from the clifftop."

"I am sure you would." Aylee's voice dripped with sarcasm. Changing tone and smiling devilishly, she added, "He is quite something to look at, isn't he? But it's more than just his appearance. I don't think he's like anyone I've ever met before. It's refreshing."

"So, did he mention why he's still hanging around? And more importantly, did he bring any friends with him?"

Aylee pointedly ignored the second question. "No, only that it disappoints him to be here still."

"He doesn't appear disappointed, and even if he were, he'd be the only one. He certainly has given everyone and their granny something to prattle on about. The talk will be mad for the next few days."

Deirdre leaned back on the bench, hands behind her and face tilted up to the stars.

"A bit of excitement won't kill anyone, I'm sure." Aylee hesitated. "Did you see Ian? I was hoping by some miracle he would have decided to stay home tonight."

"More than saw him. I had an interesting little chat with our Ian," Deirdre said solemnly as she sat up straight and turned to her friend.

"Oh saints and sinners. I hate it when you get that tone. It means I'm going to loathe whatever you say next."

"It's true and I'm sorry to be the bearer of ill tidings, but you need to hear this." Deirdre's face showed no joy.

"All right. Let's have it then." Aylee had resigned herself to whatever her friend had to share.

"He looked just dreadful when he saw you dancing with Camden. I thought it odd as he seemed indifferent when you were with the other lads, Robbie included. So I asked, and do you know what he said? He only broke it off with you because Camden threatened to fire him from his job at the distillery if he didn't. Can you imagine such a thing? I was fit to walk over and slap the old man in the face myself. To his credit, Ian looked fit to be sick the whole time."

Aylee let this sink in for a moment. Rupert Camden had told Ian to break it off with her? To what end? So he could swoop in himself? Well, if that were the case, they'd be having a few words by the end of the evening. Even so, Ian must not have felt as strongly for her as she did for him. She wouldn't have allowed a job, even a good one at the distillery, to come between her and a friend—much less someone she had intended to spend her life with.

"I don't know what to say, Dee." Aylee's voice was barely more than a whisper.

From around the corner, low voices disturbed the conversation. Neither girl could make out the words, but the tone suggested a heated discussion was taking place. Not wanting to be involved in a dispute, they looked at one another and stepped back toward the hall's side entrance. As they turned the corner, the voices grew louder and more recognizable.

Graham's clipped speech echoed in the dim light of the lanterns. "But the position was promised to me."

"As I recall, nothing was *promised* as you claim. You've got none to blame but yourself." The second voice belonged to Rupert Camden. His tone was firm and unyielding, certainly not the pleasant, if somewhat pinched tone he generally used with her or her family.

"None to blame but myself?" Graham exclaimed. "I have done *everything* you have asked of me and then some. I'm not sure what more you can expect me to do."

"I really think you are overreacting, Ruthven. Why all the fuss anyhow? I pay you well enough and you're young. You have plenty of time to promote."

"The fuss is just this. I can't have my wife—the most beautiful woman on the coast—living on a bottler's wages forever. She deserves better. When she realizes how things are going to be for her sister. . ."

The men had made it around the corner, and Graham's

voice trailed off when he saw Aylee.

"By all means, Graham, please continue." Aylee was more than a little interested in knowing how that particular sentence was going to end.

Graham flushed but closed his mouth and said no more.

"Really, do continue. I'm all on the edge of my seat as well," Deirdre chimed in.

"Girls, it's nothing." Rupert smiled and put up a placating hand. "Mr. Ruthven and I were simply discussing some business matters—management at the distillery and the like."

"That's odd. It sounded as if you were discussing my sister and me." Aylee willed her voice not to wobble as it so often did when she became nervous or angry.

"Graham was just agitated. He meant nothing by it, I'm sure." Turning toward Aylee's brother-in-law and giving him a steely look, Rupert added, "Did you?"

"Of course not," Graham managed. "As Mr. Camden said, it's only a management discussion. My apologies, Aylee. Have a wonderful remainder to your evening."

"I hope to. Thank you." Before Graham could slip away, she added quickly, "Which cousin is it that's visiting?"

She wasn't sure why she asked. It just popped out.

He looked at her quizzically. "I have no idea to what you are referring."

He turned and practically fled back up the street. Away from the music and laughter. Away from the merriment bubbling out from the meeting hall.

Aylee watched him go, still speculating about what had been left unsaid. Deirdre grasped her arm in an effort to pull her back inside.

"Aylee, I was still hoping to speak with you privately this evening." Rupert had stepped between the girls and the entryway, cutting off the path inside.

He only broke it off with you because Camden threatened to fire him from his job at the distillery if he didn't.

"Unless, Mr. Camden, you are prepared to be honest with me about the discussion you were having with Graham, as it pertains to me, I don't believe we have anything to discuss." *Or if you want to tell me about a long ago conversation with Ian Cormack.* Aylee hated being rude, but she disliked dishonesty and deceit even more.

"I see. I won't pretend I'm not disappointed in your reaction. I was hoping we were on better terms than you give me credit for." Regret laced his voice.

Aylee was secretly pleased to see her words had the intended effect. "Perhaps your hope has been misplaced. Shall we return to the party, Dee?"

"Oh yes! I believe someone is still waiting for a second dance with you." Deirdre tightened her grip on Aylee's hand and pointedly stepped out and around Rupert while leading her friend into the warm arms of happy chatter and glowing lights.

The music was livelier and the crowd more boisterous—spirits raised by whiskey and wine, flirting and dancing. The air smelled of sweat and seawater, nutmeg and roast chicken. The men had loosened their collars and women had loosened their hair. Little girls ran about in their brightly colored dresses and aprons. Little boys had shucked their coats and, in a few cases, their boots. A shaggy young dog had taken up residence near the end of a serving table and dozed contentedly amid the raucous music and laughter. A small group of young men gathered in one corner, playing a rambunctious game of chance with a set of polished stones. They made small wagers and jeered and cheered each toss of the clicking tiles. Along the opposite wall, a set of benches had been pushed together and several women traded gossip—a good deal of it about the tall handsome stranger—while rocking sleeping infants and toddlers. A girl in a lovely rose-colored dress chased a young man around a table while he feigned distress at being caught. The twinkle in his eye and flush on his cheeks implied neither would be satisfied until he gave up and let her give him a quick peck on his cheek.

The girls continued in, hand in hand, toward a group of young men and women they had gone to school with. Both Maeve and Robbie Cormack mingled in the small crowd. Aylee intended to discuss her encounter outside with Maeve at some point but certainly not now. She had similar thoughts about speaking with Ian, but a conversation with him would likely be fairly painful for both of them. It could wait. No reason to spoil anyone else's good mood.

Aylee chatted politely with Robbie, discussing the finer aspects of sheep's wool. Every now and then she scanned the room for the dark head of the mysterious Cailean.

She imagined Robbie and Deirdre might end up married one day—thankfully he didn't work for Rupert. She wanted to cement her place in their life early in the relationship. He needed to understand it was almost a two-for-one deal—if he married her best friend, he'd need to expect to see Aylee quite a bit.

A commotion kicked up at the other side of the hall. Robbie stopped mid-description of the benefits of lanolin for cracked dry hands and shook his head.

"Would you look at this bastard?" He glanced sheepishly at Aylee. "Sorry for the language."

She just chuckled in reply.

Rupert Camden had cornered Cailean and seemed to be giving him a severe tongue-lashing—the subject of which she could not fathom. It was truly an odd scene. Rupert, red cheeked and flustered, was clearly struggling to maintain his composure, despite the fact he appeared to have started the confrontation. Cailean, meanwhile, looked down on the shorter man with an almost bemused look on his face. It was as if he could not comprehend anyone speaking to him in that way.

Aylee hurried over, hoping to put the dramatics to an end.

"Mr. Camden, you seem to be making a bit of a scene." She stepped between them. "Can I help diffuse things in some way?"

"I don't believe such action will be necessary. I was simply explaining to your new friend here how things are done in this town," Rupert replied stiffly.

Aylee looked nervously at Cailean, but he remained as relaxed as he had been.

"My new friend as you call him has a name. Rupert Camden," she held out a hand toward him, "this is Cailean . . . um. . ."

She had never caught his last name.

"Vann. Cailean Vann." He lifted one corner of his mouth in a half smile toward her. "Mr. Camden, is it? I am curious why you feel the need to instruct me on the ways of town. Please do go on. I believe you may have just been getting to the good part."

Rupert bristled even more at the apparent mockery. Aylee had always thought him relatively good-natured, but now she wasn't so sure. He was exuding a sense of entitlement this evening he rarely showed when visiting the shop. Was this how he truly behaved when at work or with other people? Had he simply hidden this side of himself while in her presence? He had been condescending when dealing with Graham and puffed up and territorial now. And if what Deirdre had told her really happened between Ian and his employer, she would think him quite—as Robbie put it for lack of a better term—a bastard. How had she not seen any of this until tonight?

"Sir, I am a respected member of this community and feel it is my duty to protect our interests. The 'good part' relates to those interests." He was more confident. Aylee was not sure where this was going but had the sense she wasn't going to like it.

"Do go on, please." Cailean stood with his arms behind his back and his eyes down, as if he were concentrating on the words, puzzling them out.

"We are a tight-knit community here. We take care of one another, and while we are welcoming, we don't appreciate it when those we show hospitality to disrespect this welcoming kindness." He paused as if this explained things.

"I see." If Cailean did, he was the only one. "And I am supposed to be the disrespectful clod to whom you are referring?" Cailean asked. He was trying to sound calm and upbeat, but Aylee detected the return of the hoarseness in his voice, indicative of an anger tightly leashed.

"You are indeed." If he had been taller, Aylee thought Camden would be looking down his nose at Cailean.

The small group of townsfolk who had initially surrounded the conversation had multiplied in size.

"You've done no such thing, Cailean," Aylee stated calmly.

"On the contrary, Aylee, he has quite severely." Rupert seemed to have regained a bit of his composure and spoke with a note of condescension Aylee did not appreciate in the least.

"In what way? He has been quite polite to me, and the Bryans as well."

"He may be polite, but I would also suggest he has been overly kind to you in particular. There is where the disrespect lies," Camden said.

"I have no idea what you are talking about. Since when is being friendly a crime?"

"Since it means he is flirting and dancing with my future wife. You can't think I would let this go. Have some sense, Aylee." He said the words with a soft resignation, as if it actually pained him to need to explain it to her.

Cailean looked confused, with nearly the same expression he had worn the first time they had met.

Those around them watching grew hushed. Aylee felt the heat rising in her cheeks and clenched her hands at her sides—trying and failing to control the anger bubbling up within her.

"You are..." Cailean struggled for the correct word. "Engaged? To wed?"

Aylee wasn't sure if anyone else noted how easily Cailean excluded Rupert from the question entirely—asking only her.

"No. I most certainly am not." Her voice came out with a fierceness she had not intended—no hint of a wobble anymore.

"Well, you would be if you didn't keep running off each and every time I attempt to speak with you." Rupert sounded exasperated, as if this was a simple matter that needed to be explained to her.

"No, Mr. Camden, I would not be. Despite the high regard in which you are held by most of the town and certainly by yourself, I can see now this is not the correct path for me." She found Ian's eyes as she continued. "I've been made aware of certain things this evening, and I have seen a bit more of the real you in the past three hours than I have seen in the past three months. We aren't right for each other. I don't believe I am in need of your offer, and I am asking you not to make one."

Heat burned Aylee's cheeks and her breath was faster than usual. All conversation in the hall came to an end. The only sound other than her thumping heartbeat was the tinny fading of a fiddle solo.

"Aylee, please don't be ridiculous," Rupert said mildly. "I understand this isn't the proposal a young lady wishes for. I promise to be more romantic in the future."

"I don't believe I am ridiculous, and please don't speak to me of romance."

She glanced around and noted the shock and surprise on many of the faces surrounding her. She found comfort in the expressions of those closest to her. Maeve—relief. Deirdre—amusement. Ian—shock. But the look on Cailean's face surprised her the most. He looked almost proud of her. What sense did his expression make?

"Shall we have that second dance now then?" His

smile, while lopsided, exuded warmth and charm as he extended his hand to her and swept her out onto the empty dance space.

After several moments, others joined them and the band took up a joyful tune. The tempo increased, and the drama of the moment melted away like ice in the spring sun.

As the music faded and the couples left the floor, Aylee tried to catch Maeve's attention from the other side of the room. Cailean looked in the direction Aylee was waving, and the smile faded from his face.

"Is something the matter?" Aylee asked, looking where his gaze fell. "My sister. Always the most glorious woman in the room."

"Not at all." She wasn't sure which he was denying. "Care for some fresh air?"

Aylee took his proffered arm and let herself be led into the cool air.

The party rolled on into the night.

SEVEN

"Mr. Camden used to only come into the shop on occasion. He'd stop in to pick up a last-minute item once every month or two, nothing regularly. He would send a boy from his distillery for the majority of his purchases and to place his orders—meticulously written out to ensure they were clear. Several of the wealthier families in town do the same. We know their maids and cooks much better than the families themselves.

Aylee was sitting outside with Cailean enjoying the slight breeze blowing in off the ocean. She had already explained the situation with Ian to him. He sat quietly and listened as if he truly was interested in the story, brow occasionally furrowed. He did not press for details or ask questions, just listened.

"Shortly after Maeve—that's my sister—got married, he began to come in a bit more regularly. At first, he only placed orders with Da and still had some boy pick things up. After several weeks of this, he retrieved his purchases himself. He routinely only dealt with Da, never speaking to Momma or me for long, but he was always polite. I thought him to be not unkind, but I guess you could say a bit stiff.

"Over time, I caught him looking at me. I didn't think much of it at first. Then it became more and more obvious—every time he came to the store he would look for me first, smile, and then speak with Da about his business. Before he would leave, he would pleasantly ask me about my health, or the weather, but never much more than that."

Aylee took a sip from the mug of tea cooling in her

hands.

"Then Ian broke things off, unexpectedly and without any explanation. I'm still not sure if I was in love with him, but I think I wanted to be. It hurt so much at the time. Not because of what I thought I was losing, but because I was so embarrassed. I thought we had this thing, and he clearly didn't feel the same way. The following weeks were a bit of a fog. I worked and helped out as much as I could, just trying to keep my mind occupied. I eventually got past it enough to properly function. And then I was just so angry. I wanted to be in the shop as much as possible because I could focus on simple tasks and not have to worry about my personal life.

"Soon I began to feel like Mr. Camden's visits had another purpose. I mentioned it to Momma, and she told me she meant to speak to Da about it. I know growing up they were friendly, but now, for some reason, she and Mr. Camden don't often speak to one another.

"The next day she told me he'd expressed his interest to Da earlier that week at the pub. Da had kept it to himself, unsure how to proceed. Rupert Camden wanted me to marry him.

"I thought it a lark at first and laughed. Momma assured me it was not a jest but they—my parents—weren't going to make any choice for me. My mother thought I should consider saying yes.

"This was about a month ago, I guess. I can't really express how I felt in that moment. It felt like shame, but now I think it was more confusion. I had never even spoken more than a passing word to him, never taken a walk on the beach, shared a lunch at the pub, nothing. Why on earth would he want to marry me?"

Aylee paused. To this day she never understood why Da had not just simply said, *"No, of course not. The idea of you marrying my daughter is absurd."*

She drew a breath and smiled up at Cailean.

"I suppose none of it matters now though, does it? He

finally has my answer, and we can both move on."

"How many years are you, Aylee?" he inquired quietly.

She caught the peculiar phrasing but let it pass. "Don't you know it's impolite to ask a girl her age?" She smiled at him but could tell he really wanted to know. "I'll be twenty in two months' time."

"He has got to be . . . twice your age? Is that common among your people? To marry someone so much more your senior?"

"No, it isn't. I think perhaps it's why I was so bothered by it. It happens occasionally, of course, but there was no reason for it with me. And yet, it was almost as if I should be happy or grateful or something."

Aylee stared back down at her hands.

"Grateful to whom? You're a beautiful woman, and from what I can tell, you are kind and have a level head. People here seem to like you. Any man should be happy you would even consider him. You could have your pick." He looked genuinely affronted.

"You are very kind, but I am not entirely sure that's true. It didn't take much to sway Ian now, did it? At any rate, I suppose I'm to be grateful to my parents for giving me a choice and grateful to Mr. Camden for offering his wealth in exchange for a wife."

"In exchange?" His eyebrow lifted. The clouds passed over the moon, and the shadows shifted.

"Some people, not many thankfully, still think of marriage as a financial transaction. People are commodities. Some marry for love, but others for comfort, prestige, or wealth."

"I see." His frown deepened. "Do your parents really feel this way? Do you?"

Despite what she had told him, or maybe because of it, the words stung.

"No, I don't. And neither do my folks. Maybe it has to do with Maeve. We all felt she could have married a little higher than she did. I still can't figure out her intentions. I don't know."

"So then, let me ask you this. Why did you not simply tell him sooner you weren't interested?"

"I've asked myself the same thing so many times, and the answer is I'm not sure. I suppose I didn't want to embarrass myself or him. He had never actually asked me, and it felt a little conceited to turn down a proposal I hadn't yet received. For that matter, we still have never had a real conversation. Not about anything more serious than the price of clams or how long it would take the ferry to arrive in bad weather.

"I felt I misjudged my position with Ian so severely, there was no way I could really ever know what a man was thinking until the words were expressly put out there for me." She smiled sadly. "If I am ever to marry, I want to be able to talk to my husband, not be talked *to* by him. But I also didn't want to upset my parents—they'll be happy when I'm settled. And really, I didn't want to be the source of unhappiness for Mr. Camden either."

"And your own happiness? Where does it come in?"

"I'm happy. Generally."

Cailean scrubbed at his face, but it didn't hide his smile. "You *may* be the sweetest, kindest person I have ever met. You would be content in your unhappiness if it prevented someone else's moment of pain."

That might have been the nicest compliment she'd received in quite some time, despite the fact they'd only just met.

"It's important to be kind. There is a shortage of it in the world." She nodded as if to cement her point.

"I don't disagree, but maybe if Mr. Camden had known from the start it was a hopeless cause, he would not now be so very angry. Watching a blossom of hope shrivel before your eyes is a hard thing. Men are dangerous when they feel they've been made a fool. I honestly can't decide which of them I despise more right now, Ian or Camden."

Aylee liked Cailean a little more every time he spoke.

"I never thought of it in those terms before. Obviously I've made a mistake. Do I now spend the rest of my life atoning for it? I'm not sure I can."

"I would advise spending the rest of your life making yourself as happy as you try to make those around you." He looked up at the stars. "It is easier said than done I'm afraid, but I think those around you will be all the better for it."

The crowd had thinned, and it was getting quite late. The time to be getting home was upon them.

Aylee looked at him as he studied the sky—this strange man who was wrapped in mystery. It felt as if she'd known him all her life and could already anticipate the sorrow that would descend on her when he eventually wiped the village mud from his feet and found his way home.

She sighed as she rose from the bench and stretched. She caught sight of her parents chatting with Mr. Bryan and the proprietor of a local pub. They would be strolling back down the street to their home above the shop soon, and Aylee knew it best to join them.

"I appreciate you listening to my tale of woe and apologize for drawing you into my folly."

"No apologies necessary. Thank you for the most entertaining evening. I'll be sure to work on my dance steps." He bowed slightly, a tip of his head really, and turned in the direction of the inn.

Aylee watched for a moment and met up with her parents for the short walk home. She was already dreading the conversation to come.

EIGHT

Something needed to be done.

Cailean had tarried too long already and still was no closer to a resolution to his troubles. Those troubles would be mounting exponentially if he continued to fail. He could feel the pull of the sea and knew the longer he was forced to remain in town the worse it would become. Others before him who had remained where they did not belong were eventually driven mad. He had no desire to share their fate.

The previous days had been a collection of frantic movements and disjointed errands with no real destination or reason. His thoughts focused on an end goal with no precise strategy of how to achieve it. He hadn't known with whom to speak or in which direction to move. His destinations were haphazard and full of ill-conceived choices. Blindly he poked about, hoping chance would intervene and he would somehow stumble upon what he needed, the part of himself stolen away.

Today, however, he had a direction—a plan born from his mingling with the townspeople during the jubilee.

Despite being out quite late the evening before, he rose with the sun and quietly exited the inn.

Wearing the borrowed clothing he had slept in, he stopped in the yard and scratched Penny's cat behind the ears.

"Wish me luck."

The cat's only reply was a soft purr as it sauntered away.

He walked down to the shoreline and stood at the water's edge. The saline air was cool on his cheeks, and the lull of the waves calmed his mind. Closing his eyes, he tilted his head back and drug in a lungful of briny air. Condensation collected on his coat and in his coal and silver hair. He savored each droplet.

A lone fishing boat floated out past the breakers. It was odd for a coastal town to have such a small fleet of fishing vessels, but it seemed only the bravest were willing to sail these waters.

"I'm coming home soon. Wait for me. Please." The plea was made to the water. The wind.

He expected no reply and none came. The desire to dive into the waves was a prickling itch beneath his skin. He fought the need to scratch and instead turned away from the surf.

Leaving the beach behind, he headed into town.

His next stop was the bakery. The food here tasted exquisite, but it never seemed to sustain him for long. Mrs. Bryan had not yet served breakfast, much less risen, before he had departed the inn that morning, so finding a bite was his top priority. The baker and his wife kept much earlier hours, and smoke was rising from the chimneys in the back. The smell of fresh-baked bread was warm and comforting. He couldn't fathom how he had previously lived without experiencing the simple pleasure baked goods could provide.

Inside the shop, Cailean pulled one of his few remaining coins from his pocket and exchanged it for a mug of strong hot tea and a warm dense scone dripping with gooey jam.

His first inclination had been to visit the Garrows' shop for his breakfast. He had not yet been inside the tiny store and was curious about the life Aylee led. Caution had won out however, and he opted for the bakery instead. It was best not to delay his plans further, and he was concerned he would find an excuse to stay and chat with her. That was the problem. He enjoyed talking with her. Enjoyed her smile. Enjoyed watching her eyes twinkle. Most of all he enjoyed the way she treated those around her with respect and dignity. He was discomfited by the prospect of not seeing her again. Last evening had been a treat for him. She was the sole bright point in this whole misadventure, but the more he became attached to her, the worse it would be for them both in the end.

Knowing where he wanted to go but unsure how exactly to get there, he decided the best course was simply to ask. This too would have been an awkward question for Aylee and her family, one more reason to have skipped the mercantile. Many of the villagers recognized him, so there was no use in hiding. As the shop assistant handed him the steaming mug of tea, he asked her where he might find Maeve Ruthven.

"I've something to discuss with her," he added.

The girl smiled prettily at him and explained the directions to the cottage at the end of town.

"I'd offer to take you there myself, but well, I've got work to do. I'm sure Aylee could have given you the way or walked you there herself. You two seemed to be getting on well last night."

"We were," he agreed. "This is something of a surprise though."

He didn't elaborate on whom the surprise was intended for.

She smiled her understanding and then added, "My name's Jenny. If you have any trouble finding the place, come on back and I can walk you down at lunchtime."

He thanked her but hoped it wouldn't be necessary to take her up on her offer. He threw back the remaining tea, enjoying the warmth the bitter drink gave him, and returned the mug. As he left, he thought she murmured something about Aylee's luck. Scone in hand he headed back into the bleak grey morning.

At the end of the main street, the shops gave way to

grasses and pasture. The road forked—north toward a row of cottages and southwest toward the distillery. When Cailean approached the fork, he had the sudden urge to abandon his plan and venture down the road to Rupert Camden's establishment. He could just make out trails of steam rising from the flues along the roofline. When the breeze blew up from the coast, he could detect the barest trace of sweet-smelling fermented malt. He tamped down the desire to visit the distillery and turned right onto the cottage road. In the distance, fields of gold—barley having recently been harvested—provided a lovely contrast to the green and grey. He passed a few folk traveling on foot into town and a small group of tired looking men together in a wagon. It was still early following the night of revelry but life did need to get on. Work had to be done in the small coastal town.

The girl from the bakery, Jenny he reminded himself, had instructed him to look for the cottage surrounded by bright blue and white hydrangeas. While he did not know what a hydrangea was, he was sure he had come to the right place. The front garden was a riot of periwinkle and greenish purple flowers growing on plants almost as tall as he was. Overhead a small flock of blackbirds flew from tree to tree. They settled in the top of an oak only to be startled aloft once more by the swoop of a crying gull.

Cailean brought his attention away from the birds and focused on the small cottage, thinking how best to proceed. A thin trail of smoke issued from the brick chimney. Maeve must be awake. Aylee had mentioned her sister's husband worked for Camden, and the man should have left for work at the whiskey plant an hour or more ago.

Deciding again for a direct approach, he walked the short distance from the road and knocked on the heavy front door.

Maeve answered quickly, tying an apron around her waist as the oak swung inward.

"Can I help you?" She was questioning but not rude.

"Actually, yes. I am hoping you can."

Her face turned wary for a brief moment, but she covered the expression with a bland smile.

"Cailean right? Come in please." Her smile deepened.

Cailean was struck by just how lovely Aylee was in comparison to her sister. Maeve did have a classic beauty, but when she smiled, it did nothing for her features. The smile didn't reach her eyes, making her look sad—almost tragic. Her face held a glimpse of what it might be if it had been lit by an inner light, but the lack of warmth and grace made for a certain dullness.

Ducking his head in hopes of hiding his thoughts, he stepped through the threshold into the snug cottage.

The space was tidy, with shelving along one wall holding a collection of books and various ephemera. A large overstuffed chair, its arms slightly threadbare and worn, took up the corner next to the window, and a small olive-colored couch sat opposite the door. The smell of wet wool hung in the air along with a floral scent he couldn't identify.

Maeve showed him to a small table with two wooden chairs, their paint chipped in spots, just off the kitchen. Weak sunlight filtered in through the cream eyelet curtains and fell on a pot of tea in the middle. Maeve fetched a second mug and offered Cailean the pot. He thanked her and fell quiet watching the steam drift lazily above the pale brown liquid.

After she had served herself, he finally spoke. "I believe you may have something of mine, and I've come here today to kindly ask for its return."

Maeve looked first confused and then a bit startled. She recovered after a moment and lifted her chin. "I'm sorry, but I have no idea what you mean."

"I believe you do." The look on her face assured him he was right.

He continued to speak evenly, no hint of the anger or

frustration he felt tinting his voice.

"I saw you that day. Down by the water." After seeing her with Aylee last night, he was sure he had spied her previously on the shore.

"Which day is this? I am down by the water frequently. It is a coastal town after all."

"Six days past. Early in the morning. Before the sun had risen. You were there." The gravel in his voice was thicker, emotion pouring into his words. "I am asking no questions. Surely you aren't even aware of the..." He sighed, fought for the word—found it. "Repercussions. Please return it to me. Please. I'm begging you."

"Again, I have no idea what you mean." She paused. "Perhaps it was my sister you saw. She goes to the shore each morning, almost without fail. She looks for clams. People occasionally confuse us for one another."

Maeve's voice was shaking, and she wasn't looking at him but rather above his shoulder, eyes fixed on something in the distance.

"Only a blind person could confuse you with your sister. Aylee was there, true. *After* you had gone. She does not have what I am seeking."

"Maybe some other then? Children often look for treasures on the shore."

A lie and not a very convincing one. He had yet to see a child alone near the water in this odd little town. Was this a game to her?

"No." He stared at her, willing her to meet his gaze.

"How can you be sure? What is this possession anyhow? You haven't said." Flipping her hand to the side, she finally looked at him and added, "Perhaps it was tucked into a pocket?"

"It is a treasure, yes, but one no child would want, and you know as well as I, if it got tucked into anyone's pocket it was yours." His anger was rising, his voice growing coarser by the moment. "Stop this nonsense, Maeve. Please."

He reached out and touched her hand. His voice quieter. "As I've said, I am asking no questions."

Maeve looked from his hand into his clear aquamarine eyes. She narrowed her eyes at him and tilted her head to the side.

"Please."

Water rose to her lower lash line, threatening to spill down her cheeks. "I. . ." She took a deep breath. "I didn't know it was yours."

"So you do have it?" He couldn't control the eager hope in his voice as relief rushed through him. But in the next breath, Maeve dashed his hope once more.

"No. I'm sorry. I can't return it. I did have it, but now it's gone."

NINE

Fury consumed Cailean while he sat quietly inside the tiny cottage surrounded by flowers. A flame was burning bright in his core, and as such, it did what all flames do—burned searing bright for a short time, but given no more fuel, it settled into a low glowing ember. The heat was steady and eager, waiting to flash once more. He carried this radiant bit within him, using its energy to move him forward.

Thinking back on his conversation with Maeve, he was irritated more with himself than with Aylee's older sister. He should have forced her to give him more details, to spill the whole ugly truth. Instead, he'd listened to some bits of foolishness and prideful imaginings, all while the inferno in him grew. Eventually the rage at its highest, he had stormed from the small house with only scant more information than he'd arrived with.

Fool. He was a fool. Perhaps he deserved all of this—punishment for countless stupid mistakes. The first of which was taking the medallion from his neck to begin with.

He was losing time and he knew it. He would need to be clever and quick. He needed people to stop looking at him as if he were either an imbecile with no ability to speak or a creature to be feared. He needed to be himself again.

Maeve hadn't said much, and what she'd said hadn't made any sense other than one thing. Her scheming had not been directed at him. It had been a mistake of identity along with a lapse in judgment. The other details were lost on him in the haze of his fury. This was no help to him now.

What did give him some hope was in what she had *not* said. She never told him she had willingly parted with his prize. This implied someone else knew she had it and wanted it gone. It gave him one more person to speak to at least—a new lead to follow.

Rubbing absentmindedly at his neck and taking a deep breath to calm himself, he set out toward the smell of malting barley and aged oak.

TEN

Things in the shop were off to a slow start for Aylee. While many folks slept off the previous night's fun, she was halfheartedly stocking shelves and arranging parcels for pickup later in the day. Many of her friends were still dreaming of the dances and flirtations while trying to forget the many drinks. Others were awake but were rubbing sore muscles and sipping strong tea to clear foggy heads. The urgent need for canned goods and notions was limited, and for most, the weekly shopping could be put off for at least one or two more cycles of the sun.

Aylee's mother had walked down the road to pick up some fresh cream and butter and had returned with their dairy but *without* the usual smile on her face.

"What is the matter, my sweet?" her husband asked when she returned, storm clouds on her face.

"You will not believe the tall tales I heard while I was out."

"Try me." He wiped the grime from his hands with his apron and pulled up a crate to sit on.

"I ran into Candice Bryan while I was at the dairy. It seems Aylee is quite the talk of town today."

"Me? Why?" Aylee stopped in the act of straightening the boxes of biscuits and looked at her mother. Realization dawned. "Oh . . . It's all to do with Rupert Camden, isn't it? How I turned him down and made such a ridiculous display of myself?"

"Well, Love, yes and no," Una replied.

Aylee waited for her mother to continue.

"It isn't so much that you've turned him down. More the why of it," Una said fretfully.

Aylee and her father sat in stunned silence while Mrs. Garrow relayed the town gossip. While a marriage between Rupert Camden and Aylee Garrow was atypical, no one had a good reason it should not take place. Aylee was, after all, a kind and sweet girl blessed with an exterior quite as lovely as her nature, and Rupert was a wealthy hardworking man who was handsome enough. *No one mentioned the considerable difference in age or the fact he had used his power to threaten and intimidate.* Most folks had known about his plans to propose for weeks, and everyone agreed, if Aylee had plans to rebuke him, she would have done it before last night.

All these things together begged the question—what had changed? An outsider with startling eyes, silver streaks in his hair, and strange customs appeared out of nowhere the night of the jubilee and wouldn't you know it? Aylee Garrow was bewitched.

By all accounts, this was their first meeting. Only a few people knew otherwise. Surely this stranger was full of mischief and meant to do ill during his brief time in the village. Whispers had begun. He was a demon. He was a practitioner of dark magic and had woven some sort of spell over her. Or worse yet—he was fey. Whichever version of the story was told, all ended the same. Sweet, pretty, kind, *foolish* Aylee Garrow would fall into a trap unless she saw sense and married Rupert.

"This is all nonsense. I told you both last night how I came to my decision. About Ian. It had nothing to do with Cailean." In actuality, she *hadn't* told them the whole truth. She had left any mention of Graham or Maeve out of it, not wanting her parents to also fret over her sister.

"Yes, we know, Love. However, it's not likely Ian is going to want his side of this thing told as it paints him in a less than flattering light. You do see how it looks—having just met the young man at the jubilee?" Una asked her daughter.

"I . . . It wasn't the first time we'd met." Shame flushed

across Aylee's cheeks, and she could not bring herself to meet her parents' eyes.

"Oh?" Devon crossed his arms. "Perhaps you had better explain."

"Well, he's been in town several days now. He seems to be having a bit of trouble on his travels and needed some assistance. I gave him some old boots from the donations and a few coins to help him on his way. We bumped into one another again two days ago and he thanked me for my help. I invited him to attend the jubilee if he was able." Aylee felt a twinge of guilt over not giving additional details, but she simply was not up to the questions those details would raise.

Saying it aloud did nothing to comfort Aylee. How could any of this help her case? If one night was presumed enough to bewitch her, what would several days' time allow for?

"And why did you not say something sooner?" her father asked.

"I told Dee when we were berry picking. I didn't think it would be of interest to anyone. It was a small thing and not all that exciting. Had I known it would blow up in this manner, I would have informed not only you, but the town in its entirety."

"Hmm." Her father didn't seem impressed with her answer.

Swiftly switching the subject, she added, "My acquaintance with Cailean is a small matter, and my response to Mr. Camden isn't anyone else's business as far as I'm concerned. How has everyone in the entire town decided he must be some dark, otherworldly creature? The fey stories are just silly superstition. No one actually believes they're real." She paused and added, "Well, except maybe for Maeve. She might think they're real."

She ignored the fact demon and wizard had also been trotted out as possibilities.

"Superstitious stories to keep little ones on the straight

and narrow, I agree." Devon looked at Una and seemed to read something in her face before continuing. "But some folks in town believe they might be a bit more than stories. Some think the faeries and nixies and the like used to dwell in these parts and now just hide when people are around. Old Sean, a friend of my da's, used to tell a tall tale about a kelpie trying to drag him into the sea when he was a kid. We all just laughed it off as a joke, but Da wasn't so sure. Said Sean would get animated like he was pulling fun, but the look in his eye was too haunted for it not to be true.

"Anyhow. Lots of folks think loads of fey are just waiting for their chance to return to the open."

Aylee chewed on the thought for a moment. Sometimes she'd thought a pixie or will-o-wisp followed her at night, and other times she had hoped for a changeling to replace her sister. Folks in town, too, talked about vengeful sprites and handsome elf kings, but they all said it in jest. Why start taking it seriously now?

"You don't believe all this, do you?" she asked her parents.

"Curious things happen all the time, Love."

Aylee looked at her mother with not a little surprise on her face.

It was odd to hear her mother voice this. If it had been her sister, Aylee would have taken it much easier. Maeve knew all of the old stories—each legend and detail. She knew where the elves lived and with whom the wraiths spoke. She knew what gifts to leave the little people to gain favor and which berries to wear at night to avoid mean tricks and spells. Aylee always thought it was a fun hobby for her sister, nothing more.

"Cailean isn't a faerie king! He's just a normal man." *A normal man who happened to show up in her storeroom naked and mixes words up and listens when I speak.*

"He may be an outsider, but he is still just a man."

Devon looked at his daughter with something close to pity in his eyes. "Of course he is, Love, but you should steer clear of him all the same."

She needed some fresh air.

Aylee grabbed a basket and jammed things into it—a fresh container of meat stew, a pot of jam, several scones, some dry tea, several handfuls of fresh carrots, and a wedge of cheese. She added a skein of beautiful goldenrod yarn and some new knitting needles to the pile and headed out the back door.

Every week or two she liked to stop by the home of Shelby Abbott and her elderly aunt Violet. Shelby was a year younger than Aylee but, due to either fate or simply unfortunate circumstances, had the mind of a much younger child. Her mother had perished during childbirth, and her father, devastated by the loss, had jumped from the high sea cliffs shortly after the delivery. With no one else to care for the baby, his aunt, a childless widow, had taken Shelby in and raised her.

Early in her toddler years, it became evident she would not grow to be like her peers. She was slow to both talk and walk but loved the world just the same. She found joy in the simplest things and always wore a smile. She hugged friends and strangers alike. If her difference ever occurred to her, no one could see it.

Children could be cruel, and Shelby had received more than her share of school-yard insults and degradations. One morning, when she was perhaps seven years old, a group of boys surrounded her on the small road to school. They taunted her and called her vile names. She only wanted to be friends and didn't understand why they would be so mean. Just as she'd been about to cry, Aylee Garrow had strode up to the group, blocking Shelby with her body from the foul words and cruel faces. Aylee, a relatively popular child, shamed them only slightly, but it was enough to end the taunts. Since that day, Shelby had been enamored with Aylee, with Aylee quite fond of Shelby in return.

Violet was too old to work any longer at the seamstress, so they often relied on the kindness of the town. Aylee brought them baskets from the shop not as an act of charity but because she enjoyed visiting with them and knew the groceries were both needed and appreciated. She worried what would become of Shelby when her aunt passed away.

The pair had a small garden room just behind the tailor's storefront, adjacent to the town brewmaster and his family. A shared walkway led down past a few other homes and to a beautiful stretch of land running parallel to the sea. Aylee enjoyed walking along this strand and chatting with the Abbotts when the weather permitted. From it, the expanse of beach and water could be viewed for miles down the coast.

She walked behind the shops, Pepper racing along behind her, and tapped lightly on their front door. The wood creaked as it opened a crack and was then thrown wide in a clamor.

"Aylee!" Shelby cheered, holding her arms wide for an embrace.

"Hello, sweet Shelby. Did you stay out of trouble last evening?" She stepped into the hug, and the air was immediately squeezed from her lungs. "Oh dear."

Shelby released her and clapped her hands, bouncing up and down on her toes. She bent forward to peek at the contents of the basket, the delight illuminating her face.

"Of course I did! You brought presents! Thanks, Aylee." Her smile, Aylee thought, was worth ten times the value of the basket's contents.

"Not presents really. Just a few things I thought you and your aunt Violet might enjoy."

"Hi, Peppy Pepper!" Shelby was down on her knees, letting the dog lick her face, almost strangling Pepper, her arms so tight around the beast's neck. "Are there sweets, too?"

"Hmm? I don't recall. Do you think I should have

brought some?" she teased gently and reached into the pocket of her apron to pull out a handful of sticky toffee chews, individually wrapped in waxed paper.

"I knew you had some. I love you, Aylee." Shelby squeezed her friend again and hurried inside to share the basket with her aunt.

After the girls returned from their pleasant afternoon stroll along the shoreline, Aylee made her excuses and promised to return in the next few days. Not wanting the confines of the shop on a slow day just yet, she wandered down to the water's edge. As was often the case, particularly this time of year, the beach was deserted.

She found a quiet spot and lay on the sand, Pepper snuggled in next to her. Within moments she was dozing.

Aylee wasn't sure how long she napped, but when she awoke the sun had moved further toward the horizon. Her parents had probably already closed up shop, so she took the opportunity to stay out a little longer.

Gentle waves hit the pebbled shore, and the ocean air filled her head. She meandered up the waterline and around a small stone pier to a rocky outcrop jutting into the surf. Wanting to reach the tide pools on the far side, she climbed the rocks, careful of her hands on the sharper bits. She made her way to the small collections of seawater and the myriad of living creatures inhabiting them. Pepper splashed along the surf half a pitch down the beach. Sea birds called in the air overhead, and the waves sent fine layers of spray into the air. Aylee lowered herself to touch starfish and tiny crabs, urchins and miniature fish. She balanced on the craggy rocks, mindful of her hem getting wet and not much caring.

The sound of splashing out beyond the rocks caught her attention, and she looked up into the setting sun. The golden rays danced off the water and into her eyes. She raised a hand to block a bit of the light but still had to squint to make out the shapes in the water. A head bobbed up and down, bottling at the surface. Long kelp grew just off shore, and the harbor seals liked to hunt and play among the long tendrils. Soon the silhouette of several more seals joined the first, their sleek forms dark against the setting sun. They swam back and forth beyond the rocks. The largest seal splashed into a dive, then surfaced and barked into the ocean air. The noise grew louder as one and then two more of the animals joined the first in barking. If she didn't know better, she would have thought they were barking at her—berating her presence here on the shoreline.

"I beg your pardon." She laughed. "I believe I've just as much right to be here as you."

In that moment, she would have liked nothing more than to strip off her sweater and boots and swim out among them. The autumnal air and frigid water kept her firmly on the shore, however. With a sigh, she gathered her things. It was getting late, and the remaining chores at home would not do themselves. She climbed back up the rocky crop. At the top, she turned back to the sea for one more look at the glorious sunset. She was astonished to see the smooth white torso and thick black hair of Cailean cutting through the water. She couldn't see his face but was certain of his identity all the same.

He was approaching the small bob of seals from the opposite direction—much as she had imagined herself doing only moments before.

He's going to die of hypothermia. The thought echoed in her head.

Just as she was going to run for help or call out to him, she realized he did not seem to be in the least bit of peril. She watched for a moment more, feeling only slightly guilty about admiring his smooth skin and firm muscles. He looked quite well. He swam as if he were born to do it—gliding smoothly through the swells and waves. The seals seemed to take little notice and had gone back to their own frolicking. Shaking her head in amazement, she left him to his swim and trudged back to the store.

ELEVEN

Monday morning, she was on her way to the bakery for a few loaves of bread when she spotted Cailean heading up the main street. She smiled and waved, and he quickly crossed the busy street to meet her. He smiled wearily at her, the sunlight catching the thin streaks of silver in his otherwise pitch-black hair.

"Good morning, Mr. Vann," she chirped.

Several passersby looked on as the pair stood on the sidewalk outside a small candlemaker's shop.

"Ms. Garrow." He tipped his chin. "Where are you off to this early in the day?"

"Just to fetch some bread. Momma wants me to make some cinnamon bread puddings for the shop today. Would you care to join me?"

"I'd love to walk you, but then I'm afraid I'd better be on my way. I have somewhere I need to be shortly." He ran a hand along his throat down below his Adam's apple. Aylee had noticed this movement in him before and assumed it was a nervous habit.

"How mysterious." She winked at him. "Anything I can assist with? I may have some free time later in the day."

"As much as I wish you could help, I don't think so."

Her smile faltered briefly, but she recovered quickly. "Well then, perhaps you might be tempted to come to dinner later this week."

Knowing he would likely demure, she added, "If you're still in town, that is. I'd love to introduce you to Maeve and my parents."

If her parents could simply meet Cailean properly, she was sure they would warm to him quickly. Unlike many others in town it seemed.

To her surprise, she suspected the look on his face meant he was happy with the invitation. Poor soul didn't know what he was agreeing to. Her parents could be the loveliest people, but they did a fair amount of interrogation when they saw fit.

"Yes. I'd like that very much," he replied.

"Let's say Friday evening then. What's your favorite dish?"

He shrugged. "Not sure I have a favorite. Anything you like will be more than fine."

"Be careful. Giving me free rein might not be in your best interest." She smiled even more brightly, if such a thing were possible.

They'd reached the front of the bakery and paused outside the door.

He reached up and tucked a blowing strand of her coppery hair behind her ear. She had to suppress the urge to shiver as his fingers brushed the back of her neck.

"As I said. All things . . . I mean, *anything* will be more than fine." His voice was just barely audible at the close distance.

She blushed and looked down at her toes.

"Might I ask you something?" She sensed him nodding, but feeling the weight of those cerulean eyes on her, she didn't dare look up.

"When I met you—the first time I mean—you seemed agitated when I told you town is simply town. No name." She lifted her eyes and was hit by the full force of his attention. Her blush deepened.

"I don't believe you've asked a question yet," he teased.

"Well, is that not normal? Town is just town and the city is the city? Why does it bother you?" She left the other part unspoken—*why does it bother you when you can't think of half the words you want anyway?*

He seemed to think on it, and once more she felt the weight of his gaze. Felt it all the way to the tips of her toes.

"I suppose it's because names have meaning. Words have meanings, but *names* even more. They carry importance. Your lovely name speaks volumes. Your parents, your sister, and friends. Me. All of us are called something. Are given a distinction which becomes part of who we are. Lots of places have names as well. Other towns. Other cities. Other seas. Those titles tell stories, give details, or reveal how people who live there think of themselves. Even your sister's small cottage has a name. Hydra . . . whatever. The flower cottage. Do you not think it odd your town does not?" His voice was husky and deep but so full of emotion it was made beautiful.

In actuality, she hadn't ever pondered it. But now the idea was in her head, she had to admit it. Yes. It was odd, wasn't it? More than that. Obscene almost.

She couldn't hide her frown. "Yes, I suppose it should be called something." He was about to leave when she asked quickly, "What of your name? What's its meaning?"

"In the old language it means young warrior."

"Hmmm." She smiled. "I think it suits you. And where you come from, home? What name does it go by?"

"That, lovely Aylee, is a story for another day."

Her smile faltered at the evasion, but she chuckled. "See you Friday then."

"I will be counting the days," he replied and turned and walked back up the main street.

Only after he'd gone did she notice Deirdre, Robbie, and Ian standing across the cobbles. Deirdre had a smile plastered from ear to ear. Robbie was looking adoringly at Deirdre and her glorious smile. Ian simply looked at Aylee and turned away.

TWELVE

The following two days, Aylee didn't lay eyes on Cailean a single time. If not for the ongoing town gossip, she would have assumed he did leave town. Despite never seeing him, she heard about him dozens or perhaps hundreds of times.

It seemed every patron who entered the store had a question or an opinion or a bit of advice.

"Here are your bobbins and jars, Ms. Chadwick, and no, I have not met Cailean's family."

"Thank you for dropping by with the post. No, I have not noticed his ears are especially pointed, Mr. Crenshaw."

"Have an extra sweet drop, Ruby. I am very seriously, positively, and extra quite sure I am not bewitched. Now go and find your mother."

On and on it went. At first it was funny, followed by annoying, then infuriating. Now Aylee was merely resigned that she could not escape the topic. She noted many of her neighbors found it to be little more than fun gossip, something new and novel to discuss. Several people, however, took the whole matter much more seriously. These were the ones she dreaded speaking with. They gave her dire warnings and crossed themselves before they entered or left the shop. They sent ugly glances her direction or extolled the virtues of Rupert Camden. In a few cases, she had been outright threatened, and her father had needed to step in. It was really altogether too much.

She distracted herself from the chattering of the town's inhabitants by coming up with different names for their little village. Cailean was right; it did seem odd the town didn't have a proper name. She thought on the attributes it possessed and kicked around several ideas. *Seaside. Littleton. Quiet Shores.* None really felt right, and perhaps that was why it hadn't been given a name in the hundreds of years it had been there. No one ever found the right one. She thought about how the people got along mostly well and how some men like Rupert Camden seemed to direct life just by their mere presence. Maybe it should be called *Camden Square* or some other such thing to make important people feel more important.

Thinking about names brought her mind back to the sea, and thinking of the sea brought her mind back to Cailean and his ocean-colored eyes and unusual silver-streaked hair.

Despite what her parents thought, she had not been avoiding Cailean. She simply had been too busy to actively seek him out. Her mother's concerns stayed with her, and while she might be stubborn, she'd be more than happy if he bumped into her on the road. But she had no reason to pursue trouble when she had other responsibilities. Factoring in his imminent departure and the pain she'd experienced last spring, she thought it best to wait to see him as they'd planned rather than tracking him down.

She was thinking about Cailean's eyes and pain and names as she carried a crate of empty green glass jars out of the back of the shop. A familiar voice startled her.

"Hello, Aylee." It was quiet and tinged with longing.

Her hands stilled on the crate, but she didn't look up. Her whole body tensed, and after a long moment, she finally turned toward Ian.

He stood several feet away, hands in his pockets and staring at his shoes.

"What do you want, Ian?" It came out sounding less kind and more petulant than she had intended, but the memories of the hurt and betrayal were difficult to escape.

"I wanted to finally say I'm sorry." Unlike his younger brother Robbie, Ian had a rather handsome face. He pushed back the sandy curls hanging over his eyes as he looked at her.

"I appreciate the gesture, but I think it might be a bit too late for it."

He didn't respond. She stared at him for what felt like an eternity before the dam within her broke.

"How could you do it?" Her voice cracked, so much worse than the wobble she so detested. "How could you do that to me? Without even a word, without an explanation?"

He stepped forward and raised his hand as if he were going to touch her cheek. She stepped back out of his reach.

"I didn't know what to do, Aylee. He threatened to fire me. I thought he felt my work was being affected by the time I was spending here helping at the shop. I thought if I broke things off, he'd see I was loyal and maybe I could get a raise, save some money for us, and then when I'd really proved myself, he wouldn't dare take my job."

"I didn't see what his real move was. I swear, Aylee, I didn't see. And then it was too late. Everyone in town said you were going to marry him, and I just sort of gave up."

As if to match Aylee's mood, the sky's great puffy clouds were turning from white to steel.

"You gave up? That's your excuse. That's why you made me feel like I wasn't worth anything?" Tears were springing from her eyes.

"Don't cry, Aylee. Please. I never meant for you to be hurt." He raised his hand again, but the look on her face must have made him think twice. He stepped back and let his hand drop to his side.

"How can you even say those words? Everything, *everything* you did was to hurt me. I could maybe understand you slowing things down if you thought your job was at risk, but to not even respect me enough to tell me why? That's something I don't think I can ever forgive."

"Don't say that, Aylee. Please don't say that." He stepped forward again but stopped short a second time. "Don't you see now we can get back on track? You told the old bastard you didn't want him. He's got no cause now to keep us apart."

"Ian, you need to go." She turned to head back into the mercantile.

"Aylee, please." He sounded so wounded, as if this were all her doing and not his own.

"Goodbye, Ian." She closed the door and went back to work.

THIRTEEN

Business had finally started to die back down, most folks having already taken the opportunity to stop in and share their two cents. Aylee had thought she might be able to take a late afternoon stroll along the water later to clear her mind and the memory of her conversation with Ian, but the wind was picking up in an autumn gale. Her legs were itching to be stretched, and her face craved the salt spray. But no amount of longing would make her fool enough to venture out in a full-force coastal squall. More than one person had been swept off the rocks and paths by sneaker waves and crashing surf. Once in the water, the undertow would finish the job. Days like this reminded her why people feared the sea and the enormous power it contained. Tonight she would be snuggled in her bed reading by lamplight instead of enjoying the outdoors.

The bell over the door tinkled, and a gust of frigid air blew in along with Deirdre and her mother. The wind ruffled their skirts and hair into chaotic swirls.

"Sorry about that, Devon," Mrs. Sommerson apologized. "It's blown up wicked out there."

"No apologies, Gertie. All's well. What can I get for you lovely ladies today?" Her father was ever the embodiment of gentle good humor.

"I need a jug of oil for my lamps and also some laundry powder. If you've got any extra lengths of rope and a box of nails, I'll take those as well. Deirdre, grab a few boxes of sugar and some dried fruit if you will."

"We're making scones." Deirdre looked at Aylee and grimaced. On more than one occasion Deirdre had lamented about her mother's baking skills, or lack thereof.

Aylee chuckled and placed the items Deirdre handed her into a plain paper bag. No time for fancy wrapping and ribbons today. She tucked a small box of matches in on top.

"Be careful with that on your way home. It looks like it might rain."

"Oh for certain. It came in faster than normal. Looks like it's gonna be a howler," Deirdre replied.

"I spoke with Ian this morning."

Deirdre threw a quick look over her shoulder and leaned in closer to her friend. "And how did that lovely conversation go?"

Aylee just shook her head. Deirdre didn't press.

"On a lighter note, I've heard your man is still causing quite the stir." Deirdre always knew just what to say to get Aylee interested in a conversation.

"He's not my man, and I've heard the same."

"Have you heard he got into a bit of a scuffle up at the distillery?"

"Really? When?" This was news.

"So that's a 'no, I haven't heard.'" Deirdre smiled like a cat holding a mouse hostage in its mouth.

"Ugh! Just tell me!" Aylee almost shouted. She looked sheepishly around the shop. Then quieter, "Spill it, Dee."

"You know they say patience is a virtue." But Deirdre hastily continued, "Well, I've heard from some of the fellas he's been up there twice since the jubilee. Walked right in through the gate and asked to see Graham Ruthven both times. The boys on the loading bay told your Cailean to beat it, and the first time he did. But then he came back the second time and gave them a bit of cheek. Things looked like they were gonna get ugly, but that fine-looking man of yours just sauntered off peacefully. It wasn't until about an hour later they caught him round the back."

"Round the back? Was he trying to break in? That doesn't seem like something Cailean would do." Though how would she know what he would or wouldn't do? He'd broken in somewhere once before, hadn't he? She had to look at her toes as an image of him hiding in their storeroom uninvited flashed across her memory.

"No. That's just it. He was sitting there pretty as a picture. Right under an open window. Nothing on him to indicate he'd even been inside. No whiskey bottles or stolen money or anything."

"Well that's all right then, isn't it? Just sitting isn't a crime."

"Technically, Aylee, it's trespassing, so yeah, it's kinda a crime. But the boys weren't too pissed about it. Not until Mr. Camden showed up and started causing a fuss. He was apparently quite upset and yelling at your man about being a thief and all."

"Oh that doesn't mean anything." Aylee couldn't hide the distaste from her voice. "Let me guess, I'm once again the stolen goods."

"Hmm? I suppose. I hadn't thought about that, and the boys did say Camden didn't mention anything specific being taken. But still... why would he want to see Graham of all people? Ugh!" Deirdre made a face, speaking volumes about how she regarded Maeve's husband. Aylee didn't disagree.

"Anyhow, one of the boys decided to send a bit of a message on behalf of Mr. Camden. I'm afraid Cailean left with quite a shiner."

"For goodness' sake. I wonder about the men in this town. Perhaps I'll just be a spinster." Aylee was only half joking.

"Whatever you say my dear." Deirdre gave Aylee a reassuring hug and grabbed the bag of scones-yet-to-be and followed her mother out the door.

The wind was really picking up, whistling through the cracks in the windows and throwing loose debris down the cobbles in front of the shop. A length of burlap was dancing along the gutter when rain began to smatter in fat drops on the shop windows. Aylee gave a silent prayer for the sugar and matches sitting atop the other goods in the Sommersons' possession and went to check the oil in their own lamps upstairs. A few needed to be topped off, but the chore took only a few minutes to complete. Once she was satisfied with the stock of matches, reserve candles, extra wicks, and dry wood for the fire, she hurried back downstairs.

During her brief absence, Maeve had arrived and was busy helping their mother pack up the remaining perishables from the cold counter to either bring upstairs for their own dinner or store away in the icebox. Aylee was going to help them but caught a glimpse of color from the corner of her eye. Her father's maroon jacket was flapping wildly in the wind outside the front windows.

The storefront was composed of four good-sized glass panes broken up by wood trimming. Sturdy shutters folded up to either side of the panes on fine weather days but needed to be closed across the glass in stormy weather. The shutters were held firmly by thick wooden crossbars which were unwieldy but necessary to ensure flying debris didn't smash the windows to bits and allow the storm to invade the shop. They shouldn't have waited this long to put the shutters out, but the weather had been lovely just that morning.

Devon Garrow was losing the battle with the wind to cover the first of the four windows. Aylee hurried out to assist him.

The wind hit her with more force than she expected, sucking the breath from her lungs and stinging her eyes. A loose strand of hair began an unforgiving assault on her cheeks. Ignoring the bite to her exposed skin, she pushed to her father's side in an attempt to help him shoulder the wood into place. While she pressed her weight against the panel, he used a mallet to hammer the latches down firmly.

They moved to the next pane. The blue-grey paint on the wood was a perfect match to the turbulent skies. Devon yanked the panel from its holding and pulled it across the vulnerable window. Just as Aylee put her hands on the edge to help secure it, the wind gusted and the heavy material slammed her hand against the framing. Pain lanced through her fingers and into her wrist.

The wind snatched the cry from her lips as she cradled her damaged hand against her chest. Her father looked distraught but couldn't let the wood go for fear of it slamming back and causing more damage.

Despite the pain, Aylee needed to help him, so she tucked her hand gently in the palm of the other and helped wrangle the shutter into place. The pressure of the wind was fierce, and Aylee was worried she'd let the wood free again. Sweat was collecting on her brow despite the cool air slashing across her face. The shutter was bucking hard against her, jarring her shoulder. It was going to come free. She squeezed her eyes shut, focusing on pushing against the slab. A hoarse grunt reached her ears, and the pressure and movement were suddenly much better.

Aylee opened her eyes and saw strong arms extended in front of her face, keeping the wood stable enough for Devon to hammer home the latch.

Cailean had appeared out of the rain and stood between Aylee and her father. He moved to the next shutter and deftly held the wood while Devon anchored the crossbar. They maneuvered the last shutter in the same efficient way, and the three hurried inside to the relative safety of the storefront. Devon pulled the door snuggly behind him and flipped the welcome sign to read "Closed." It hung inside the small glass pane in the door, and while this could still be shattered in the storm, it was at much lower risk.

Una and Maeve looked up in unison, neither smiling as Cailean's presence registered. Aylee understood her mother's face, the same resigned expression she wore when Aylee brought home a stray cat or Devon insisted on a nip of whiskey after dinner. Maeve's expression was more puzzling. She looked almost fearful. Aylee wondered at that but placed the thought to the back of her mind. She could ask her sister later what troubled her.

The flesh on the back of her hand was already bruising. It had an angry reddish black color like overripe plums. Her fingers were sore, but she could move them, so likely not broken. The tip of her third digit was a pulsing retched thing—a mini heartbeat under the tense discolored shell of her fingernail. She went behind the counter, grabbed a small ceramic dish, and filled it with ice chips from the cold counter. Resting her hand on the surface, she winced, but once the sting dulled, she submerged the rest as far as she could. She carried the bowl back over to where her father was clapping Cailean on the back with a hearty "thank you, young man!"

He turned to Una. "Our Aylee got a bit more of that shutter than she bargained for."

Una had closed the space to peer at Aylee's submerged hand. "Oh, Love. What have you done now?"

"It's fine, Momma. I'm fine."

Realizing none of them had been formally introduced, she looked first at Cailean and then at her parents. "Cailean, these are my parents, Devon and Una Garrow, and my sister Maeve. Momma, Da, this is Cailean Vann."

"Mr. Vann here was surely in the right spot at the proper time," Devon said.

"Just glad I could be of some help," Cailean responded.

"Why exactly are you here?" Maeve's tone was nothing short of accusatory.

If he was taken aback, it didn't show. "Just on my way back to the inn. I didn't expect the weather to turn so quickly, and I guess I got caught out."

His rough voice was as calm as ever—his expression serene. And most interesting, no sign of a black eye. Deirdre must have had her story embellished along the way.

"Fast storm even by our coastal standards. That's true enough," Una acknowledged.

Maeve wasn't done though. "Back to the inn from where? The inn isn't on this stretch."

"Lord in heaven, Maeve. What's got into you?" Devon asked. "The man just helped us out of a jam, and you act as if he's up to no good."

"Perhaps he *is* up to no good. Perhaps he followed me here. We don't know him at all."

"Maeve. Why on earth would he follow you here? You're being. . ." Aylee was going to say rude, but jealous seemed more like it. She wasn't sure what her sister was implying, but this was too much.

"What, Aylee? What? You think you know him, do you? You can't actually tell me you really know anything about him aside from he's an interesting dance partner and a stranger to this town. You know nothing that matters."

Aylee could feel the heat in her face, and she struggled to contain her emotions. "I know him well enough, I can assure you."

"Sure you do." Maeve glared at Cailean as if to challenge him to defend himself.

"I think I'll just be going now. Didn't mean to kick up anyone's fire." Ire, Aylee thought, but again didn't correct him. "Mr. and Mrs. Garrow. Maeve. Aylee."

He tipped his head toward her and made a few steps toward the door.

Una gave Aylee the same resigned look and stepped in front of his tall frame, blocking the way. Una was shorter than Aylee by at least two inches, making the difference in size with Cailean that much more evident. Nonetheless, she was imposing when she needed to be.

"You'll do no such thing. The weather is just kicking in. You'll catch your death out there, and I won't have it. You are staying with us until this passes. You and Maeve both." She looked at her elder daughter. "I can't have you trying to get home in this. Besides, someone's got to eat these pies before they spoil."

Both Cailean and Maeve opened their mouths to

protest, but Una cut them off simultaneously. "Nothing from either of you. Mr. Vann, we owe you for your help and, Maeve, it is just out of the question. Graham will need to make do without you for the time being."

"Momma, don't be—" But Una held up her hand, effectively ending the discussion.

Maeve huffed a sigh. "Fine. Aylee, I'll be in your room." She marched to the back of the shop and out of sight.

Cailean helped Devon move a few heavy crates to the back of the shop while Una took a moment to look at Aylee's injured hand. Agreeing it was just badly bruised and the nail might not actually fall off, Aylee dumped the ice and helped lock up the cases. Once things were secured to Devon's liking, the three remaining Garrows retreated up the back stairs with Cailean in tow.

As they entered the cozy common space, Aylee relaxed a bit. The room provided a haven against the storm. A moderate hearth took up one wall, its warmth diffusing into the room to banish the cold ache of the air outside.

Devon dropped into a chair and immediately removed his sodden boots. The Garrow living area needed no standing on formality. What happened there in their home was different from how they would behave in the shop or with others from town.

Aylee lit the lamps, and Una handed around warm mugs of strong tea laced with a bit of honey and apple brandy. The warmth from the ceramic mug eased a bit of the pain in Aylee's hand. Devon, still in his wet stocking feet, tossed a log of pine into the fire and stoked the flames, working to build it enough to keep them warm for the long night to come. A crackling waltz took place as the flames tried to grow higher but were occasionally pushed back down by the wind coming in through the flue—up they rose only to pirouette and bend back down to the music of the storm.

They didn't make much conversation, save for the

elements voicing their fury outside. The windows rattled and drafts whistled through cracks unseen by the human eye. Pepper snored softly, sprawled out as she was in front of the fire. No amount of storm would bother her.

Una and Devon, sitting in at the small dining table adjacent to the sitting room, occasionally spoke quietly to one another, but the words were lost on Aylee and Cailean. Aylee glanced from her parents to the man sitting arm's length from her and wondered if he was uncomfortable. She certainly would have been in his position. Sitting in a strange home, in a strange town, while a gale threatened to blow the roof off.

"I've been hoping to run into you for the past two days. No bread to buy?" he asked.

She looked up at him. "I'm sorry. I've been busy with the shop, but you could have dropped in."

"You don't need to apologize. I thought about stopping in a time or two, but I decided maybe it was best not to."

"How do you mean?" She tried to keep the hurt from her voice.

"I may not be from here, Aylee, and I know the words I speak often get lost or jumbled." He smiled his teasing smile. "But I'm not deaf or dumb. I hear how people talk and then stop talking when they see me."

"It's a small town, and as much as I love my home, the people can be small minded sometimes. I'm still planning on Friday night, aren't you?"

"More than you know." He sighed. "If . . . I'm still able to make it."

Cailean sat forward on the edge of Aylee's favorite emerald armchair. He glanced at Aylee and then down to the small plate of ginger biscuits Una had placed in his hand a few moments before. He raised one to his mouth and nibbled off a corner. A small smile crept over his face, and he took a larger bite. Aylee couldn't help but notice how straight and white his teeth were—and silently added it to the list of his attributes.

"Thank you for the bite to eat. These are quite tasty." He raised his voice for Una to hear and gestured at the small plate on his knee.

"Of course you've had simple ginger biscuits before." Amusement tinged Una's words.

"No, actually, I've not. We don't have anything quite like this where I'm from." The harsh quality of his voice was so at odds with his features. It wasn't unpleasant in the least, just so different, and Aylee still wasn't used to it.

"And where exactly is this home of yours?"

If she raises her eyebrows any higher they'll disappear into her hair.

The wind chose just that moment to pick up to a screech as it raced through the exterior eaves.

"Umm . . . well . . . it's down the coast a way." He fidgeted just a little. It was the first sign of discomfort Aylee had seen from him since that first morning in the shed.

"Down the coast is not very specific."

"No. I don't suppose it is." He looked thoughtful for a moment. "In good weather, it's about a day's journey, I suppose."

"Oh, you're not from the city, are you?" Devon interjected. "Some of the lads from town get it in their head to leave and make their way to the city every now and again. Generally, they're looking for work or a new start. Not that I've anything against it. I just never took you for a city lad."

"No, Mr. Garrow. Not from the city. Close to it, I suppose, but also a world away it seems. I doubt you'd have heard of it. We call it Domanmara. I love it dearly."

He looked sad, and Aylee wanted nothing more than to reach up and place her hand on his cheek. Probably not the best plan with her folks watching.

Una looked anything but happy as it was.

"I see." Her mother stood and came a few steps into

the room. The firelight played against the lamps, causing shadows to rise and fall on her otherwise lovely face.

"Mr. Vann, I realize we appear to be a simple family from a simple town. I can assure you, however, we are not fools."

Aylee had no idea where this was coming from. Cailean had told her names held power, but what sort of power could his hometown have over her mother?

"Of course you aren't. I never—"

"Please let me finish." The wind howled, and a soft keening played back and forth in the confines of the room. Despite her shorter stature, Una towered over him as he sat looking up at her from the chair. "I don't know exactly what it is which has brought you to our doorstep, nor do I know what it is which is keeping you here. I do, however, know some of the folks here in town are already more than a bit wary of you. Devon and I don't know you well enough to judge, and clearly our Aylee holds you in some regard. Please don't think, for even one moment, we would let this affection of hers cloud our judgment. I will not allow anyone, or *anything*, to bring ill favor on my sweet girl."

"Oh, Momma. I can make some decent choices for myself you know." Aylee was simultaneously touched by her mother's protectiveness and frustrated by it. An image of a nude Cailean flashed into her mind. *Maybe not always decent choices.*

"I'm sure you can, Love. I just need Mr. Vann—from *Domanmara*—to know how things stand." Una looked pointedly at Cailean.

The way she said Domanmara, as if she knew of the place and hated everything about it, seemed odd to Aylee. She had never heard of it and couldn't imagine how her mother would be familiar with it.

"Mrs. Garrow. Please believe me when I say I have no intention of bringing any unpleasantness to Aylee or her lovely family." His earnest sincerity was obvious.

A SIMPLE TALE OF WATER AND WEEPING

The wind shrieked a long mournful bale. It sent shivers down Aylee's spine, and her heart raced in an unpleasant sickening way. That cold painful sound was full of sorrow, and she clearly was not the only one to feel it.

Una clutched at her breast, and Devon bent forward, placing his hands on his knees. Cailean took a deep breath and rubbed his eyes. He blinked and jerked into a more alert stance.

The wailing continued and took on a more song-like quality—a funeral dirge sung on operatic lips.

Pepper growled long and low, the hackles rising on her back.

It hurt Aylee's heart, this wind song. Something warm dripped onto her hands, and she realized salty tears were streaming down her face. "Oh . . . it sounds so sad."

Grief hung in the air and was broken only when Maeve rushed into the room.

"He must be dying! Don't you all hear it?" She looked around at them and cried out, "He must be dying!"

"Who, Maeve?" Una was up and wrapping her elder daughter in her arms.

"Graham. The rest of us are here. It must be Graham," she replied in anguish.

Confusion rippled through the room. Only Cailean looked intrigued rather than bewildered. Understanding dawned in Aylee. Her sister thought the wailing was a banshee. They weren't simply hearing the howling of the wind. It did continue to blow like a fiend outside, but she could pick out a soft lamenting lullaby lacing the storm with something much more powerful than Mother Nature's fury. How had she not noticed before? Her sister, who loved all the old tales and stories, thought a banshee was signaling the death of a loved one.

Maeve pointed to the window. "Can you not hear her? The harbinger of death? The banshee sings with the storm."

But it couldn't really be a banshee. They were just like

the other fey tales—scary stories to explain grief and sorrow to children.

"You can't know for sure Graham is in danger." Devon looked over his shoulder where he stood by the window. He turned back, though Aylee wondered how he could see anything in the thick rain and darkness which blanketed the town.

"It *could* be the wailing woman," Cailean admitted in his hoarse voice. "I've not heard her in some time, but it sounds and *feels* like her."

Aylee looked at him as if he had lost his mind. Cailean was buying into this fantasy as well?

"Momma, I need to go. Now. I need to get to the cottage." Maeve's voice was pitched too high and her mouth twisted with anguish. Aylee's heart broke a little for her sister.

"Be sensible, Maeve. The weather." Una's protest was feeble at best. Maeve wouldn't listen to her mother.

Devon had already grabbed his jacket and was reaching for his boots as he spoke. "I'll go to your house and bring Graham here. He may already be on the road if he hears it, too. He'll know you'll be worried. Stay here with your mother."

"I'll do no such thing, Da." The lament lulled a bit in its intensity. "I'm going, and you can't stop me."

Maeve, wrapped in a red shawl, grabbed a lantern and was out the door before Devon had even laced one boot. Something about the image of her fleeing out the door tickled at Aylee's thoughts, but she couldn't place what it was. Cailean was right behind Maeve.

"I'll try to see no harm comes to her."

The banshee's voice rose in crescendo, bringing a small sob from Aylee. Maybe they were right. No natural gale could bring such desperation to her body and soul.

She looked from the open door to her parents. Her mother started to object but sighed and waved her hand. "Go" the gesture implied.

A SIMPLE TALE OF WATER AND WEEPING

"Keep Pepper with you" was all she said.

FOURTEEN

Despite the fact Maeve was only twenty yards ahead, Aylee had a devil of a time making out her form in the wind and rain. Maeve had never been lazy, but she wasn't precisely athletic either. Aylee was surprised at how gracefully and quickly her sister ran through the night.

Cailean called out for her to slow, but it was to no avail. Maeve raced up the road with no hesitation, the wind and the rain soaking her hair and jacket.

As soon as Cailean and Aylee left the buffering presence of the town shops on the main street and stepped into the open stretch of road leading to Hydrangea Place and the surrounding cottages, the wind blowing in off the sea slammed into them. Despite the pressure of the storm in her ears, Aylee could still hear the banshee's lament, though little else. It drove into her bones—her soul—with the weight of a thousand years of suffering. She fought against the sobbing rising in her chest as if in reply.

Lightening flashed, and in the afterimage, she saw the shape of a woman huddled under an ancient oak further up the glen. She blinked the rain from her eyes and saw the silhouette of a large bird where the woman had been. She blinked again, and the darkness of the autumn night hid all of its secrets once more. She turned her head to the right, trying in vain to find either shape in the darkness. The momentary shift in her attention, along with the lightning's accompanying thunder, kept her from noticing a large divot in the road. She stumbled forward. Before her knees impacted on the hard ground, strong hands caught her around the waist.

Cailean pulled her upright and held her steady, perhaps a moment longer than was strictly necessary. She could feel him behind her as he muttered into her ear, "Have a care now."

A brief nod was all she could muster in response, and they were moving again, the sky coming down on them in fat drops of freezing liquid.

They managed to make up the distance with Maeve, and by the time she reached the cottage walkway, Aylee and Cailean were only a few yards behind. All three—four if you counted the dog—were soaked through, hair plastered to their heads and faces. Aylee's jacket weighed more than she did, and her trousers were sodden restrictive weights on her legs. Even Pepper had rivers of water streaming from her long coat. The lamps inside were lit, and soft yellow light filtered through the windows.

A sense of foreboding hung in the air. Would they open the cottage door to find Graham expiring on the floor? Or worse yet, find it empty and abandoned. What would they do then? Racing into the night, looking for any sign of his whereabouts sounded futile and dangerous.

Cailean placed a hand on Maeve's shoulder. "I can go first, if you like."

"No. I need to see." She stepped forward and put her hand on the knob, the banshee's song and howling wind seeming to nudge her forward. She turned the small iron handle and gasped as the door flung wide. The night sky came alive with the phosphorescent flash of lightning to reveal Graham—a healthy, whole, if somewhat disheveled Graham—standing in the doorframe.

Maeve threw her arms around him, the red shawl falling to the ground. Aylee watched the scarlet material land in a wet heap and opened her mouth to ask Maeve where she'd gotten it. Just as quickly she closed it—she had other things to worry about at the moment. They all did. Her sister was relieved, but the wailing continued.

"What's all this now? You'll catch your death." Graham stepped aside to let the water-logged trio into the cottage. He looked abashed as Pepper shook out her coat, sending water spraying all over the entry rug.

Maeve took in her husband. "You're unharmed." It was a statement and a question and an accusation all in one.

"Of course I am. It's only a storm." Graham was frowning at his wife.

"Do you not hear the wailing woman, Graham?" Maeve threw her hand toward the window as if the sound could be seen as well as heard.

"Is that the ruckus? I hadn't realized."

Aylee gave him points for knowing about the things which interested his wife but immediately took them back at his next statement.

"Even still, what is that to me? It's madness for you to come out in this storm. I thought you were staying at your parents."

"She's singing of death. I needed to make sure it wasn't your funeral she was heralding!" The emotion was rising in Maeve's voice. She had been truly frightened for Graham.

"You of all people should know it isn't only death she heralds, Maeve. You've all gone and put yourselves in danger just as sure as she sings." Graham wasn't exactly oblivious to his wife's suffering, but he didn't sound too consoling either.

Aylee and Maeve only looked blankly at one another. What was Graham talking about?

"But banshees aren't real. None of you are making sense. It's just faerie stories!" Aylee protested.

"Oh . . . of course." Cailean groaned and rubbed his eyes with the heels of his hands.

Aylee raised her eyebrows at him. *What now?*

"The wailing woman, or the banshee. Her lament. It doesn't only signify death. Or at least, it doesn't *always* only signify death. It can be a warning. In times of mortal peril, she may appear to warn those she has an obligation to protect or oversee.

"This may be a *warning*, not a tiding of death." The gravel had returned to his voice, adding a weight to his words.

Maeve took this in. "So I may have done nothing more than add to our danger by dragging us all out into this storm."

"Not necessarily. Perhaps the danger lay at the shop. We heard her singing there first. We need to get back and check on Da and Momma." Even as Aylee said the words, they didn't feel right to her. Was she really starting to believe this madness?

The wailing had intensified as they had raced toward the cottage. If the danger lay behind them, wouldn't the warning diminish? Nevertheless, she was moving toward the door.

"Don't be rash, Aylee." Graham said the words, but his tone implied he really couldn't be bothered to care one way or the other.

Cailean glared at him, and Aylee could feel the frost in the air.

"Graham's right." Maeve sighed. "Listen. She's still singing."

Indeed, Aylee could hear the crooning just as loudly as before, and just as it had previously, it brought a well of grief up from her core and a shiver through her body. Cailean placed his arm around her shoulders, attempting to bring a bit of warmth to her.

Graham took in the sight and turned to his wife.

"You may want to discuss with your sister just how inappropriate a picture this paints. I'm sure Rupert wouldn't be thrilled to know how comfortable she seems in *his* arms. I know I wouldn't be if I was in his place," he added pointedly.

Aylee opened her mouth to say something. The low

A SIMPLE TALE OF WATER AND WEEPING

growl coming from Cailean, however, said all she needed to say.

Maeve grew still and looked at her husband. She said icily, "I don't believe it is any concern of yours."

He simply shrugged, and Aylee could have sworn his eyes held sorrow.

"Back to the matter at hand." Aylee aimed to change the subject but did not attempt to move away from the solid wall of the man holding her. "If she is in fact real, how do we know which of us the banshee is trying to warn?"

"She *is* real, Aylee. You can hear her as much as we can. She can sing to any person who is losing a loved one in death." Maeve paused. "I'm trying to recall what the old stories say about warnings of danger."

"Well, I should think it's quite obvious," Graham said with his signature condescension.

Honestly, what does Maeve see in him?

"As *he* pointed out"—he sneered at Cailean—"she only sends portents to those whom she is obligated to protect."

The sadness in Graham only moments before had completely vanished, replaced by condescension and disdain.

"What exactly is your point, Graham?" Aylee was finding it harder and harder to remain patient with her sister's husband.

He turned once again to his wife. "Honestly, Maeve, I would have thought you of all people would know this. She is only obligated to protect those who are fey."

As the words hit their mark, all eyes turned to look directly at Cailean.

FIFTEEN

Cailean dropped his arm from Aylee's shoulder and stepped away from her. He couldn't look her in the eye. He should have explained long ago. Days ago.

"Cailean?" she asked him.

"I need to go" was his only reply.

"*Cailean?*" More demanding this time.

She placed her palm on his chest. He felt her warmth melt into his heart and knew he needed to leave before this got uglier than it already was.

"Aylee. I'm sorry." The ground glass of his voice was painful to his own ears. "Graham is right. I'm putting you in danger—all of you in danger. I didn't think. . ."

You think you know him, do you? You can't actually tell me you really know anything about him aside from he's an interesting dance partner and a stranger to this town. You know nothing that matters. Maeve's words rang through his head.

He stepped back from Aylee's touch, and a little part of his soul cried out at the loss. He moved toward the door. He needed to leave. Needed to drag whatever threat was trailing him as far away as he could.

"Once I'm gone, lock the door and stay with your sister. When the singing stops, you should be safe to travel home, but wait out the storm here just in case."

He didn't want to look at her. He needed to look at her.

"Cailean. I don't care. Whatever it is you don't want to say, I don't care. You're still my friend."

Oh lords, she was so kind. Kind and naïve. She didn't think it mattered! He couldn't bear to think how she would look at him when she realized just how wrong she was—when her feelings of friendship would surely turn to loathing and disgust.

He didn't speak, afraid his voice would betray his emotions. He shook his head in silent disagreement, grabbed a small lantern, and stepped out into the night.

If Graham was right—and Cailean was fairly certain he was—danger was following him. Short of losing his sanity, he wasn't sure what more could possibly befall him. His worst nightmare had already come true. Whatever was lurking in this terrible night, he needed to pull it as far from the small cottage, and those sheltering within, as he possibly could. He'd figure the rest out later.

He raised the lantern above his head and wiped rain from his eyes. He had no idea what kind of danger he was in so had little idea about which way to go. The part of him that loved the sea tugged him in the direction of the waves, and he let it dictate his movements. His mind tried to stay focused on the task at hand, but with every step toward the surf, a tumble of memories flooded him. Swimming in the shallows, chasing his brothers and sisters through the surf, avoiding danger, protecting his people, feeling the swells directing him, seeing the sun and the moon shimmering on the surface, having the chance to be something amazing. They flashed like bits of gold one after another, appearing and disappearing in quick succession. He could go back now. Nothing was stopping him.

A mantra began in his head, driving out all other thought. *To the sea. To the sea. To the sea.*

He quickened his pace, his body knowing the cool depths weren't far off. He would plunge into the icy waters and be at peace. He could already feel the frigid brine, sense the pull and the drag of the waves, smell the kelp and the coral in his nose. He knew the lullaby of the currents and ached, physically ached, to have the foam and the water embrace and caress every bare inch of him. He shucked his jacket to the side of the road and unbuttoned the front of his shirt. Felt the icy sting of the rain but paid it no mind. Knew in his head this would not end well but could not convince his soul to heed the warning.

To the sea. To the sea. To the sea.

The madness was overtaking him, but what did it matter? His secret was out, was it not? At least it seemed Maeve couldn't keep it from her husband, and soon the entire town might know. Aylee certainly would. And really, wasn't she all he cared about in this unfortunate village?

His steps became more urgent, and he tore into a run, rain and wind lashing him. The cry of the wailing woman grew louder and more frantic with each step he took toward the ocean. With every breath he drug into his lungs the wailing rose and shrieked. He would have liked nothing more than to find the wretched thing and silence the voice by any means necessary. Still the pull of the water was greater. *To the sea.*

Lightning seared the night, and the thunderous crash was a mere second behind. In the strobe of light he saw her. She stood perhaps twenty feet in front of him, blocking the path to the water. He skidded to a halt, not wanting to crash into her. All thoughts of silencing her wailing fled. Her long grey cloak was blowing not with the wind but against it. He could see her face as he slowly walked forward once more. Blood red lips matched her bloodshot eyes—worn crimson from centuries of weeping. Her skin was porcelain, her features delicate in their perfection. Long platinum hair, which should have been plastered to her head with rainwater, flowed and streamed behind her, perfectly dry in the deluge. In the next flash of light, he caught sight of her shadow on the ground. Enormous shadow wings stretched out to either side of her body.

She was simultaneously the most beautiful and the most abhorrent creature he had ever seen.

It made no difference. He needed to get around her. She couldn't stop him. Not when the waves were this close. *To the sea.*

The water beckoned to him just beyond her beautiful, deadly visage.

He stopped perhaps five feet from the banshee, her voice a soft caress in the frenzy of the storm. He could not make out the words, only the emotion. She raised her arms to her sides, the shadow wings spreading wide, blocking the path. She continued her lament. He understood. She was keeping him from the watery depths, saving him from himself—from what he'd almost done.

The mantra stilled. The call abated. He shook his head and drew a ragged breath.

"Thank you," he whispered.

She raised a hand and pointed at him, a long thick nail curved like a talon tipping her lovely, elegant finger. No, not pointing at him, but behind him. He turned to follow her gaze over his shoulder and heard a crack.

The world went dark.

SIXTEEN

Aylee paced back and forth in front of the cottage's small window. Her injured hand was throbbing, her eyes stung with tears, and her stomach twisted with nausea. The muscles in her back and shoulders ached with tension. Every note of the banshee song increased the strain, squeezing her heart and her spine with layers of sorrow.

Palpable tension filled the cottage itself. Shortly after Cailean had run from her—well not her per se, but that was how it felt—Maeve had looked at Graham with a frightening calmness. "We need to talk" was all she had said. He had nodded, and the two of them had stepped into the bedroom at the back of the cottage. Aylee had been left with dozens of questions and not a whisper of answers.

Graham had implied Cailean was fey, but how could it possibly be true? The fey weren't real, and even if they were somehow more than just silly superstitious stories, he held no outward signs of immortality. No pointed ears. No tail or feline eyes. And if he were in fact one of the faerie folk, why had it not come as a shock to either Maeve or Graham? If her sister had, by some chance, deduced this, why had she kept it to herself? When would she have known? And Cailean himself. He hadn't been offended or angry when the implication had been leveled. Did it mean he was admitting to the charge? But most importantly, why did he think it would make any difference to her? She could not care less. She thought they had formed a sort of friendship, and she would not abandon him if he needed her. Short of being a flesh-eating kelpie, there wasn't much she wouldn't overlook. Yet he had run out the door as if he couldn't stand being in her presence a moment longer. Presumably he had meant to draw the danger away from her and her sister, but what if it was something more?

What she did care about was that he might be in real danger. The weather was bad, and he was a stranger in town. Both the elements and some of the superstitious townspeople could pose a very real threat. He might need her assistance, and she had no way to find him.

She needed to think, to sort through the mess in her head. Being stuck in this cramped cottage was going to slowly drive her mad. It was too much to take—the sound of arguing from her sister and Graham, the crashing thunder and high surf, and the incessant wailing. . .

The incessant wailing. It had stopped. She paused and waited a moment. Listening intently, she cocked her head in the direction of the back bedroom. The arguing had hushed a bit, but the back and forth continued. They hadn't noticed the end of the banshee song, which was enough to tell her Graham and Maeve had quite a bit to say to one another. The tone of those hushed voices told her not all of it was kind.

Aylee decided it was time for her to go.

Maeve certainly was not in a position to interfere—not while she was embroiled in whatever was happening between her and Graham.

Beyond the walls of the cottage, the squall continued to rage, whipping the pale flowers lining the walkway into a thrashing mess. But with the quieting of the lament, Aylee knew what she needed to do. If the wailing woman had stopped singing, one of two things had happened. Either Cailean was safely out of harm's way and by association she should be too or whatever peril the banshee foretold had come to pass and her friend needed her help.

It was decided.

She ran into Maeve's small kitchen and grabbed a burlap bag. She wrapped some matches and candles in a piece of waxed paper and tied it with string. She placed the packet, along with a jar of whiskey, two apples, and a wedge of cheese into the sack. She also grabbed a hambone with some chunks of meat still attached and added it to the sack for Pepper. She tightened the laces on her boots and shouldered on her jacket, still sodden despite having been thrown over the hearth grate to dry.

With a quick look back at the muffled voices in the bedroom, Aylee smacked her leg to call Pepper to her. She let the dog run ahead as she closed the front door and ventured out into the storm.

She needed to decide which direction to go. If Cailean had truly intended to steer danger away, he likely would not have gone back into the heart of town or back toward the inn. That left two options. She could take the road to the distillery—Whiskey Road as it was called by the locals, another name in a nameless town—or she could search the rocky pathway to the shoreline. She knew he was a strong swimmer, but to risk the shoreline in this gale was madness. Cailean was quirky yes, but not mad. She opted for Whiskey Road.

Racing down the cobbles, away from the safety of the cottage, Aylee saw danger in every dark shadow and around every blind turn. Her world had made such a dramatic turn in the past two weeks. Gone were the quiet and occasionally dull days. All things held new possibilities, it seemed. Whoever, or whatever, Cailean was, he had brought excitement and even a little adventure to her life. She felt more awake and alive than she ever had before.

The road bent slightly to the right up ahead. One side was bordered by a low stone wall meant to keep sheep off the road. The other held a large stand of birch trees obscuring her view of what lay beyond. She slowed at the curve, meaning to take a moment to catch her breath and soothe the ache in her shoulder from holding her lantern aloft. She also needed to decide how far to go before turning back.

The birch leaves had mostly fallen and littered the

ground in great soggy clumps. A few still clutched the spindly limbs of the trees, and in the wind and rain they shook with a slurping wet rattle. Far off, she could hear the waves crashing against the rocky outcroppings along the shore. She picked up traces of what she thought might be voices under the other sounds but couldn't be sure. Her mind might be playing tricks on her, with the haunting voice of the banshee no longer filling it. She was still reeling from that cruel keening wail.

She raised the lantern away from her face, hoping to gain a few extra feet of eyesight. A creeping feeling shot through her as if she were being watched. She lowered the light and blew out the flame.

She stepped off the road and into the cover of the trees, whistling low to Pepper. The dog came to heel next to Aylee. Listening. There it was again. Definitely voices.

Ears straining, she could tell they were coming from the opposite branch of the road—from the direction of the shoreline—but still she could not decipher the words or the identities of the voices.

She wiped the rainwater from her eyes with the back of her hand, trying to see into the darkness. A bobbing light was making its way up the lane. The pace was slow and steady, no sense of urgency in the steps despite the arcs of lightning continuing to scorch the sky.

As the voices grew louder, she thought about calling out or stepping from her hiding spot. Perhaps whoever this was had seen Cailean and could point her in the correct direction. Something in the pit of her stomach, however, had her stepping back further into the cover of the trees. Who would willingly be out on a night such as this? Likely not someone she wished to bump into.

The rain continued to come down in buckets, dripping from the leaves and branches above her to soak through the thick layer of her jacket. Without the motion of her muscles to generate heat, she was shivering. She wouldn't be able to stay in this position for long.

A SIMPLE TALE OF WATER AND WEEPING

The light bobbed closer, and a small group came to the bend in the road. Two men who appeared to be carrying a third between them. Drunk perhaps? Shadows still kept their faces hidden, and the sounds of the storm distorted their voices. The third man's legs were dragging in the road behind his limp form. He must have been out cold.

A chill raced down her spine, having nothing to do with the frigid rain driving into the exposed skin of her neck and cheeks.

Aylee followed the trio with her eyes and shifted her weight from foot to foot, careful not to lift them, lest she make more noise and alert the men to her presence. She shifted again, attempting to bring some circulation to her aching toes. Why couldn't they move along faster, for saints' sake? She would be numb if she stayed hidden much longer, but to step out into the road would be awkward at best and dangerous at worst. She shifted again and the burlap sack fell from her shoulder. The sodden piles of leaves muffled the sound, but one of the men must have heard. His head snapped up, and he turned toward the stand of birches. Aylee leaned back, hoping to dissolve further into the shadows. She placed a hand on Pepper's head, willing her to remain silent.

"Who's there?" the shorter man asked. Aylee stayed still and silent as death.

"I said, who's there. Answer me damn it!" The voice was muffled but harsh.

Both men had thick knit caps pulled low on their heads and thick wool scarves wrapping around the lower portions of their faces. Only the one in the middle was uncovered, his shirt open to the navel. Rain drenched his bare chest and head, which hung at an angle that obscured his face.

"This ain't right. We should just leave him," the other man said.

"For shit's sake. We can't just leave him here. That isn't what the boss wants. We need to bring him farther up before we dump him," the first voice argued.

"He ain't my boss, and I'm tired of you acting like he is. There's someone or something out here. I'm too damn cold and tired to think about what it is. You can drag him farther up by yourself. I'm going home." Voice two was clearly done arguing.

"Let's at least get the bastard to the far side of the wall. We can tell him the bloke fought and got away."

This was not just some drunken friend the other two were dragging home after a night out with a bottle of spirits.

They hoisted the limp body over the low stone wall and unceremoniously dumped it into the grass and mud of the pasture. Seemingly satisfied, they walked off in the direction Aylee had just come, back toward the row of cottages and the rest of town beyond. Aylee waited in the shadows until they were out of sight and then ran to the abandoned man.

Mud squelched under her boots as she swung her legs over the wall. She knelt beside his limp form as her eyes tried to make out his features in the darkness. Somewhere behind her the sheep huddled together against the storm, their occasional soft noises rising to mix with the noise of the downpour.

Pepper ran back and forth on the other side of the fence. She could likely sense Aylee's tension.

Aylee placed her hands on the man's shoulder and attempted to roll him over. A low moan escaped his lips. As his face turned away from the wall, she made out the dark waves of hair framing the alabaster face and swore.

It seemed the banshee's warning hadn't been enough to protect Cailean after all.

SEVENTEEN

Aylee's attention was caught by a dark shadow obscuring a good portion of Cailean's face and neck. The rain caused the shadow to run in rivulets and drops from his skin. Not a shadow at all, but blood, made to look not red but black in the absence of light.

Who had done this to him? She fought the urge to race down the road and confront his attackers if only to know who they were. It would be foolish of course, and she might end up worse than her friend. Plus, she couldn't leave him here lying in the rain and the muck.

"Cailean. Can you hear me?" she whispered fiercely. "Please wake up. We need to get you inside. Somewhere safe."

His response was another soft moan. She pressed her fingers, made frigid by the deluge, gently against the side of his head and became nauseous when she felt a spongy soft lump above and behind his left ear. The movement elicited another louder moan.

She ran her fingers blindly down the back of his head, lifting it gently from the ground to do so. She searched his face and upper body for other signs of damage. After completing her quiet palpation, she decided the lump on his scalp was the only obvious injury. Not wanting to risk the continued exposure and possible hypothermia, she would need to get him indoors.

"Cailean. We need to move. I need you to wake up and help me. Please." She didn't like the pleading in her voice.

His eyelids fluttered, accompanied by another groan. He blinked once, twice. His eyes began to focus on her face.

"Aylee?" he rasped. "Why'd you hit me?"

Simultaneously giddy with relief and terrified at what had happened to him, she huffed out, "I didn't hit you!"

And if she hadn't spooked his assailants? What would have become of him then?

"My head certainly feels like you hit me." He closed his eyes again briefly.

"It was voice one and voice two." She helped him sit up, back braced against the wall. "Or rather a couple of men. I watched them drag you up from the shoreline road and dump you here and run off back toward the village."

"That makes more sense, I suppose." He shook his head slightly, as if to clear his thoughts, and winced in pain.

"You suppose? We need to get inside. This rain isn't letting up." As if to emphasize her point, a crack of thunder crashed through the night. "Do you think you can stand?"

"Let's go." He began to stand but wobbled on unsteady legs.

Aylee immediately scooped his arm over her shoulder and steadied him. She shifted her small bag and grabbed the lantern with her free hand. At this point it was useless. Even if she dared to light it, the wick would be drenched. She couldn't leave it behind though. It might be needed later.

Where to go? The cottage seemed the quickest, but she was still unsure about the accusation Graham had leveled at Cailean, in addition to whatever tension existed between Maeve and her husband. She absolutely did not want to be in the middle of it right then. Whiskey Road ended at the distillery, but she'd be damned if she was going to ask Rupert to help them. It was likely only the night watchman at the distillery anyhow. Then there was town. She could make it home relatively quickly, but the men who had knocked Cailean unconscious had gone in the same direction, and she couldn't risk running into them. To the shore then? A small cave near the base of the cliffs would give them space. It would be damp and cold but would provide some shelter.

It hit her then. She'd been within a stone's throw of a warm, dry place this entire time. The shearing shed. Not more than a hundred yards up into the pasture was a small wood-framed shed used by the folks in town when they needed to collect the wool from their flocks. It wasn't perfect, but it would do.

She had to raise her voice to a near yell to make sure Cailean heard her over the howling wind. "We can duck into the old shearing shed! It's not much, but the roof is solid and there's a hearth. We can wait out the worst of it there."

In the short time it took to help Cailean through the grassy pasture, Aylee's boots and trousers became thoroughly caked in mud and manure. The rain had finished its progression through her jacket, blouse, and underclothes as well. She hoped the waxed paper parcel was faring better.

The worn pine door opened with a creak. When they stepped inside, the darkness was absolute. She fumbled along the wall until she felt the small hearth with her foot. She bent down and felt the pile of kindling waiting there. The shepherds were good about making sure things would be ready for the next occupant. Her fingers closed around a blessedly dry tinderbox sitting beside the stone fireplace. She struck a match and nearly cried with relief when the flame lit up the immediate area. She placed the match to the kindling, and within a few heartbeats a small fire crackled in the tiny shed.

Her body was shaking violently with cold, and her damaged hand did not want to cooperate, making it difficult to unfasten the buttons on her jacket and boots. After a few minutes of struggling, she finally got them off and placed them on the hearth grate to begin the drying process. She looked to Cailean, expecting him to be doing the same. Instead of removing his soaked clothing, he was simply watching her. She blushed slightly at his gaze.

"Give it here. It'll dry faster by the fire." His shirt was already unbuttoned when she'd found him, his jacket missing completely, yet he hesitated to remove the saturated garment.

"So now you're shy?" She chuckled. "Have you forgotten how I found you the day we met?"

He sighed and pulled the shirt from his torso.

He was glorious without his shirt. She only realized she was staring when he smirked at her—a smaller version of his lopsided grin. She turned away quickly, needing to focus on something else.

She tried to take quick stock of the shed. She'd only ever been inside once before when she'd gone with Deirdre to take some lunch to Robbie. At the time, she was too distracted by the sight of the sheep being sheared to really notice what the shed contained.

A low bench sat along one wall near the door opposite the hearth. It was a wonder she hadn't tripped and gone sprawling as she entered the space. Cailean rested there, leaning his injured head back against the wood slat wall. A table with various tools used for animal husbandry took up the far corner. Aylee searched the small cupboard next to it and found little of use other than a thick woolen blanket, ripe with the musty odor of years without washing. She placed it on the floor in front of the fire, and Pepper promptly claimed her space on it. She put her face on her paws and sighed out a breath.

Aylee sat next to her dog, her back to Cailean, and tried to control her shivering. She ran her hands up and down the wet sleeves of her blouse.

Cailean's voice held no note of humor or teasing. "I won't look if you want to take it off."

She thought about it but sighed. "Probably best if I don't."

She sensed rather than heard him as he pushed off

from the bench and came to sit beside her on the floor.

"Let me take a peek at your head." She touched his scalp gingerly, and he winced again. The rain had washed away most of the blood, and it didn't seem to be oozing. Thank the saints for small favors.

He didn't look at her as he said stiffly, "It'll heal soon enough. Don't fret."

She glanced sidelong at him. "What happened back there?"

It was many questions rolled into one. What happened at the cottage and why had he not denied the accusation of being fey? Why had he run off? What had become of the banshee, and who had delivered the blow to his head?

He blew out a long breath before he spoke. "When I left, I thought it best to avoid heading back into the village. I've always felt safest by the sea and made my way in its direction. I was almost to the tide wall when I saw the wailing woman. Her singing was more frantic than it had been, and she stopped me before I could . . . do something rash." He paused and took another long breath. "Anyway, I saw her standing there and, Aylee, you can't imagine it. She was . . . destroying? No, not right. She was . . . devastating . . . in her beauty but also so terrible at the same time. I've never seen her before, and I hope never to see her again."

Aylee didn't think many people had ever seen a banshee, but she kept quiet.

The fact he chose not to address what Graham had said did not slip past her. She'd let him talk, and if he didn't acknowledge it, she'd ask him when he was done.

He looked haunted. "I thought she was protecting me from myself."

She remained quiet. She hoped, whenever he was ready, he would tell her what he meant by that as well.

"I let my guard down. It's not something I do in general. I can't let my guard down. But tonight I did. And someone decided to bash my skull in. I think maybe with a bottle? Not sure. The next thing I knew, I woke up to a face full of grass and a demon of a headache."

"And you don't know who did it? Who hit you?" she asked.

"No. I didn't get a good look, but even if I did, I only know a handful of the people in town. You said you saw them too. You couldn't tell?"

She shook her head. "Their faces were covered, and I can't think of anyone who would deliberately attack you."

Her teeth were practically chattering, but at least her feet were getting warm, stretched out in front of her toward the fire as they were. A small spider crawled along the front of the blanket. She gently nudged it into a corner of the room.

She grabbed the small sack and removed its contents. The waxed paper had held up remarkably well, and it took only two tries before Cailean removed the matches from her trembling hands and lit one of the candles. He placed it in a tin holder and set it on the bench behind them. It helped illuminate the remaining darkness in the small space.

Aylee placed the apples and cheese on the bench as well, tossed the hambone to Pepper, and held onto the jar of whiskey. It probably wasn't wise to drink too much, but a few sips would help warm her from the inside.

She unscrewed the lid and took a quick sip of the fiery liquid. Hands still shaking, but less violently, she handed the jar to Cailean. He looked quizzically at her and then tipped the glass to his lips, wincing as the liquid slid down his throat. She smiled at his expression as he returned the whiskey to her.

Taking another slightly large drink, she sighed. "I'd love nothing more than a hot bath right now."

He frowned a bit. "A hot bath? Really, why?"

"Why?" she asked. "Are you serious?"

"Very."

"Aside from the fact I'm freezing to death and smell

like manure? Because a lovely hot bath is one of the most glorious things in the entirety of the world. Some salts and a little lavender oil . . . it's just heavenly." She closed her hazel eyes and smiled; just thinking about it made her warm and content.

"I see." He cleared his throat and smiled at her. "You love a good hot bath. What else do you love?"

The rain had steadied into a persistent cadence on the roof, but thunder still boomed outside.

"Well, I suppose I love my parents. I love Maeve."

"Doesn't count. Of course you love them. They're your family."

She frowned. "I think it counts. Not everyone loves their family."

"I suppose. *Beside* your family, what do you love? And not Pepper—that's also a given." He asked as if he genuinely cared. The earnest expression made her want to answer him truthfully.

She thought for a moment, chewing on her lower lip.

"I love thunderstorms. Or at least I did, until tonight. Now I'm not sure how I feel about them. I love warm scones with thick cream oozing out the sides. I love to snuggle into my bed after a long day and quietly read without anyone interrupting the fantastic images the words conjure in my head. And the sea. Most of all I love the sea." She could tell him these things so easily. Partly because she wanted to tell him, but partly because he was actually interested in the answer. She smiled but felt a tear slip from the corner of her eye at the same time.

"Don't be sad," he said quietly, his voice low and hoarse. "You love the sea? Why?"

She didn't answer right away.

He cleared his throat. "Most folks I've encountered around here at least fear, if not outright hate, the ocean. I can't understand it."

It was true. She imagined it was because of how small the vastness of the ocean made people feel, how quickly it could sweep you out and away from land. How easily it could pull a person under, stealing the very air from their lungs. But she also thought it had something to do with the superstitions and the scary stories of kelpies, mers, and sirens waiting to pull a hapless person to their death.

Rather than all of those truths, she told him a different set.

"The sound it makes when the waves crash on the rocks. How it can be temperamental—calm or raging depending on its mood. The smell of the salt and the sense of stillness it brings me. The feel of the water on a warm summer day as it slides over my skin. But most of all, the endless expanse of beautiful color—teal, slate, and cobalt—and aquamarine. Colors just like. . ." She stopped before she finished.

"Just like?" he prompted.

"Nothing." Heat had risen in her cheeks, and she looked down at her hands.

"Obviously not nothing," he said quietly. "Just like what?"

She debated for a moment and softly said, "Your eyes. Just like your sea-colored eyes."

"Aylee. . ." He had turned to face her while she spoke and raised his hand to cup her face. His thumb stroked over her bottom lip, and those beautiful cobalt and aqua eyes drank in every inch of her face. She wasn't so cold anymore.

The firelight was flickering in her strawberry waves, making them flash golden and amber and red all at once. He blinked and took a deep breath. "I really would like to kiss you right now."

"I really would like for you to kiss me right now." Her voice was a breathy whisper.

"I would like to . . . but I can't." He dropped his hand from her cheek. She felt the absence like the sting of nettles in her skin.

"You can't kiss me?" Aylee looked at him with a mix of

amusement and incredulity. "Dare I ask why? You seem to have a set of perfect lips." Her face flushed with embarrassment. "Perfectly working I mean. Well, except for the words, but I imagine that hasn't anything to do with your actual lips."

He chuckled, and with the hoarseness in his voice, it should have been an unpleasant sound. It wasn't unpleasant at all.

"Mechanically speaking, yes, I am capable of kissing you."

"More than capable I'd wager." Her voice almost too low for him to hear.

"You aren't making this easy," he chided her. "I am capable, but I have promised myself not to engage in any romantic endeavors while I'm here."

Her face fell. "Oh. I see. You're spoken for." When he didn't seem to understand, she added, "There's someone else. Back home?"

"No. It isn't that. I just. . . It might be easier if there were."

She waited. Patient. Expectant. Hopeful. It all flashed on her lovely freckled face.

He cleared his throat. "I need to tell you something first." He carefully took her injured hand and raised it, giving the bruised flesh just the barest brush of his lips, and placed it back in her lap.

"I'm not sure that was the kind of kiss I had in mind," she grumbled, causing a slight smile to curve his mouth.

"If after I tell you what I need to say—if then you still want a different kind of kiss—I'll be more than happy to oblige." Something in his tone told Aylee he didn't believe she would.

"Deal."

He ran his hand through his hair. "I'm not sure where to start."

She handed the whiskey to him, an offering of liquid courage. "I find starting at the beginning, before the hard part, sometimes helps."

"That's just it. The beginning *is* the hard part." He looked at her and seemed to gain a bit of strength from whatever he saw on her face. "Okay. The day we met—the first day we met—I was lost and confused. Do you remember?"

She nodded. Of course she remembered. How could she forget?

"I imagine I seemed like some sort of raving lunatic. I'm still shocked by how well you handled finding me in your storeroom, given my state of, well . . . my appearance. I mean it when I say I will never forget your kindness to me. Not just because you were decent and helpful, but because I was so completely out of my mind and I needed to be reminded of how good people behave."

Aylee must have looked confused because he shook his head and tried again.

"I was lost that morning, physically and mentally and emotionally. I had a very important part of my soul taken, and I was completely at a loss for what to do. I wanted to track it down and kill whoever had stolen it from me." Not one misspoken word. It had to be a record.

"Cailean, you aren't making any sense. You told me that morning you were seeking a way home, but you kept mentioning your coat? Start there."

"Right. Let me back up a bit. The night before we met, I had been down on the shore with my family. My brothers and sisters brought me to the beach as a kind of celebration. Back home, I had just received some good news. I had been chosen to serve our ruler as a personal guard. For my people, it's a great honor to be chosen, and I'm one of the youngest guards in the past three hundred years. I've spent much of my life training and serving as a guard in lower courts, always hoping I would be chosen to rise to the rank of Queen's Guard. My brother has been a Queen's Guard for a long time, and I wanted nothing more than to serve alongside Declan. I am to begin my service on the winter solstice.

"I was having perhaps the most magical night of my life. I don't get the chance to visit the shore too often, but I have always loved it, and I wasn't sure when I'd get the chance to do so again. So I ventured off to look at the rocks and caves. We had a tight timeline, but I was distracted by the lights of the town and the feel of the night around me. As the night turned silvery in the dawn light, I made it back to the beach just before the sun rose. My family members were already dispersing as I went to fetch my *cotabonn*—my coat—from the sand where I'd left it. It was gone. Just gone.

"I was frantic. I never take it off, not for long. We're taught from an early age not to. That night I just wanted to feel free, and I left it lying in the sand like a—what is it your lads in town say? A *pissing idiot*." He said the phrase clearly enough.

"I couldn't find it anywhere, and I wouldn't be able to return to Domanmara without it. All I have ever worked for, everything I am, was gone in the blink of an eye. My life would be forfeit. I followed you home that morning, Aylee. I thought perhaps you knew where it was. I was prepared to retrieve it anyway I could."

Aylee still felt confused. "You followed me home, naked through the streets, for a piece of *clothing*? I don't understand how a jacket can make the difference in when you return home. Is it a uniform or something you'll get in trouble for?"

"Not a jacket, Aylee. A coat. *My cotabonn*." His eyes pleaded with her, willing her to understand what he was saying without it actually being said.

When she still did not understand, he said in a dry soft voice, "I'm a selkie, and without my coat I can *never* return to my people. *Never* return to the sea."

EIGHTEEN

Aylee was quiet for a moment, letting his words sink in. A selkie? Of all the scenarios she'd played in her head in the past several hours, Cailean being a selkie had not been one of them. Her mind went back to the conversations with Maeve and Graham.

You think you know him, do you? You can't actually tell me you really know anything about him aside from he's an interesting dance partner and a stranger to this town. You know nothing that matters.

Honestly, Maeve, I would have thought you of all people would know this. She is only obligated to protect those who are fey.

And then Cailean's own words came back to her. *If after I tell you what I need to say, if you still want a different kind of kiss. . .*

Aylee ran through the list of Maeve's favorite stories in her head. Banshees were terrifyingly bleak. The faeries were cunning, cruel, and beautiful. The sprites and pixies mischievous. The trolls wicked. The kelpies eaters of flesh. And the selkies? Well . . . Aylee did not remember many of the fey stories to the same degree as her sister, but she did recall most of the details of the selkies. Most of the young people did. They were lurid and scandalous.

Selkies were seducers, coming ashore to steal the virginity of young maidens and to lure husbands away from faithful wives. They provided release for those who sought their company, often gifting illegitimate babies to barren women only to return to the cold waters after the seeds had been planted.

These weren't the sort of stories told to young children to keep them on the path and away from the cliff's edge. They were the ones mothers whispered to blushing brides the night before their weddings and the kind drunken boys fabricated when boasting to their friends. Tales of stolen kisses and ruined lives.

Cailean couldn't be a selkie. He just couldn't be.

Cailean saw the frown on her face and in her eyes. His heart broke just a little. He'd known it was coming, but to see it so plainly was worse than he'd anticipated.

"And now you know my dirty secret. I've been washed up from the sea and left here to flounder and dry." He turned away from her, and his shoulders slumped even more.

Aylee couldn't know the toll the confession took on him, but she sat up straighter and asked quietly, "Why didn't you tell me sooner?"

"Because of the expression on your face, Aylee. I did not want to see that particular expression on your face. Not when you look at me." His voice was hard.

"I'm sorry. It's just a shock. I thought you were just a normal person. A person I'd like to get to know better. Then Graham made his fey comment, and I thought, 'This can't be right. He's not fey, he's just Cailean.' And now I learn you're not only fey but a *selkie*?" Her voice cracked on the last word.

"The worst of the worst," he agreed.

"Don't say it like that," she snapped at him.

"Like what, Aylee? Should I just pretend I don't know the stories you've obviously been told? Right now you are thinking I am the worst kind of wicked, aren't you?" His normally alabaster skin was flushed a deep rose as his anger flowed. "You're thinking how all this time I was just waiting for my chance to get under your skirt."

"Why are you being such a horse's arse? You drop this on me, and I'm just supposed to accept it with a sweet dumb smile on my face?" Her temper was flaring as well.

"I never said you had to accept it. In fact, I know you shouldn't accept it. Why should you? My people are the debauchers of innocents. As far as you know, you were next on my list. Never mind the fact I don't even have a list."

"What does that even mean?" she cried.

"Forget it. I just didn't want you to think I was after more from you than I am. You were so damned kind and sweet, and I didn't want you to be disgusted by me."

"I never said I was disgusted!" She threw her hands up in the air.

"Not with words, you didn't. You have a very expressive face."

Aylee turned her *expressive* face away. "You'll need to forgive me my face, I suppose! If I were fey and not human, maybe I could hide it better."

He stilled. "You don't think I'm human?"

"Fey aren't human."

"I'm just as human as you are." He sighed, all the fight leaving him. This was worse than even he thought it could be. "Aylee. Look at me."

He gently turned her to face him again. The heat of her skin on his hands was both soothing and torturous.

"Really look at me. I am just as much a man as Ian or Rupert or your father for that matter. Being fey—banshee, warlock, naiad, even faerie or selkie—doesn't make me not human. It just makes me a different kind of person."

The non-human creatures, the sprites, trolls, goblins, and the like were a whole other story, but he didn't have the energy for that at the moment.

Aylee looked at him skeptically. He was concerned she would think this was just some other trick or half-truth.

"It's about the magic we wield, not the blood in our veins," he said.

She crossed her arms over her chest and looked at him from the corner of her eye. "If you had just told me."

"When should I have told you? The day I showed up naked in your home? I doubt that would have gone over too well. Or maybe the night you broke it off with the old man you were going to marry?" Hurt flashed across her face as if he'd struck her, but still he couldn't stop. "Or how about the time you watched me swimming in the ocean with my family? Should I have crawled on shore with the tears still in my eyes, knowing I would likely never get to go back where I truly belong, and told you then?

"I'm telling you now. As much as I hate the way you will forever look at me, I'm telling you now." His voice broke as the wind went out of him and with it the blossom of hope he'd carried the past several days.

He could tell by her expression Aylee had not known he'd seen her the day on the shore or that he had been in such pain at the time. Her words from earlier in the evening—was it really only a few hours ago—came back to him. *I don't care. Whatever it is you don't want to say, whatever it is you are, I don't care. You're still my friend.*

Could she live up to those words?

"I know it was unrealistic of me, but I had hoped you would be different." Would she hear and feel the anguish and disappointment in his voice?

The tension didn't leave her exactly, but it softened like grass in the morning dew.

"I hope I am, too. Different, I mean." She faced him again. "Thank you."

He tilted his head. "For what?"

"For trusting me enough to tell me." Her face was contemplative. "I don't know exactly what to say . . . but I do know I am happy to listen. And for the record, I am not disgusted by you."

She was so matter of fact. Could it truly be so easy? He didn't think so, but he hoped so. A small pressure was building in his chest.

"I should have told you before. I'm not sure what to say now. You humble me."

"You know, you didn't stumble on your words at all. You said everything you needed to and never lost the words. I wonder if it's because you were talking about you.

About who you truly are. In here." She placed a hand on his chest but drew back quickly.

"I do have questions. Soooo many questions!" Her beautiful hazel eyes lit up, and he knew, just knew, his voice would be a gnarled wreck by the time he finished answering everything she'd want to know. Perhaps he'd get lucky and the storm would let up sooner rather than later.

NINETEEN

The storm did not let up quickly. The small clock hanging above the tool table had read nine when Aylee first lit the fire, and its hands were well past one when she was satisfied enough in her queries to place her head on her arm and shut her eyes. Cailean had been as truthful as he could as he told her all the things she wanted to know.

He stood and stretched, twisting his back from side to side, each movement making the muscles of his sleek torso move in the firelight. He grabbed another log from the side of the hearth and tossed it into the flames, hoping it would burn long enough to keep them warm until daylight. He grabbed his now-dry shirt and shrugged it on just in case the fire died out while he slept.

Pepper whined, and her paws fluttered as if she were chasing rabbits in her sleep.

"They'll be so worried. My parents." Not asleep yet then.

"Maybe not. They might just think you stayed the night with your sister." He settled back down on the ground next to her, leaning back on his hands.

"You don't know my da," she huffed. "The minute the singing stopped, I'm sure he was off to Maeve's. By now, they probably think I've thrown myself into the sea or something."

"We can go now if you like."

When she yawned and her eyes drifted closed, he amended, "Try to get some sleep. First light we will get you home. I promise."

He brushed the strands of coppery hair from her face.

"You haven't fulfilled your end of our bargain yet." She

looked up at him through thick lashes and smirked. "You still owe me a different kind of kiss."

"Oh? Oh!" Realization dawned in his eyes. "Really?"

"Really."

He waited only a heartbeat to lean down, and slowly, ever so slowly, brushed his lips across her forehead, each closed eyelid, behind one ear and up the line of her jaw, stopping before his lips brushed hers. She sighed softly, and he pulled back and murmured, "Get some sleep, Aylee."

Just before she drifted off, he heard her softly whisper, "I've decided I still love thunderstorms." Then she was out.

The rain finally ebbed sometime in the early hours of the morning. The fire in the hearth had gone out too. Aylee woke as the first light of dawn slowly crept into the shed. Her muscles were stiff and sore from sleeping on the cold ground. Cailean remained slumbering beside her.

She let him continue to rest as she cleared out the remains of the fire and laid a new set of kindling in its place, ready for the next person in need of the space. After she was satisfied things were in order, she gently ran her fingers through Cailean's hair. No trace of the lump from the previous night remained. *Must be nice.* She stretched her own bruised fingers and grimaced at the plum discoloration of her fingernail.

Pepper stretched and yawned and rubbed her cold nose against Cailean's exposed neck.

He awoke with a start but smiled up at her.

"I hate to wake you, but I need to get back to the shop." Dread filled Aylee when she thought of her parents waiting for her.

"Right." He rubbed the sleep from his eyes.

Aylee tucked the woolen blanket back in the cupboard, and Cailean shouldered her small burlap sack. The morning air was fresh and clean, the smell of the wet grass and trees mixing with the ocean fog. It was just this side of cold but not biting.

When they reached the back door to the shop, Aylee suggested she handle her parents alone. She didn't think the sight of Cailean would in any way help her with the questions they were sure to have. If they'd been up all night as she'd suspected, she didn't think they would be in good humor at all. She just didn't anticipate quite how livid they would be.

TWENTY

Ian Cormack stood in the alley behind the mercantile. He had come early to catch Aylee when she inevitably went to the beach to gather clams and was surprised to hear her voice coming from up the lane rather than from the back of the mercantile. When he'd walked the short distance from his home, he'd planned exactly how this conversation would go—each thing he would say and precisely how Aylee would respond. The voices caught him off guard, and his carefully planned dialogue flew from his mind. He panicked and ducked into the shadowy space between the Garrows' storage shed and the neighboring shop.

He knew deep down he'd hurt her last spring, but he also knew—in his heart—she would forgive him eventually. It was the kind of person she was. What he had done might have seemed unacceptable at the time, but it had been done with her in mind. She simply hadn't understood the pressure he was under. If he gave her just a bit of time, he would make her see his side of things. Inevitably she would realize these past months had been difficult for them both and they would not be repeated. When she finally understood, he would be able to win back the girl he wanted to marry.

He had planned to ask her to let him help with the clamming. When he saw her round the building with the bloke from the jubilee, he wasn't sure what to think. The dark-haired stranger laughed low, and Aylee elbowed him in the ribs, laughing in return. She looked happy, and the sight of it made Ian distinctly *unhappy*. He stepped back further into the doorway, all thoughts of a pleasant morning evaporating with the ocean fog.

A SIMPLE TALE OF WATER AND WEEPING

"Where the hell have you been?" Devon Garrow's face flashed a brief moment of relief before the anger overtook him. "We've been frantic all night!"

Una just hugged her daughter quickly and turned away. She seemed too upset to speak.

"I know. I'm so sorry. We just got caught out in the storm and—"

Devon didn't let her finish. "Caught out in the storm, my ass, Aylee. I went to Maeve's, and she told me how you chased out after Cailean. You could have been killed."

"He needed help—"

"And where exactly have you two been? I asked Ned, and he says not at the inn. Not at Violet's. Not at Maeve's. So tell me. Where?" Her father's face was a sort of puce color. A small pulsing vein stood out on his temple.

"I'm trying to tell you, but you keep interrupting me." She'd never seen her father so angry. Her mother didn't even look at her. She knew it would be bad, but this was terrible. Aylee swallowed the acid rising in her stomach.

Her voice was small. "You asked around at all of those places?"

"Of course I did. By the time I got to Maeve's, the storm was really picking up and you were gone. She said you left without even telling her."

"I was going to tell her, but she was . . . preoccupied. Half the town must know by now. I'm so sorry." Aylee's stomach churned. Her mother was pacing back and forth, looking at the ceiling, the floor, out the window, anywhere but at Aylee. Pepper just lay in the corner, head on her paws.

"Where were you, Aylee?" her father ground out one more time.

"Someone attacked Cailean. I wasn't sure where to go, and I was scared they'd come back so we went to the shearing shed to wait out the storm." She wanted her parents to understand.

"What do you mean attacked?" he asked, a hint of concern in his voice.

"Someone struck him in the back of the head and knocked him out. They were dragging him off somewhere when I found him."

"Who would do such a thing?" His voice, while inquisitive, implied he might not believe her.

"I don't know. Two voices. I couldn't make out the faces. I thought to bring him here, but they had come this way. I needed to get him somewhere out of the rain so he could rest. I was scared and couldn't think of anywhere else that might be safe."

"The shearing shed was the safest place you could think of?" Finally, her mother spoke, her voice soft and tired. "Safest from prying eyes at least?"

The words stung.

"What's that supposed to mean?"

"You know exactly what it's supposed to mean."

Aylee did in fact know exactly what her mother was implying. That was what they thought of her?

"You aren't a child any longer. I suppose we should have seen this coming."

"I. . ." She was at a loss for how to respond.

"We spoke to Maeve. We know what he is." Her father's voice had lost some of its anger.

Aylee frowned. She had surmised Maeve and Graham both knew Cailean was fey—but hadn't imagined they knew what particular form of fey.

"And what precisely did she tell you?"

"The truth. She told us he's a selkie, as if I *needed* her to tell me that. He's from Domanmara after all." Her mother practically spat the words out.

How could she possibly know anything about Domanmara or selkies or fey in general? All this time Aylee supposed everyone thought the stories were tall tales and granny stories just like she did. Obviously, her family had other ideas or knowledge. Her head was spinning.

Either way, it didn't change the fact her parents thought she and Cailean were doing things they shouldn't be.

"I see. So just like that I'm not the daughter you thought I was? Everything I have ever done means nothing?" Aylee tried to control the wobble in her voice. She was going to break down if this didn't end soon. "I was trying to *help* him. He *needed* my help. Why is that so difficult to believe?"

"Whether or not we believe you is not the point," her mother bit back.

"To me it is." Aylee looked at both of them. In this place, where they had always supported her. Always been loving. Always taught her about the kind of person she should be.

"All those times you told me how important it is to be caring and respectful to others, to be compassionate because you may not know what someone was going through. Did you mean only to be kind to people from town? People like you?"

"Of course not. We want you to be who you are and to do the right thing, but we also know how the world works. How people react in particular situations. And I don't mean just young people such as you and Cailean. I mean we know how people will talk and how they will act toward you both," Devon said. "Not everyone in town is understanding of outsiders, and once they know the kind of outsider Cailean is . . . It won't end well, Aylee."

"It seems you and Momma have already decided the gossips are right." Her voice sounded as dejected as she felt.

"If you say nothing happened, we'll believe you, Love. But you know it's going to be tough for you and worse for Cailean."

Aylee was thankful her mother had calmed a little.

Una added, "Rupert certainly won't have you now."

Aylee's temper rose again. "I don't care what Rupert Camden thinks of me." She didn't raise her voice, but the strength of the words held a venom unlike any her parents generally heard from her. "I thought we were done with this discussion. I don't love him. I am not going to marry him. The idea of being his breeding mare is revolting."

"Aylee..." Caution laced her father's tone.

"And I can't imagine what poor Ian will think," her mother added.

Poor Ian? Clearly Aylee had never really grasped how important it was to her parents that she get married off soon. Her future was never really supposed to be her own. They hadn't even liked Ian all that much and had as good as told her they thought she could do better. Was better richer, or did they actually care if she was miserable and unloved for the rest of her life?

"Ian broke my heart for a few extra coins in his pocket" was all she said.

"That's not fair," her father replied.

"No. No, it's not. I deserved better." She deliberately misunderstood her father's words. "Cailean is more decent a man than I've met in this town. And he didn't even have to seduce me for me to think so."

A hush fell. She didn't typically speak so crassly and certainly not in the presence of her parents. Her mother looked mortified, and her father's face had turned a brighter shade of scarlet, the vein furiously pounding in his forehead. She'd gone too far. Too late now.

"I'm going for a walk." She strode to the door, leaving her parents in stunned silence. "Come on, Pepper."

TWENTY-ONE

The conversation with her parents would not leave Aylee's mind as she plodded toward the stretch of beach know as the strand. Misunderstandings, old prejudices, fear and love and magic—they had combined to make a strange brew that neither Aylee nor her parents knew how to stomach. Once she allowed the salty air to bring her temper down, she could understand their concern if not their harsh reaction. She hoped upon her return to the shop they would be able to talk more civilly and vowed to mend what she could with them.

The strangest bit was how wrong they were in thinking Cailean was anything less than the respectful man he had presented himself to be. She was certain it was no act, and if she were honest, they should fear her motives more than those of the young fey stranger. Perhaps they'd been right to assume the worst of her, but certainly not the worst of him.

The entire history of the situation was intriguing. Cailean had spent a good portion of the previous night enlightening her to some of the more interesting slices of the selkie histories as well as the general fey stories she'd grown up thinking were just that—stories.

According to Cailean, however, all of the stories were at least partially based in fact, if not entirely accurate. Centuries ago, magic was as common as grass on a hill or pebbles in a stream, and people learned to harness the magic for specific purposes. The faeries used it for power, wealth, and beauty, while others—including the selkies—shaped it to allow them freedom and adventure. Over time, the magic became so ingrained in the wielders it was

A SIMPLE TALE OF WATER AND WEEPING

passed down from generation to generation.

Despite its common use, many people remained wary of magic and never dabbled with it. They were content to live without the powerful influence—preferring to rely solely on their own strength, wisdom, and character. A divide began between those non-magic humans and the group commonly known as fey.

Several hundred years ago, the magic began to dry up. Many speculated it was like any other natural resource—if used with good stewardship it might have stayed abundant, but when wasted and taken for granted, it became scarce. Those fey who were the strongest were able to keep their magic by limiting its use and tightening the lines of succession in their families. Many went into hiding for fear of being attacked and having their troves of magic stolen. Brutal killings and kidnappings of unguarded wielders ensued, by those who sought to take and use the magic—much like a starving man might kill for bread for his family.

Many of the water fey—the selkies, merrows, and the like—had taken to the oceans during these times. Knowing many who sought their power would be unable to battle them at sea, they were content to live mainly in the waters, only coming to land when necessary. A hierarchy developed over the years, with the strongest of the water fey elevated to royalty and the others happy to serve as their subjects.

The selkie population had always been limited, and in time, the bloodlines needed refreshing. Many visited the shores to take lovers and produce offspring. Once the numbers increased sufficiently, the practice was frowned upon. For some, though, it became a game—a sport—and over the generations it led to the characterization of the selkie people being little more than wicked debauchers. In truth, the vast majority of the seal people remained a quiet, temperate bunch—content to swim the world's oceans, enjoying the natural wonders of the waters.

Over time, as the wells of magic faded, the histories of most fey faded along with it. People were happy to change fact to fantasy, and the truth became little more than whimsical superstition and tall tales.

The old sport of selkie men and women washing ashore to seek entertainment of the more carnal variety had ceased for the most part. Certain members of the royal line continued to take part in these activities, but it had become more of a rare delicacy than an everyday occurrence. Cailean found the practice particularly distasteful but was more than aware of his duties as a Queen's Guard and suspected he'd be on watch—silent and protective—during some of these trysts in the future.

Aylee was interested in the stories and the politics, but it wasn't what had really fascinated her during their discussion. She wanted to know all of the particulars about the transformation itself. How did he go from being a lithe creature of the sea to an elegant human in the blink of an eye?

Cailean had explained as best he could, but it was as natural to him as breathing so he wasn't able to explain it in a way she would easily understand. It would be akin to describing how one fell asleep and dreamed. What was clear was that the coat of a selkie was more than just a skin, a pelt, or a garment. It was a bit of the soul of the selkie in physical form and contained the magic. Similar to merrows, nixies, and kelpies, the selkies could reside in either their aquatic or terrestrial form depending on their location. Like other animal shifters, selkies were humans gifted with the ability to take on animal shape. They needed to be in possession of and wrapped in their *cotabonn*—and only their *own* coat—to go from one form to the other.

The *cotabonn* itself was a tidy bit of magic, created specifically for each newly born or made selkie. This magical garment was fashioned of elements from the sea in addition to a piece of each individual's essence.

A SIMPLE TALE OF WATER AND WEEPING

In human form, the coat transformed into a medallion worn around the neck on a leather thong. Should a selkie's coat fall into the possession of another, the selkie would be trapped in terrestrial form until it was reclaimed.

Cailean had explained his own loss and his fear of never finding it. Most selkies needed to make the transformation back to seal fairly frequently or the loss of the magic would eat away at them until they were slowly driven mad. An overwhelming urge to return to the sea could make him do unimaginable things—the most disastrous would be throwing himself from the cliffs or drowning himself just to be in the water again. Aylee had felt the whiskey churn in her gut at that nugget of information.

He was running out of time.

No wonder he had been frantic. She wondered how he could remain so calm and composed. Some unknown enemy was in possession of his *cotabonn*, a piece of his soul and the source of his magic.

Cailean tried to describe the medallion itself, but the right words eluded him. The best image she could muster was something akin to a pearlescent grey sand dollar, strung on a thick leather cord.

He'd alluded to having an idea who had taken the medallion from the beach but had evaded her when she'd pressed him further, saying it made no difference as the original thief had let it slip out of their grasp days earlier. Aylee had been puzzling over the murky details and an idea was eating at her. One she hoped she was wrong about.

Deep in thought, she came down the lane nearing the strand. She was torn from her thoughts by the sight of Shelby Abbott bounding toward her.

"Hi, Aylee and Peppy Pepper!" She smiled jubilantly at the pair.

As ever, Shelby was dressed immaculately. Her frock was simple but well made, and the marigold hue matched her disposition wonderfully. Her chestnut hair had been pulled back in a lovely braid, and her youthful face was clear and vibrant.

"Hello, sweet Shelby," Aylee returned. "Hello, Violet. How are you both this morning?"

"Lucky the storm didn't blow us into the sea last night," Violet replied.

"It really was quite something, wasn't it?" Aylee asked.

"The beach is a mess!" Shelby added. "I've seen the cute man you danced with playing in the waves. Maybe he made the beach a mess. I'd like to play in the waves with the cute man. Maybe you could take me, Aylee. To the beach."

"You'll do no such thing. You know I've told you to stay away from the water, Shelby." Violet rarely raised her voice to her niece, but when she did, everyone knew she meant business.

"All right, Aunt Violet. I'm sorry. I won't play in the waves, I promise." Turning her chastised face to her friend, she asked, "Did you bring me any sweets today, Aylee?"

"I'm so sorry, lovely girl, but I'm afraid I left the shop in a bit of a hurry and didn't think to grab any." The crestfallen look on Shelby's face hurt Aylee's heart. "But I'll tell you what. I'm going to head back home in just a little, and I will definitely return by the time the sun goes down with a treat or two for you."

"There's no need for it, Aylee," Violet said, her voice softened. "Our Shelby will survive the day without a toffee, I'm sure."

"I'm sure she would, but it'll give me an excuse to come visit."

Shelby stood from where she had been sitting on the damp sand to rub Pepper's belly. "Thanks, Aylee. You're the best."

They parted, and Aylee walked to the water's edge. The beach was indeed a mess. Debris and kelp littered the sand.

A SIMPLE TALE OF WATER AND WEEPING

She stood for a long while and stared out at the calm waters. The teal and aqua depths hid many things it seemed.

Aylee didn't return to the shop until midmorning. She entered the bustle and normalcy of an average morning. A few patrons were picking up supplies, and the smell of savory pies and blackberry preserves filled the air. Her mother must have had time to put some things on the stove. Despite their row, life went on.

Mrs. Matlock gave her a little smile as Aylee tied on her apron. Her mother was busy in the back, so Aylee helped the older lady with her bag, the entire time deliberately avoiding her father's eyes. The other patrons had finished their purchases, and the store was nearly empty. After Mrs. Matlock paid for her parcel and left the shop, Aylee took a small pile of order slips from the counter to pack up the items requested on each. She grimaced slightly as she read the name of Rupert Camden on one of the last slips.

A jar of pickled onions nearly slipped from her grasp as the bell over the door rang, and she looked up to see Ian enter the shop. This day just kept getting better and better.

"Hello, Aylee. Mr. Garrow." Ian tipped his head after he removed his cap.

"What can I help you with, Ian?" Aylee asked quietly. "Shouldn't you be at work?"

"Mr. Camden gave me the morning off to take care of a few things for him. The stills are empty right now, and most of the whiskey's been barreled already." His voice held a hard edge quite unlike the pleading tone from their last conversation.

"I see. Are you here for his order then?"

"No. Well, yes, I suppose I could take it with me. But that's not why I came in." He removed the wool cap from his head and looked down at his worn leather boots—unhappiness etching his face.

Mr. Garrow continued sweeping up nonexistent dust from the back corner of the shop.

"Ian. . ." She sighed and looked away from him.

"Aylee, please." He was going to rip the brim clean off if he wrung the cap any harder. "Just let me say what I've come here to say."

She could do this. She nodded and gave him a look that meant she was listening.

"I was hoping maybe we could go for a walk later. Just to talk. Nothing more." He stopped again and instead of looking at his feet, he stared at the ceiling. "I know you hate me now and maybe I deserve it. I just . . . I just want us to be friends again. I'm not asking for anything more right now. Just friends. All right?"

He didn't deserve her forgiveness, but she could at least extend a bit of kindness to him. Life was too short to hold onto the anger.

"I guess, Ian." She sighed and shook her head.

"When will you be free?" The hope in his voice was a little more than she could take.

"I told Shelby I'd bring her some sweets this evening," she said in a resigned voice. "Let's say six o'clock, and you can walk with me to Violet's. But you need to know, I can't ever go back to the way things were before."

She couldn't and *wouldn't* go back. She'd felt firsthand how easy it was for him to break her heart, and she knew good men—better men—were out there in the world, if not here in town. If her parents and the rest of the world were so hell-bent on her marrying soon, the least she could do was find someone who would respect her and treat her like a person—not just a pretty face. Ian would never put her first, and Rupert would likely never let her be more than just his young pretty wife. She would hold out until she found someone who would see her and need her just as much as she saw and needed him.

"I'll see you at six." Gone was the hard edge to his voice and the misery from his face. Ian practically danced to the door before she could change her mind.

As she stared after him out the front windows, her da

came up behind her and placed his arm around her shoulder. "You handled that nicely. I'm sorry your mother and I didn't give you the trust you deserve. We were worried is all."

"I know, Da. I know," she replied as he went back to his work. Dragging her attention away from the window, she took a deep breath and huffed out a sigh as she crossed her arms.

"I suppose I just don't understand. If you and Momma can't accept Cailean as the decent man he is, how are we to expect the rest of the town to accept him? You might say all the right things, but when it comes down to it, how are we any better if we hold the same prejudices they do?"

Devon picked up a stack of fabric bolts, moving them to the side to run his broom behind them.

"That's a fair question. I suppose even the best of people make mistakes when those they love are involved. I promise not to act rashly and to take my time to get to know the man."

Time. Cailean didn't have time.

She nodded. "That's all I'm asking."

"And don't judge your mother too harshly. She has her reasons for her reaction. As for me, well, my only excuse is that I love both you and your mother. Double the mistakes."

He looked like he wanted to say more, so when he didn't elaborate, Aylee asked, "What sorts of reasons?"

He waved a dismissive hand in the air. "Oh, you know. A load of rubbish from when she was younger. Nothing for you to fret on. Give her a day or two, Love. She'll come around."

Aylee didn't want to speculate on whether or not her mother *would* come around, so she didn't respond. Her father went back to his broom. She had grabbed the next order slip when another thought occurred to her.

"Have you ever wondered why the town doesn't have a name, Da?"

He didn't even look up from his sweeping as he replied, "No, Love. I haven't."

TWENTY-TWO

Maeve arrived just in time for lunch. Thankfully Graham was not with her.

They ate a light meal of roasted potatoes with bacon and sprouts. The conversation was limited and strained. Aylee had much she wanted to say to her sister, but none she wished to say in front of her parents. The truce between them following the morning's squabble was still tenuous.

After the sisters cleaned up the dishes, Una and Devon asked Aylee if she could mind the store for bit while they took a short nap—it had been a late night after all.

As she wasn't needed at home for anything in particular, Maeve agreed to stay and help.

They walked down the shop steps and flipped the sign back to open, but this time of day, the foot traffic would be light. The tension lingered.

"Da was beside himself last night," Maeve ventured, looking at Aylee from the corner of her eye.

"So I gathered."

"You shouldn't have left like that. I was worried as well."

"I would have told you, but you and Graham seemed to be having a fairly intense conversation."

Maeve remained silent, so Aylee added, "I'm trying to figure out how you knew about Cailean."

"It wasn't hard. You know how much I've always loved the old stories." Maeve still wasn't looking at her. It wasn't a lie exactly, but Aylee knew it also wasn't the truth.

"Cailean's coat has been stolen."

Maeve was the sort of person who knew the power she

had over just about everyone. She wasn't malicious about it, just astute in how she was regarded by others, her family members included. Today, she was using the power of silence to infuriate her younger sister. Aylee knew she'd only talk when she was good and ready.

"I found your red shawl at the beach. Are you going to tell me it was just a coincidence?"

Maeve looked slightly surprised.

It has been tickling at Aylee's brain, the red shawl. She hadn't recognized it as her sister's when she'd picked it up on the beach the morning Cailean mysteriously appeared in town. When her sister had it on the previous night, the recognition finally came. Maeve must have seen it in Aylee's room and thought she'd left it at her parent's home one night by accident.

"So you dropped your shawl on the beach the same morning Cailean's coat went missing and you just so happen to know he's not only fey but also a selkie? What's really going on here, Maeve? If you have his coat, he needs it back. You can't let him suffer like this." Aylee was angry, but the words came out more controlled than she felt.

"It's not like that, Aylee. Honestly, it's not. I don't have his coat, I swear. If I did, I'd give it back! I made a terrible mistake."

Tears were welling in her sister's eyes, and despite herself, Aylee embraced her and held tight for a moment. Perhaps her sister was finally ready to talk.

Maeve shuddered with a few quiet sobs while Aylee stroked her head, the auburn hair in a messy braid down her back.

"Shh. It's all right. Just tell me what you can."

Maeve, red-eyed and weepy, pulled back from her sister's embrace. *Even crying, she's breathtaking.* The red in her eyes served only to make the green flash a brighter, more brilliant emerald.

"It's all just such a terrible mess. I've been selfish and careless, Aylee. I'm a fool." She wiped the tears from her

A SIMPLE TALE OF WATER AND WEEPING

cheeks.

Aylee waited. Prodding would not help. Once she had composed herself, Maeve began a tale almost too strange to believe. Except Aylee did believe it. After all she had seen and learned in the past few days, what else *could* she do?

"Two summers ago, before Graham proposed to me, I was down on the beach with a group of friends. Silvie, Angus, and Graham were there . . . as well as Ian and Robbie. It was the same night you had that horrible fever. We had gone down to have some fun and share a few pints of ale. We were all having a grand time, and Silvie and I were feeling daring. We wanted to show the others we weren't scared of the ocean, so we decided to go for a little moonlight swim. We'd shucked our clothes and were in the water before the boys even noticed. We swam for a few minutes, and Silvie started getting nervous because she'd had a bit too much to drink. She swam back, but I stayed out a little longer. I was just thinking about heading to shore when I felt something brush against my legs. I yelped, thinking what a fool I was for being out in the waves alone, and I started to panic. I went under briefly but came to the surface quickly. I felt the same brush against my legs and then at my hip and waist. I batted it away, and my hand fell on the body of some large animal. I turned to swim to shore, and this large grey seal was swimming beside me. It looked at me, and I swear it sounds crazy, but I felt like it was looking into my eyes—as if it could communicate with me in some strange magical way. Instead of increasing my terror, it made me feel at peace and safe. It swam all the way back to shore with me.

"Aylee, I can't describe it. It was the most amazing thing I'd ever experienced." Maeve took a long breath.

"I fetched my clothes from the beach, careful to stay out of the sightline of the boys, but couldn't drag my eyes from the seal as it just floated there in the waves. Watching me watching it.

"Anyway, Silvie stumbled back to where I'd been watching the water. She needed to be getting home before her parents began to worry. I needed to get home too, and I let Graham walk me back to the shop. I didn't sleep well that night or the next. Two nights later, while I tossed and turned, I decided to go back to the beach and look for my seal. I snuck out without telling Da and Momma and made my way back to the shore.

"It was as if the seal *knew* I would come back. As I came over the bridge and down the steps to the sand, I looked out into the waves. Sure enough, there it was, swimming back and forth. It was magnificent. I sighed and just sat down on the sand and watched it gracefully play in the waves. Within a matter of minutes, I'd taken off my dress and boots and was walking to the surf's edge when. . ."

Maeve's voice turned soft and tentative, a fierce blush creeping over her face to match.

"And then what?" Aylee prompted. Maeve was ashamed or embarrassed to go on, but Aylee had a feeling where this was heading, and if Maeve's seal was in fact who she feared it was, she needed to know. Now.

Still, her sister hesitated.

"Maeve. Tell me," Aylee demanded. "Was it Cailean?"

"Cailean?" That drew a shocked looked from Maeve. "No! Saints no, Aylee."

Aylee sighed a long breath of relief. Saints indeed. Thank them for small mercies.

"But, well. You won't think quite so highly of me if I tell you what happened that night." The crimson stain on her cheeks deepened and a small tear trickled from her eye.

"I'll always think highly of you, Maeve. There isn't much you could say to turn me."

Maeve gave her sister a small smile. "Thank you, Love."

She went on. "I made it to the edge of the water and

then a man—that's not right—not just a man, but the most beautiful man I had ever *seen,* was walking out of the surf directly toward me. I was startled and confused and, well... only half clothed. I didn't think. I turned and grabbed for my dress to cover myself. He walked right up to me, and the look in his eyes was mesmerizing. I stared for a moment, my hands trembling. His eyes were a rich golden caramel color, and even dripping with sea water I could see the gold and silver streaks in his hair. He was absolutely the most wondrous creature I have ever beheld."

Maeve had a far-off look in her eye and a smile on her face as if in some amazing daydream. Aylee thought it likely her sister visited this particular daydream rather frequently.

"He reached up and cupped my face with one hand and, Aylee, I was lost. Just lost. I dropped the dress I was holding, and we stood there as if it was always meant to be this way. He dropped what he had been holding in his other hand alongside my things and kissed me.

"This was before Graham. I'd only ever kissed one other boy, and it had been nothing, *nothing* like this. As I said, I was lost. We did things that night. Things you aren't supposed to do with someone you just met, and while I knew all of it was wrong, I couldn't get enough of how right it felt.

"I stayed there on the sand all night. I slept on and off in the arms of a total stranger. As dawn started to come up, I told him I had to get home, and he smiled and handed me my dress. He told me his name was Declan, and he would come back the next night if I wished it. I just dumbly nodded, and then he did the most extraordinary thing. He picked up the object he had dropped. It was some sort of large pearlescent locket, but when I blinked, it had transformed into what I took for a tunic. Then I realized it wasn't clothing at all, but a kind of pelt. A seal pelt, and the entire thing became clear. He was a selkie. I had just spent a night in the arms of a selkie, and I wasn't the least bit sorry."

TWENTY-THREE

Saints and sinners.

"Declan? His name was Declan?" Aylee's head was trying to process Maeve's story, but when she heard the selkie's name, a bolt clicked home. It was Cailean's brother.

"Yes. Does the name mean something to you?" Maeve frowned.

Aylee shook her head. "No . . . it's not important. Go on."

"Well, you had just been sick, so it was easy for me to claim to be ill as well. I stayed in bed the next day to avoid helping in the shop. I napped for most of the afternoon and went back to the beach at night. I did the same thing for the next three nights. Declan would wait for me in the surf and walk up the beach when I arrived. Each night was just as splendidly sweet as the first. I was worried I'd get caught, but I couldn't help myself. For the love of all things good, can you imagine if Momma or Da had found out? It'd be the end of me."

Yes. Aylee could imagine. Hadn't her parents just accused her of doing the very same thing with Cailean? It didn't seem to be the correct time to mention this, so she kept her mouth shut and willed Maeve to continue.

"I needn't have worried overmuch though." Here her eyes lost their spark, and her mouth turned down at the corners. "On the fifth night, Declan wasn't there. I returned each night for a week and still no sign of him. It was hard to admit to myself what I had done, but the draw kept me going back once or twice a week. He would likely never be there again, and I got nervous about what we'd done. I didn't know if it was possible, but the stories seemed to make out ... well ... what if I had been with child? The thought never occurred to me while we were ... enjoying ourselves. The reality of it hit after he'd left, and I was paranoid. How would I possibly explain such a situation?

"Graham had been flirting with me all summer, and I knew he was interested in me, so I encouraged his affection. Within a month we were married."

Aylee was stunned. She had never understood why Maeve had agreed to marry Graham, but the truth was shocking. If she hadn't learned about Cailean and the selkies, she never would have believed Maeve's fantastical story.

It did bother her how much Declan played the part of the wicked selkie. Cailean had insisted it wasn't in the nature of the seal people to make sport of seducing folks, but Maeve's story reinforced the lore.

The bell over the door jingled, and Aylee turned, a smile automatically placed on her lips, to find Jenny Black, the bakery shop assistant. Jenny was dying for a lamb pie, it seemed. While Maeve hid behind the counter halfway to the kitchen, Aylee chatted pleasantly with the girl. She had to lie and tell the nosy thing she had no idea if Cailean was staying in town or planning to leave and that she did not in fact know if he had a special someone back home. Jenny eventually got tired of not hearing the answers she wanted and paid for her pie, shuffling back through the door and up the street in the direction of the bakery.

The door had barely shut, and Aylee spun to her sister. "Well, it's all a bit much to take in, isn't it? Does anyone else know? Silvie or Graham? And what has all this got to do with Cailean if this was moons ago?"

"No one knew," Maeve responded emphatically. She played with the ends of the long auburn braid running over her shoulder. "At least, no one knew until recently."

She didn't need to elaborate for Aylee to understand.

"How did Graham figure it out?" The weird friction between Maeve and Graham was making more sense.

"Oh, Aylee. I have been so incredibly stupid." The tears were back in her sister's voice and in her eyes. "You need to understand, before I tell you this next bit, you need to understand I really truly thought I was doing what I had to."

"I believe you, Maeve. What precisely did you do?" Aylee wasn't sure she really wanted to know, but they had come this far, and Cailean needed some answers.

"First, let me say, I know I didn't marry Graham for the right reasons. I know I was greedy and foolish and deceitful. I know all of those things. But in the last months, I've come to feel more for him than I thought I would. Back when we were first married—and although I know it makes me horrid—I thought I would never really love him. I didn't think I wanted to ever really love someone at all. My heart still felt as if it were left on the beach and pecked apart by the gulls."

Aylee stared at her sister, who winced. Aylee imaged Maeve knew it sounded ridiculous to claim to love someone she had only known for a total of four days. The fact he had clearly used her and discarded her would make her feel not only small but also like the world's biggest fool. She might hate herself for it, but she would own the love and the self-loathing. Maeve was different from Aylee—she would embrace the emotion rather than run from it. Maeve had a confidence Aylee would always envy.

Aylee tried to remember Maeve's demeanor in the weeks preceding her marriage to Graham but couldn't recall her being either sad or happy or nervous. If anything, Aylee recalled her sister being a smidge flat and had just chalked it up to the stress of the wedding. Now she saw it as something more—self-preservation.

"Believe me. I know how absolutely *horrid* and *dirty* it sounds, but it's true. I had no interest in living happily with Graham, and on some level I think he knew my heart wasn't really in it, but he married me anyway. Sounds like a match made in heaven, right?

"Obviously, no babe came after we married, and I thought about asking him to leave me.

"Things *did* start to change though. I thought of Declan less and paid more attention to Graham. One morning I woke and felt the first twinges of what some might call love for him. About a year ago, I decided I wanted to start a family. When things never materialized, I could feel Graham getting frustrated. I think he's had some trouble at work, and the combination was making him miserable. I've been trying to be patient with him, just as I know he was patient with me, but having him withdraw is a lot harder than I ever thought it would be. I was quite angry with him for pushing me away just when I began to want him to pull me closer.

"About a month ago, I woke in the middle of the night, and all I could think of was Declan. After all the months, it hit me again what those few nights had been like. I snuck out while Graham was sleeping and went to the beach. I don't really know what I was hoping for exactly: that he'd be there and we could run away together or just have one more amazing night on the sand...I don't know. Whatever it was, it didn't matter. No handsome seal or stunning man was waiting for me.

"Things just got worse after that. I became more frustrated and Graham so withdrawn. I care for him but almost can't stand to be around him. Being miserable just reminds me of how happy I was for a few nights.

"I started leaving the house more and more. One morning, just before dawn, I was down on the beach, and I was walking with my eyes closed enjoying the spray on my face, and I kicked something. At first I thought it was an unusual shell. Then I saw the leather thong, and my heart almost stopped. The medallion looked so much like the one Declan wore I thought for sure it was his. I was shocked and relieved and ecstatic all at the same time. I called for him and looked for him, and when I couldn't find him anywhere, I made a snap decision. I grabbed the medallion, tucked it in my skirt, and headed home. I knew he couldn't return to the sea without it, and I hoped, stupidly, if I held onto it long enough, he would come to find me. I went back to the beach the next few mornings but left the locket hidden in the bottom of my linen chest.

"It never occurred to me it could be anyone's other than his."

Aylee interrupted. "That's who you were looking for the night of the jubilee." It was a statement, not a question. "When you asked me if I'd seen Graham's cousin? You thought Declan would come in search of his coat?" *But you needed it to look innocent.*

"Yes. That night I also realized I must have made a mistake. I saw you dancing with Cailean, and I couldn't be sure, but I had a feeling the coat might belong to him and not Declan after all."

"So why didn't you return it then?" Aylee cried to her sister.

"I was going to, Aylee. I swear I was. I went home that night with a plan to bring it to the shop or the inn the next day, but when I opened the trunk it was gone."

Aylee felt her heart plummet to her toes. "Gone? How could it just be gone?"

"I wondered the same thing. Someone must have known I had it. So then I thought maybe it was Declan's after all and Cailean was sent here to retrieve it. I didn't want to ask Graham for fear he knew nothing about it, and then a whole pile of questions would need to be answered. I just didn't know who to talk to or what to do. Cailean showed up at the cottage the next day. He knew I had taken it."

Maeve must have seen the confusion on her sister's face. "He saw me on the beach and figured it must have been me."

"But I was down on the beach the same morning,"

Aylee said. "He never asked me if I had taken it."

She remembered Cailean mentioning following her home and his muddled plans to fetch his coat at any cost. She shuddered at how wrong their first encounter could have gone—*would* have gone, if he hadn't been the kind of person he was.

"So, if Cailean didn't steal it back from you, who do you think has it now?" Aylee asked.

"Once I realized your friend couldn't be responsible I had to think who might want the coat."

"*Cotabonn*," Aylee said absently. "Its proper name is *cotabonn*."

Maeve was twisting and twirling the end of her braid again. "Last night, it finally hit me. Graham knew without me saying *anything* Cailean was fey, and if he knew he was fey he must have had reason to suspect which particular kind of fey."

Ahh . . . Graham. *Of course*. Graham had no issue calling Cailean out for what he was. Presumably because he thought his wife was keeping the coat for reasons of her own. Which of course Maeve was, just not the reasons Graham had suspected. Maeve had no love or adoration for Cailean, but how was Graham to know that?

"Graham took the *cotabonn*, didn't he? He thought you and Cailean were involved." It explained quite a bit of the unpleasantness Aylee felt while at the cottage last evening.

"He did, or maybe he still does. I told him everything, and I wouldn't blame him if he didn't believe a word I spoke." Maeve's expression was hard to read. Aylee's perfect sister, not so perfect after all.

"So does he have it? When can we give it back to Cailean?"

Maeve bit her lower lip, and Aylee felt her heart sink.

"That's the worst bit. He gave it to Rupert Camden."

TWENTY-FOUR

The store was quiet—the closed sign facing outward. Light filtered in through the front windows, a peachy grey-green, brought on by the combination of a setting sun and low-hanging patchy clouds. Above her, a floorboard creaked, and Pepper snored softly in the corner.

Aylee sat on an empty crate, her head against the wall, eyes drooping closed against her will.

Maeve had left an hour ago, and Una and Devon Garrow remained upstairs. Aylee enjoyed the peaceful quiet and thought about her current situation. Had it really only been days ago she had longed for more adventure and excitement in her life? She wanted to live a life of independence and excitement, but she was thinking more along the lines of a few trips down the coast or to the city, perhaps the ability to make her own wages without depending on a husband. This was a tad more extreme than she had in mind.

Only last month, she had lived her life free of the knowledge which now pressed in on her from all sides. Fey were real. Magic was real. Her family knew of these things and had let her live her life thinking it all whimsy and make-believe. Everything she thought she knew to be true was a mere shadow in the light of the real world.

She let her mind drift toward the power of words and names. She imagined names for the town—some fanciful and some mundane. Imagined herself giving this place a name and others not only accepting it but adopting it with affection. *Bleak Meadows. Splendor. Osprey's Roost.*

None seemed quite the right fit.

She let her eyes close again and listened to the quiet

sounds around her—the soft in and out of Pepper's breathing, the squeak of a hinge on one of the signs out front, the groans and thumps of footsteps above her head as her parents walked from spot to spot upstairs. The quiet sounds filled her. She drifted on a gentle ocean of feeling, mute sensation rocking her in waves and—not unlike a seal transforming into a man—she drifted into slumber.

In her dream she was surrounded by water warmer than any ocean she'd ever been in before. It was as if she floated on a swell of bath water, and as if the bath had been laced with her favorite oils, the sea smelled of peppermint and lavender. She lay on her back and let the waters cradle and rock her. Flotsam brushed against her skin, tingling and tickling as it did so.

Above, a periwinkle sky dotted with thick white fluffs of cloud; below, deep teal waters. As she floated staring at the sky, she sensed movement below her. A dark shadow obscured the sandy bottom. She mustn't look at what swam in the depths. Dream Aylee could feel in her marrow to look would be the end of her. The waters began to feel less calming. She wanted to peek at what caused such swells around her but didn't dare. She squeezed her eyes shut in her dream, afraid to see the thing lurking below her, if even for only a moment. She had no name for the great hulking thing below and thus no power over it. The waters grew increasingly violent. The nausea of fear had her whimpering. *Don't look, don't look, don't look.* She would drown before she looked.

The shadow gained weight and substance. It pulled itself from darkness to form, gravity swelling as the enormous body took shape, pulling the waves, and her, toward its maw. It would have teeth. Teeth big enough to take a great chunk of her flesh if it chose to.

The shaking increased, and she opened her mouth to scream only to have it filled with the warm briny water. She gagged and choked—the salty water tinged with iron. Gone were the soothing peppermint and lavender scents.

In their place a thick carrion smell. Blood. She was floating in blood. Not water at all. The rocking turned to thrashing.

"Aylee!" Strong hands shook her shoulders. "Aylee, wake up! You're having a nightmare!"

Her eyes flew open, and it took a moment for her to register Ian's face above her. She coughed and sat up, catching her breath. A dream. It had been only a dream.

Slowly her heart rate settled, and she wiped a hand across her face, feeling the saline tracks of tears on her cheeks and lashes. Pepper was sniffing at Ian's feet as he absently scratched between her ears.

"Ian." She wiped her hand across her face, scrubbing the imaginary blood from her skin. "Sorry, I must have drifted off. Is it six already?"

"A few minutes after." He looked at her with something close to concern. "The back door was unlocked. Are you all right now? It must have been ghastly—you still look a little shaky."

"Yes. Fine, thanks." She let him help her to her feet. "I haven't had a nightmare quite so intense in some time."

She dusted off her trousers and slipped her feet back into her shoes. She picked up the small brown paper parcel of treats she'd put together for Shelby and forced a smile on her face.

"Shall we, then?"

TWENTY-FIVE

Ian kept a respectable distance from Aylee as they walked toward the strand, her dog running ahead and then back to them repeatedly. His palm itched, so strong was his desire to grab her hand. He fought that magnetic pull, knowing it would only cause her to push him away. So he would bide his time instead. He would work bit by painstaking bit to rebuild the trust she had lost in him all those weeks ago. He cast around for a neutral topic, just to get her talking to him again.

"The winter barley planting is set to start soon. Should be a good crop for the next reaping." It wasn't that he really cared about the crop, but at least it was a safe first step.

"It seems so. I know Dee's da has been busy with the fields. The recent harvest was a good one too. You're sure to have a fine mash next go around." She didn't cringe away from talk of the whiskey distillery. It was a small victory, but he would take it.

"I expect we'll be getting top dollar from the city in the next few years. The aged bottles look quality."

"It's good to hear. Not just for Camden, but for you too. You'll be a foreman before too long or even have a distillery of your own one day," she said as she followed Pepper with her eyes. He knew she meant it, and it gave him a little pang in his chest.

"Maybe, but that would mean moving from town, and I'm not sure that'd be the best thing for me." *For us* he wanted to say but held back.

Most villages of their size could only support one distillery, maybe two, if they were both small or family run.

Camden's operation was already pushing the boundaries of what the town could sustain, providing little to no room for competition.

"Perhaps getting out on your own and away from town is just what you need." She didn't mean it to be hurtful, but it stung just the same. He knew she would never leave her family or their shop, so clearly she had no intention of sharing in any future with him in another spot. "Getting out from under Rupert Camden might be the smartest thing you could ever do."

"I don't know about smartest, but it certainly wouldn't be the stupidest. Given as I've already got that covered."

She made a small sound he took for agreement.

He needed to change the subject and get back on good footing. "So what have you got in the bag for Shelby this evening? It's got to be something Violet won't be happy about."

She chuckled softly. "You might be right. Let's see. There's a handful of hard licorice, some cherry jellies, and a good amount of toffee. You don't think she'll approve?" She smiled slightly at him, and his heart did a little flip.

"If it was the *only* bag of sweets you brought to her this month, maybe. I'm guessing, however, this isn't the first time you've been to see her in the past week."

"The third I believe." She laughed, and this time he felt it in his toes.

"Damn, Aylee. You're lucky she has any teeth left after all that sugar."

"Her teeth are fine. She deserves whatever small bit of happiness my little gifts give her. She doesn't have an easy life, you know." Her voice carried a trace of sadness.

"Of course I know, Love."

Aylee stopped walking. Damn it all. He was a pissing idiot. It had been going relatively well.

Her cheeks were flushed, and she looked on the verge of either tears or blows; he couldn't be sure which. Just like that, the mood had shifted.

"I think we both know you don't get to call me that anymore." Her voice held a coldness which stung as much as any winter wind.

"Sorry, Aylee. It just came out." Only her family called her Love. Her family and—until last winter—him. He hadn't used the endearment since the terrible day he'd asked her to leave his home—somehow thinking it was wise to convince her he had never felt for her the way she had supposed. She surely wasn't going to let him slide right back into using it again.

"I'm trying to accept what happened between us, and I am trying my level best to get past it. Please don't make it harder than it needs to be." Her voice was wobbly, but she started walking again. Minor victory number two.

"I'll do my best, I promise," he replied. "I can't say it won't happen again, but hopefully the next time it'll be because you want me to call you Love."

She looked at him from the corner of her eye. "I think you shouldn't hold your breath."

He half laughed, half sighed in reply.

They were nearly to the entry gate of Violet and Shelby's small yard, when two men appeared from around the corner. Ned Bryan raised a hand in greeting. It was Ned's companion that sparked Ian's ire. The bastard who'd walked Aylee home this morning from wherever she'd been. Pepper was all too happy to see them both and was excitedly circling the pair of tall men.

"Mr. Bryan, Cailean! It's lovely to see you both!" She smiled at both men with a warmth he hadn't received from her in months.

"Darling, Aylee! We were just on our way to your shop!" Ned gave her a quick warm hug. "I know your folks have likely closed up for the night, but I was hoping to ask them for a quick order to be brought by tomorrow. The missus is in dire need of some honey and chestnuts. I was meant to get them picked up today, and it completely slipped my mind. She gave me quite the tongue-lashing as we were to have a special bread for the guests this week. Cailean here agreed to join me on my journey down the lane. I'm not sure if his intentions were to see you or simply to escape Candice's wrath for a few moments."

"I merely wanted to enjoy the crisp air and your fine company, Mr. Bryan." He threw a quick smile to Aylee. Ian scowled.

"I'm afraid my parents are likely in for the night, Mr. Bryan, but if you want to give me your list, I'd be happy to pack things up and bring them out to you in the morning. I'll be heading to the beach for clams early, I suppose, and swinging up to the inn first won't be any trouble."

"Oh, I don't know, Aylee . . . I can't say I'm much of a fan of you going down to the shore so early in the morning. You sure your da is okay with you being so close to the water all by yourself?" the big man asked.

She smirked at him. "I go there each morning and have yet to meet my doom."

When he still looked skeptical, she added, "Fearing a thing, Mr. Bryan, only gives it power over you. I refuse to give the sea such a gift."

"Aylee Garrow, you are a gem among rocks. Don't you lads agree?" He looked at Ian and Cailean in turn and chuckled to himself. Shaking his head, he handed Aylee a small scrap of paper with a list of desired items scribbled in his wife's tidy handwriting. "If you're sure, I'd be happy to tell Candice you'll be round in the morning."

Once Aylee assured him it would be fine, he turned to walk back home. Almost as an afterthought, he called over his shoulder, "Try not to make too much noise when ya come back tonight, Mr. Vann."

Ned Bryan let loose with a hearty laugh, as if this were a private joke the two shared, and moved back up the lane at a pace not easily accomplished by a man of his size.

"We were just going to deliver a nip of a treat to my good friend Shelby. Would you care to join us?" Aylee asked.

A SIMPLE TALE OF WATER AND WEEPING

Ian forced himself to suppress the groan of displeasure rising in his throat. It wouldn't do to have her think him uncharitable to the stranger.

"I suppose I could use a little more fresh air. Thanks." He extended his hand to Ian. Aylee smiled then, and Ian couldn't imagine why. "I don't believe we've met. Cailean Vann."

Ian noted the subtle strength in the handshake and replied calmly, "Ian Cormack."

"I'd forgotten you two hadn't met yet." The smile on Aylee's face turned more bemused. She whistled for Pepper and started walking through the small yard once more.

The men hung back as she knocked at the door and was smothered in a long embrace by Shelby. Violet clicked her tongue once she observed the pile of sweets in the small package, and Aylee had the good grace to shrug sheepishly as the older woman shook her head. Shelby beamed and waved at Ian and Cailean as Aylee walked back to where the men waited.

"Well, it was nice to make your acquaintance," Ian said to Cailean as she approached. "I suppose we should be getting back."

Aylee looked down at her toes, but Ian caught her smirk just the same. He had intended this to be a dismissal, but Cailean was having no part of it. Rather than taking the bait, the stranger smiled congenially and looped his arm through Aylee's. Mischief lit his ocean eyes.

"Oh, I've got the evening to kill. You heard Ned. They aren't expecting me back just yet and my room can be so dull."

"I see. I'm sure you won't find our conversation to your liking. You might even think *it* dull. We were just discussing the barley crops and the malting coming up." Ian needed to salvage this and couldn't afford to seem rude, but the last thing he wanted was another man around while he was still trying to get on Aylee's good side.

A SIMPLE TALE OF WATER AND WEEPING

Especially not a man who stood a head taller and was fairly well built.

"You work at the distiller's then?" Cailean asked.

"I do. I've been there the last four years. I started out cleaning and stacking barrels and bottles. Now I help with the distilling and the bottling. A little of everything, I suppose." Ian was proud of his work. *Proud enough I let Aylee slip through my fingers like grains of sand in the wind.*

"Sounds like you enjoy your work," the other man observed, his voice rough but not attacking. Ian thought he sounded as if he had the croup. It was wretched.

"I do." Ian added a bit sheepishly, remembering Aylee was with them, "But it does have its downsides."

Aylee winced slightly at the statement. Surely she had to know it wasn't her he was referring to but the position he had been put in. This was a damn field of sheep dung he needed to traverse carefully. It would make her feel slightly better to have him admit to someone else he had behaved badly of his own accord, instead of laying the blame solely on Camden's shoulders. But he would do no such thing in front of this bastard.

"Most things in life have downsides, I'd wager. It's how we deal with them that's important. Don't you agree?" Cailean looked to Aylee with a gleam in his eye.

"Completely." She smiled back as if this were a game they were playing.

"Yes, I suppose, but sometimes we get what's owed us and sometimes not," Ian responded slowly.

"You may not be owed anything, but I feel like I am." Aylee said the words quietly, the emotion in them causing a pressure in Ian's chest he didn't want to acknowledge just then.

"Perhaps you could do something to help settle the debt."

Was she agreeing to take him back if he did something for her? Ian might be able to get her back after all. If he played his cards correctly, that was. If not, he felt he still had a little insurance on his side.

"Do you think you might be willing to help us?" She looked at him with those lovely hazel eyes, tucked a long copper strand behind her ear and gave him a hopeful small smile.

"I can't make any promises, Aylee, but I can try. What is it you need?"

"Cailean has had something stolen, and we think it might be hidden somewhere at the distillery."

Ian was shocked but quickly schooled his features into a more neutral expression.

"All right then? Do you want to tell me what this item is?" he asked cautiously.

"I'll let Cailean handle this part."

Ian looked warily at the dark-haired stranger. Some sort of silent conversation seemed to be passing between his former flame and this unusual outsider. Ian almost thought Aylee was willing the other man to play along with whatever game she was at.

Cailean, for his part, didn't flinch as he said, "You'll be looking for something like an unusual seashell. Flat, round, and iridescent, smoke colored—about yay big." He held his hands out, forefingers and thumbs creating mirrored L shapes roughly four inches apart. "It should be strung on a length of black leather. It won't look like much to you, but I can assure you it's . . . valuable."

"No offense, mate, but I don't feel like losing my position for a cheap bit of ocean debris. The beach is full of shells after all. Why's it so important?"

"It just is," Aylee said firmly. "If you don't want to have a look around, then don't. We can manage fine on our own."

Ian raised his hand in what he hoped was a soothing rather than aggressive gesture.

"Relax, Lo . . . I mean, Aylee. I haven't said no yet. I'm just trying to get an idea of what I might be getting involved with." Ian looked from Cailean to Aylee, a mix of curiosity and something like dawning anger on his face.

"Well, see, this is the tricky bit," Cailean said. "I can't exactly tell you more. It's an important piece of 'debris' to me. I cannot really give you particulars about why it's important, only just that it is. If it's retrieved and given back to me, I can be on my way and leave this rubble little town behind. I would think this prospect alone would be enough to pique your interest."

"What do you mean 'rubble little town'?" Ian pressed.

Cailean looked to Aylee.

"Adorable. I believe he said adorable," she supplied.

Cailean looked knowingly between Aylee and Ian. Aylee, for her part, set her mouth in a firm line. She didn't dare argue about him leaving, but the expression on her face told Ian everything he needed to know.

"Interesting..." Ian mused. "And if I were to go in search of this important bit of junk, where would you suggest I look for it?"

"Well... is there anywhere within the warehouses or offices where one could hide something without every employee on the lot bumping into it?" Cailean asked.

"Loads of places. Depends on who was hiding it. Are we talking about a cooper, a bottler, or someone with more authority to be about, such as one of the foremen?" Ian asked.

"Not sure," Cailean replied. "How about someone such as Graham Ruthven?"

"Graham?" Ian looked to Aylee. "What's Maeve's husband got to do with this?"

Aylee took a deep breath. "Nothing. Look Ian, do you think you could take a glance in Rupert's office? Just casually. I'm not suggesting breaking into his safe or anything, but maybe when you speak with him next? Just to see if anything fitting the description Cailean gave you is lying about?"

Halos of light were spilling out from various home and shop windows—ghosts of color dancing on the wet cobbles.

Ian crossed his arms over his chest. "I don't know. I don't want to get sacked, even for you, Aylee."

"Believe me. You've made the point clear before." He took the jab. "Just if the opportunity arises? Fair?"

Ian could feel the color rising to his cheeks. Maybe this really was a fool's errand and he should just say so and move on. *Is she really worth it?* Yes. Yes, she was.

They reached the back of the shop by the time Ian agreed to keep his eyes open for an odd bit of material hidden away at the distillery. She said goodnight to both men. Ian bristled when she gave Cailean a quick peck on the cheek before going inside. Cailean didn't seem to mind Ian's presence at all. It was as if he knew her former flame held no spark for her any longer, so why be bothered enough to care.

TWENTY-SIX

Aylee was up and out of the shop before her parents made it out of bed. She'd left them a note about getting to the inn with the Bryans' order before clamming on the beach. Pepper grumbled her dismay at the early outing, but once Aylee produced a chunk of cold pheasant, any complaints seemed to be gone.

Stars were still visible to the west, but a peachy light had crept into the horizon. Winter was a cat crouched, waiting to pounce. Town was the mouse. She'd needed to bundle up in a thick warm coat and wool knit cap to keep the air from biting too sharply. Frost limed the cobbles, and ice threatened to send her sprawling more than once.

While she walked to the inn, she pondered yesterday's conversation with Ian. She hated herself just a little for leading him to believe she could forgive him if he helped her and Cailean find the coat. She was also none too pleased with Cailean for his implication that with him out of the picture, Ian would have a straight shot back into Aylee's heart. She wasn't nearly so capricious, she told herself, and didn't want anyone to think she was.

For a time, shortly after Ian had ended things so abruptly, she would have done anything in her power to get him back. That time had been brief, and she loathed the memory of how she had behaved. When she thought Rupert Camden was going to propose, she hadn't wanted to lead him on, knowing she would never agree, but hadn't been strong enough to say so directly. She vowed not to be so spineless in the future.

When she delivered the parcel of goods to Candice Bryan, they chatted for a bit. Apparently Mrs. Bryan really didn't *need* the hazelnuts today, but she had asked her husband to get them and he'd forgotten, so it was his fault Aylee had to be drug out at such an early hour. Simple as that.

Cailean stood in the corner, arms crossed over his chest as he leaned against the doorframe. She winked at him as she handed a small packet of cherry jellies to Penny Bryan—Candice none the wiser. He smiled in response, but Aylee could swear he looked almost sad in the moment.

She raised her eyebrows at him—a silent *why so gloomy?* He seemed to shake off what he was thinking and dusted his hands against each other.

"Mind if I join you on your quest for clams?" His cerulean eyes never left her face.

"I'd like it very much, Mr. Vann," she answered. "There's a bit of information I wanted to chat with you about, and last night didn't seem an appropriate time."

Inappropriate was an understatement. No way in all the world—magical or otherwise—would she have brought up the details of his brother and her sister in front of Ian. Cailean looked intrigued and more than a little wary.

They strolled down to the sand in companionable silence. Cailean knew when she was ready to talk, she would.

The dawn sky was bleak—pregnant steel clouds hung with a weighty oppression over the water, and a thick hazy fog was creeping onto land. The waves left the sand a dark murky brown, but soft enough the digging would be easy.

Cailean set down the bucket he'd been carrying for Aylee and took her hands in his, rubbing the cold flesh in an effort to bring the blood flow back. She smiled at him appreciatively, and she closed her eyes and tilted her head back, inhaling the damp air deep into her lungs. The moisture caused the hair around her face and neck to curl slightly, and Cailean thought the contrast between the creamy skin of her neck and the wet copper of the curls might be the loveliest thing he had seen in quite some time.

He removed one of his hands from hers to let a stray curl wrap around his finger. The brush of his hand on her neck made her shiver. Aylee took another deep drag of the air and wrapped her arms around his waist.

He held on for a few moments and begrudgingly reminded her the clams weren't going to shovel themselves. As if on cue, Pepper arrived and shoved her wet nose directly between his legs, causing a most unromantic yelp to escape him. Aylee simply laughed and grabbed the shovel.

"I had an interesting discussion with my sister yesterday," she stated, eyes raised from the soggy ground to look at him.

"Good interesting or bad interesting?" he asked.

"Both, I think." He could hear the shrug in her voice. She dropped a sand-covered chunk into the bucket and moved to another spot on the waterline. "She told me how she knew what you are, and the details got more than a little uncomfortable."

"I'm listening." He took the shovel from her and dug, trying to allow her to focus on the story instead of the clams.

"She confessed some things to me I'm not sure I should share." She hesitated a moment. He let her pause and didn't push or pry, already aware of the direction this was likely heading.

"The other night, you told me not all the old stories of the selkies were true. Or at least not wholly true for *every* selkie."

"I did."

"Do you know if your thoughts on the matter might be shared by your brother?" A deep flush spread across her cheeks. He could only describe her expression as embarrassed for asking and hopeful of the correct answer.

"I have several brothers, but I assume you mean

Declan?" He was the only brother which he had mentioned specifically. "What's he got to do with this?"

"Well, you know Maeve is the one who plucked your *cotabonn* off the sand, and obviously she knew what it meant to be in possession of it. You also know it wasn't you she was looking to keep on shore. Have you not wondered who it was she wanted your coat to belong to?"

"You're saying Maeve believed the *cotabonn* belonged to Declan specifically." Not a question but a statement of fact. "Maeve has met Declan before and was hoping to refresh her acquaintance with him."

"*That* is what I am saying, yes."

He pursed his lips and looked up at the sky. "Damn, Declan. I should have put it together."

"So he does enjoy his time on land frequently then?" Aylee looked crestfallen at the implication his brother had taken advantage of her sister without a second thought.

"No, Aylee. I didn't mean to imply. . . It's just the night we came ashore, Declan did mention how much he enjoyed this particular beach, and the entire night he seemed retracted." He took a deep breath and tried again. "Distracted. I assumed he was worried about something else. I never guessed he might be hoping to see someone."

Aylee had bent down to dig in the damp ground. She gave him a brief retelling of the events as Maeve had told her. Cailean noticed she didn't mention specific intimate bits, but he could fill in the blanks well enough.

"She made it sound as if she loved him. I think she had some misguided belief that if she could keep his medallion long enough to get to see him, she might at least get an explanation of why he left and never came back to her." Aylee stared out at the waves. "I know it has caused you immeasurable harm, what she did. I hate that anyone in my family—someone I cherish so completely—has brought this grief on you. But I also kind of understand. It's horrible when someone you think might care for you just leaves. Without even a goodbye.

"She wondered if it was because she wasn't pretty enough or kind enough or good enough. If she had been bolder, would he have come back to her?" Her voice cracked and she swallowed. "It doesn't make sense I know—this wondering. But I've wondered the same thing. Not about Maeve of course, but about me and well. . . What is it about me that wasn't enough?"

Cailean squatted down next to her and placed his fingers under her chin. He gently raised her face so she was looking him in the eyes.

"Know this, Aylee Garrow. That spineless ass *was* never, and *will* never, be worthy of you. You are all of those things. Kind, generous, courageous. And certainly beautiful. Here," he touched her chest above her heart, "and here," he cupped her cheek. "Anyone who has had the good fortune to spend a minute in your company would say the same."

Tears welled in her eyes. "That's lovely to hear, but at the end of all this, you are going to do the same. Leave, I mean."

It felt like a punch to the gut, hearing those words from her, but he knew they were true. "Aye. I am. Hopefully you at least will understand why, but even though you might understand, know this—I don't deserve you either."

She wiped the tears from her eyes and immediately swore at herself. She had managed to bring a handful of gritty sand into her lashes. She laughed so she wouldn't continue to cry and used the edge of her jacket to clear away the grains. She allowed him to take her hand and pull her to stand.

"Well, then. I suppose we will just need to make a date now." Aylee tried to sound upbeat even as the idea of him leaving hung between them. "I vote for the first full moon of autumn each year."

He looked at her, brow furrowed.

"The first full moon. I'll happen to find myself on the

beach if you happen to drag your splendid seal hide from the water."

"Oh Aylee. . ." He blew out a long breath. The morning light caught him just right, the waves matching his aqua and cerulean stare. The barest trace of saline lined his lower lashes. "I'm not sure. . ."

She felt a catch in her chest but refused to acknowledge it. She could pack it away and examine it at another time.

"You don't have to commit. I understand."

"It's not that I don't want to agree. Believe me. I've rarely wanted to agree to something so much. I just. . ." Real anguish crossed his face.

Aylee spared him. "Can I ask you another question?"

It was more for her benefit. Another small self-preservation. An avoidance of the rejection she was sure to come. Despite his earlier words, despite the way he looked at her, he would never be able to stay. Could never choose her, even if he wished it.

"You know you can." His voice was still tinged with the rough edge of emotion.

"How old are you, Cailean?"

He laughed quietly and turned to look out to sea. "Of all the questions in all the world, my age is the most important?"

She stepped back and grabbed a stick proffered to her by Pepper. She hurled it as far down the beach as she could and watched her dog chase after it, sand and water kicking up behind her.

"I have loads of other questions which are more important, but I thought this one was easy. You look to be just a few years older than me, twenty-four, twenty-five maybe. But sometimes when you don't think anyone is watching, there's this certain look in your eyes. It makes you seem much, much older."

He took a deep breath.

"Would you be dismayed if I was older than your Rupert Camden?"

A SIMPLE TALE OF WATER AND WEEPING

She stared at him wide-eyed.

He smiled devilishly. "I'm only joking. I've been on this earth longer than you for certain, but I am still a young man."

Not exactly an answer. She didn't push.

"One more."

"Of course." He smiled again.

"You told me before, you don't have anyone back home. But since you are a *young man*—have you. . .?" She felt more than awkward asking, but part of her needed to know. It was silly, but even though he would never be hers, the idea of him being someone else's made her feel sick in the pit of her stomach.

"I have had . . . acquaintances in the past, yes. But my heart has never belonged to anyone."

The tension released from Aylee's shoulders.

"I need to get back to the shop." She stepped away and trudged through the sand, clam bucket in hand. "I'll see you tonight."

"Tonight?" he called after her.

"It's Friday, remember. You're coming to dinner with my family," she yelled over her shoulder. She whistled to Pepper and left him standing near the water alone.

TWENTY-SEVEN

With the pheasant roasting merrily in the oven, the root vegetables peeled and bubbling in a sauce rich with herbs and butter, and the quick bread cooling on the sideboard, Aylee finally found time to set the table. She used their best dishes, painted with clever pasture scenes in a rich burgundy glaze, to offset the beautiful bunches of red and gold mums she placed in two matching pewter pitchers. The silver was polished and the napkins pressed. She set the table for six, not knowing if Graham was coming but deciding to err on the side of caution just in case.

Really Aylee wasn't sure why she was fussing so over appearances. Cailean had been in this room before and seemed perfectly comfortable, but after this morning, she wanted to give him a pleasant evening. It was wrong to suggest he was abandoning her. Clearly he couldn't stay in town even if he wanted to, but still it felt wretched to know she would likely never see him again.

As far as his age, he'd done a fantastic job of avoiding telling her a hard number. Perhaps the magic in his blood helped him remain young. She couldn't blame him for not telling her the truth, when she all but retched at the notion of marrying Rupert Camden based on his age.

She was setting out the last of the goblets when she realized they had no wine to go with the meal. She had time to run to the pub down the road to get a couple of good bottles. She grabbed her coat and left Pepper sleeping by the fire as she hustled out the door.

The main street was quieting down as the patrons in town finished their errands and went home for the evening. The pub was the busiest establishment on most

Friday nights, so it was no surprise clumps of people were heading in the same direction. Up ahead, she could just make out Robbie and Deirdre as they crossed the street along with a few of Robbie and Ian's friends. Deirdre raised a hand in greeting and said something to Robbie. He turned and smiled at Aylee and joined his friends inside while Deirdre waited for Aylee on the corner.

"Hi there, lovely," Deirdre greeted her friend. "Care to join us for a cider? Robbie's meeting a few of the fellas here, and I thought I'd tag along. I could use a female companion."

"As fun as it sounds, I have other plans this evening. Cailean's coming to dinner."

Deirdre raised her eyebrows and made a whistling noise. "I see. Maybe I should invite myself to your place instead."

"You're always welcome to join us. You know that. I can add another setting easily," Aylee said. "I just came to buy a bottle or two of wine for the meal."

"Ladies." Aylee turned to see a friend of Ian's saunter past. Calvin Murphy was a bottler at the distillery too.

"Hi, Cal. The boys are inside. Tell Robbie I'll be there in a tick."

"Will do, Dee," he replied. He turned to go but not before he looked Aylee up and down, a leer on his face.

She ignored the flush at the unwanted assessment and prodded Deirdre into agreeing to come to dinner. "You can bring some cider along if you want, but my parents would be happy to have you there."

They walked inside the small building and were assaulted by the raucous noise of happy patrons. A lone fiddler was playing in the corner, and the pub tables were full of men and women laughing and talking.

Deirdre left Aylee at the bar to inform Robbie she was going home with Aylee instead of staying for drinks with him and his pals. A loud roar of laughter issued from the table they were at, and Aylee assumed the boys were giving him some kind of grief.

Aylee stood next to the bar and had to shout at the pub owner to get his attention. She dropped a few coins on the bar and asked for three bottles of wine. As he turned to leave, she felt someone press up behind her, pushing her body harder into the counter at her front. She tried to push back, but the wall of body behind not only did not yield, but came closer.

"Yeah, go ahead and wiggle some more." The voice near her ear was harsh and smelled of whiskey.

An arm wrapped around her waist and turned her to face Calvin Murphy, Ian's friend from the distillery. He pinned her once more up against the bar. She put one hand on his chest to push him away, the other against the sticky surface of the counter to keep her balance.

"Let me go," she hissed at him.

He stepped back, and she turned to push around him. For a brief moment she thought he was going to let her pass, but he only used the opportunity to reposition himself, caging her against the bar, an arm on either side of her smaller frame.

"Not just yet, sweet girl. I'm just getting comfortable. Ain't you?" He bent his head to kiss her, and she turned her face away from his thick wet lips.

"Now that's not very nice." He squeezed her closer, crushing her hand between his chest and hers. "Am I not good enough for ya? Ian told me you've been pushin' him away, so I thought you might be looking for something else now that you're not Camden's anymore."

His voice. Something in his voice triggered an image of lightning flashing and the smell of wet leaves and earth.

"Let. Me. Go." Tears were in her eyes, and she wondered how no one in the crowded pub could see what was happening.

"I also heard that new friend of yours might be dealing in things he shouldn't. Poking around up at the distillery and such. You should be more careful who you associate with."

"I have no idea what you're talking about. Now, get off me." She tried to bring her knee up between his legs, but he had her pinned too tightly.

His only reply was to run a hand up her side from her waist to her breast, his meaty fingers under her coat and groping her through her blouse.

"Hey now, leave that girl alone!" the pub owner yelled as he returned.

That at least garnered some attention, and within a blink Robbie was there, pulling the vile man away. "What the piss are you doing, Cal?"

Aylee thought she might be sick.

Robbie's eyes were fiery, and his fist was clenched at his side. He placed a half-drunk pint on the bar and grabbed Calvin by the back of the shirt, hoisting the other man away from Aylee. Robbie never shied from a fight, particularly if it meant sticking up for someone he cared about. Saints bless him.

The noise in the pub had never fully receded, but within moments, the laughter and music were back full force as if nothing out of the ordinary had happened.

She tried to settle the shaking in her arms as Deirdre wrapped her in an embrace and ushered her out the door.

"It's okay, Aylee. Take some breaths. Robbie'll be beating the shit out of him any minute now." She rubbed her hands up and down her friend's arms and then wiped the tears from her cheeks. "Breathe. In and out. There you go."

Aylee took the breaths as directed, and after a minute or two she was composed enough to remember the wine.

"I'll grab it and then we'll be on our way. Are you all good out here by yourself?" Her chocolate eyes looked worried as she peered into Aylee's face.

Aylee nodded and Deirdre hurried in. As she walked away, Aylee caught her friend huff out "Piece of shit" once again. She returned in a blink and they were back at Aylee's house before her heart rate returned to normal.

Deirdre initially objected when Aylee asked her not to discuss the events at the pub with her parents.

"I just don't understand why you wouldn't want them to know," she'd said. "They should bar him from coming in the shop and have the council look into it."

"They've got a good bit to worry on right now, and I don't want to add to the mounting pile."

Deirdre still looked skeptical.

"Look, Dee. If you can keep this one secret for me, just for tonight—not for the rest of eternity—maybe I can share another secret with you."

"Is it a juicy one?" Deirdre asked, light glittering in her eye.

"The juiciest," Aylee affirmed, and like that, the matter was settled.

Graham did indeed decline to attend dinner with Maeve so the setting for six was perfect.

Cailean arrived right on time, and Aylee could have sworn Deirdre swooned at the sight of him. She did have to admit he looked even more handsome than usual. He had taken care to borrow a clean shirt and jacket from Ned and had a sprig of evergreen in his buttonhole. It brought out another shade of blue-grey in his eyes.

Those brilliant ocean eyes clearly saw more than she gave them credit for.

"What's wrong? Did something happen?" He was through the door and next to Aylee in a heartbeat.

"Something happened all right," Deirdre murmured. Aylee shot her a withering look, but she didn't stop. "You said I couldn't tell your parents. You said nothing about keeping it from Cailean."

When Aylee just frowned, Deirdre continued, "That arsehole Calvin decided to get a little handsy with our Aylee."

"It was nothing. Just a little incident at the pub." The smile Aylee wore was clearly not very convincing.

Color flared on Cailean's cheeks, and his face stilled into a mask of pure darkness.

"Please," Aylee said. "Please, I'd just like to have a nice evening. I don't want my parents to know right now."

Cailean didn't say anything, just studied her face for a moment.

"Please, Cailean. We can talk about it later."

Deirdre shrugged and gave him a look that spoke of many years of long suffering at her friend's request.

"Fine, Aylee. We can talk later."

He smiled and allowed Deirdre to show him into the apartment.

Dinner went smoothly, and Aylee was pleased to see her parents engage Cailean in conversations both mundane and fanciful. Topics ranged from how many men would undertake a cooperage apprenticeship to how the water fey hunted for fish in the depths of the icy sea.

At one point Aylee asked the group if they thought the town should be named. Cailean smiled at her but remained quiet while her parents, sister, and best friend laughed at various ideas the others floated. For some strange reason, Deirdre's favorite appeared to be Barley Bottom. She giggled for minutes after suggesting it, and Aylee couldn't help but laugh along as tears seeped from her friend's eyes at the idea.

Only once did the conversation steer into more dangerous waters.

"Why is it Aylee should marry so soon?" Cailean asked once the dinner dishes had been cleared from the table. "She seems independent and smart—fully capable of running the shop for you on her own if the need should arise."

Aylee sensed rather than saw her mother stiffen.

"I'm not suggesting she grow into a spinster just yet. Only why not allow her some freedom if she so chooses?"

Deirdre leaned over to Maeve and whispered, "Oh, this might get good."

Maeve only smiled and affectionately brushed Deirdre away.

"Well. . ." began Devon. "Of Aylee's abilities there is little doubt. If there were, Maeve and Graham could certainly assist with the shop. I, and her mother, only want her to be happy."

At Cailean's skeptical expression, he added, "Why is it you believe she wouldn't be happy if she were to marry? Is there not something to be said for having a partner to carry life's burdens? To share in one's joys as well as their sorrows? Having someone to chat with about the ordinary and to have a fierce ally when the world's darker moments come calling?"

Aylee looked at her father. Really looked at him, as he sat misty eyed and watching her mother. She felt selfish then, thinking the worst of them and not ever really taking the time to see they wanted her to marry someone she could love and hold dear. What if she never found such a person? Or worse, what if she'd *already* found them?

Cailean spoke. "Mr. Garrow, if we are all so lucky as you in life, the world will become a better place indeed."

"I've no doubt our Love will find the right man. It's just a matter of her mother and I being a bit more patient, I suppose. Now, who wants dessert?"

Deirdre and Maeve left shortly after dessert, both eager to get home before the rain picked up. Cailean stayed to help clean up the dishes.

As Aylee walked him to the door, she quickly told him of the events at the pub earlier. He seemed to grow colder and more distant as she finished.

"I'm sorry I wasn't there to assist your friend Robbie."

She smiled sadly. "I'm sorry, too. But if I am to be as independent as I would like to believe I can be, I can't have a tall dark bodyguard with me every moment. I'm not

A SIMPLE TALE OF WATER AND WEEPING

the queen of the selkies after all."

"No, I don't suppose so." He took her hand and squeezed it. "I'm running out of time, Aylee. I can feel the water calling to me. I don't think I have many days left. One way or the other, I'm afraid I won't be here much longer. I won't be able to fight the call."

His face was a grim mask. With the lamplight playing in his eyes and the shadows dancing in his hair, he looked so much older. Wearier than she had ever thought he could look.

"When I'm gone," he began, but she cut him off.

"Let's not talk about it now."

He ignored her. "When I'm gone, you need to promise me you'll at least try to be safe and happy."

"Cailean..."

"Promise me, Aylee. Say the words."

"I promise. When you are gone..." Her voice cracked. "When you are gone, I will try to be safe and happy."

"And you'll be confident and kind and all the other things in here"—he tapped her head at the temple—"which I adore about you? You'll embrace those things for the strength they are?"

She looked into those lovely eyes, and afraid her voice would break, she nodded.

She knew he didn't believe her. She wasn't sure if she even believed herself.

TWENTY-EIGHT

That night, the ocean called. He answered.

He didn't remember leaving his bed in the night or the walk to the shore. He didn't remember taking off his boots and leaving them by the rocks or how he stripped his clothes in the moonlight. He vaguely recalled the delicious feeling of the icy water on his feet and then his thighs. He had a sense the bracing liquid had felt welcoming as it came up over his chest and head.

His first clear thought was when his muscles froze up and he nearly inhaled a lungful of the brine. He kicked to the surface, desperate to get back to the shore in the distance. How had he gotten out this far? How would he get back in?

Without the thick layer of fat and the tough seal hide, the frigid temperature was draining his body.

He was a strong swimmer, but the leaden feel of his limbs not cooperating wasn't something he was accustomed to. Panic threatened to consume him, but he couldn't let it.

Out of the depths, a large male seal appeared. He knew this beast, this man in disguise. Declan was followed by a small colony, or bob, of his kind. They swam beneath and next to him, pushing and supporting him as he made his way back to the shore. Without them, he surely would have drowned.

As he hauled himself onto the sand, he looked up and blinked a mix of seawater and tears from his eyes. He was most certainly running out of time.

TWENTY-NINE

The Saturday afternoon rush had just begun to pick up when the front door banged open to reveal a frantic Violet Abbott. It had not yet banged shut before Aylee was moving toward her. Something was terribly amiss.

"Have you seen Shelby today?" The words ripped into the air with chilling clarity.

Violet's face was ashen. Her mouth a tight trembling line.

Placing a hand on her shoulder and looking her intently in the face, Aylee responded, "No. I've not. What's wrong, Violet?"

"She's gone. I was doing some mending earlier this morning. In the front room. By the fire. I must have drifted off in my chair. She knows not to leave the house without my say so." With each word out of Violet's mouth, Aylee's heart rate increased. "When I awoke, she wasn't there. I've been up and down by the strand and around our street, but she's nowhere to be found. I thought maybe she came here to see you."

She was stricken.

Una Garrow had come quickly when she heard the terror in the old seamstress's voice.

"We'll get some of the boys to start looking about. She can't have gone far." She called into the back for her husband. "Devon, get the Cormack boys and Graham and start looking for our sweet Shelby. Seems she's wandered off."

Violet, not young by any estimation, appeared to have aged a decade since Aylee last saw her.

"It's going to be fine, Violet. We'll find her. She

probably went for a walk and just didn't realize the time." Aylee tried to sound reassuring, but it was feeble even to her own ears.

"I'll never forgive myself if anything happens to her." Tears were streaming down her aged cheeks.

Una said, "Now, Aylee. You go on down to the beach and take a look around near the tide pools. I'll just close up and run over to the Sommersons' and ask Deirdre to head up toward the inn and the dairy. Maybe she can ask Ned and Candice if they've seen her."

"You can't think she would have gone down by the water?" The terror in Violet's voice broke Aylee's calm.

"Probably not, but best to check anyway, Violet." Her mother gave Aylee a grave look, which sent her running out the door.

Aylee knew Shelby had no fear of the sea, despite the numerous times she'd been warned—not only by her aunt but by just about every other person in town—to stay away from the water. While Aylee knew part of her lack of fear had to do with her simple innocence—Shelby couldn't imagine danger anywhere—she herself was partially to blame. Shelby was aware Aylee went to the shore nearly every day, and if Aylee could do so and not be afraid, then surely Shelby could as well.

But where another young woman would see crashing waves and a dangerous undertow, Shelby would see a sand piper that wanted to be chased into the surf. Instead of a drop onto treacherous rocks, Shelby would see only a lovely bunch of fuchsia seaside daisies wanting to be picked.

Aylee raced down the main street and past the churchyard, quicker than she would have thought possible. The lovely young woman meant so much to her; she wasn't sure what she would do if something happened to her friend.

As she crested the small stone bridge leading to the shoreline, the image greeting her was so unusual she thought she might be imagining it.

Shelby was indeed on the small sandy beach, just above the waterline and next to the outcropping of rock leading further down the coast to the small pier. It wasn't her friend in her wet skirts and windblown hair which caused Aylee to stop short, however. It was the beast standing next to her. Shelby had a dreamy look on her open face, a smile spread from ear to ear, as she ran her fingers through the long white-gold mane of the most glorious palomino horse Aylee had ever seen. The horse leaned into the touch as Shelby stroked the perfectly formed neck and shoulder.

The horse stood taller than a Clydesdale and had at once a wild fierceness and a hypnotic calm. Aylee wanted to run from its immense power but felt herself so entranced by its beauty, she needed to touch it. Riding such a creature would be like riding the wind. It would be ecstasy.

The closer she got to the pair by the water, the faster she moved. Somewhere deep in the back of her mind, a voice was screaming at her. *No. No. No. This is not right*, the voice shouted at her. *Not right*. She hushed the voice and kept approaching.

Aylee couldn't remember a time she had envied anyone more than she did Shelby in those moments. There her friend stood, touching the creature. She could think of no other word than creature as it was so much more than a simple horse. *Touching it!* Aylee should be standing there, not Shelby—stroking the magnificent steed.

As if in response to her thoughts, the horse turned its face toward her, and she could sense it speaking to her. *Come, lovely. Come closer. Come run your hands in my mane. I'm sure your friend can share. She has soft hands, but I bet yours are softer. Come closer.*

Something in the horse's face didn't seem altogether right. Despite its beauty and power, there was a *wrongness* to it.

The voice in her head was now screaming. *No. NO.*

NO! She didn't want to listen to the screaming. She wanted the calming lull of the creature to wash over her. Her brain was a pleasant misty sort of foggy—as if she'd drunk too much spiced wine.

Aylee stepped up next to the glorious animal. The beast swished its tail, and the hairs rose to curl around Shelby, embracing her. The girl had a vacant look in her eyes. From the corner of Aylee's mind—the corner not coated in a sodden blanket of calm—registered a thin line of drool coming from her friend's smiling mouth. Her fingers continued their endless twirling of the creature's silken hair. Shelby was making a soft noise, something between a giggle and the mewing of a kitten.

Aylee knew this too was wrong, but the moment her mind turned toward it, the hypnotic call of the horse grew louder. *Place your hand in my mane. Feel how soft and comforting it is. Feel me. Be with me.*

Aylee reached a tentative hand to the horse. *No. No! NOOOO!* The voice was screaming louder than the crashing waves of the surf. She hesitated.

Feel me. Be with me. This is all you want. Here. Now. We can ride the wind and the waves together.

Still she hesitated. The words were oily and vile in her mind, yet she *did* want to run her hands over the creature. She wanted to feel its powerful body beneath her. It was disgusting, but the desire was nearly impossible to resist.

Do you prefer this version of me then?

The fogginess of her mind thickened. She blinked, and where the horse had been now stood the figure of a man. Skin the caramel of cooked sugar and hair the same white-gold of the palomino. A painful beauty—features too perfect, lips too full, teeth too white. His body was a work of art, and his posture all seduction and grace. His eyes. His eyes were wrong. Repugnant. Rancorous. Black depthless pools where no light escaped.

Feel me. Be with me. Why do you resist? The golden man wrapped his arm possessively around Shelby.

A SIMPLE TALE OF WATER AND WEEPING

Aylee took another step closer. Her body was responding to the depthless pools of those eyes. The fullness of those lips.

Closer, lovely. Closer. Come with me. Together we will find pleasures you've never dreamed of. Come with me. Be with me. Even as the voice drew her in, her body resisted. The voice turned into a hissing, slithering entity in her mind.

No. First one foot then the other dug into the wet sand. She panted against the strain. Her mind splintered between desire and revulsion. Her muscles waged a war of self-preservation.

The creature broke eye contact with Aylee and hugged Shelby tighter to its sculpted chest.

I would have preferred you to join me, but I'll settle for her.

No. No. NO! Aylee embraced the screaming in her head. She tied herself to that voice like an anchor and let it drag her mind up out of the fog. The creature shifted once more into the form of the horse, its eyes the same inky depthless pools. The sense of wrongness was so clear she didn't understand how she could have been lulled. Its face, once beautiful, was stretched and cadaverous. Its once lush mane hung in clumps like seaweed upon the shore of its shoulders.

The creature shifted, Shelby on its back, and set off straight for the waves.

Aylee lunged to grab her friend. The beast was tall and strong. It took all of Aylee's power to jump up and wrap her arms around the other girl. Shelby made no effort to free herself, even as the profane beast splashed into the water. Aylee pulled with one final burst of energy, and Shelby's hands flew from the mane, her body toppling off the creature and into Aylee. Shelby's arms found Aylee's waist and clung to her as if she had just awoken from a nightmare. Perhaps she had.

The monstrosity below them bucked and turned, an unnatural scream rising from its throat—so clearly not a horse now as its face continued to contort. The wrongness of the thing amplified. The entire face became something wicked and other. Its mouth stretched to accommodate an overabundance of teeth more at home in a creature from the deep—long and needle sharp.

With a speed she would not have thought possible, it struck out at Aylee. The creature's lower jaw opened so wide, it might have been unhinged, and then slammed back in an attempt to capture her arm. Its teeth raked over her skin. But those strong jaws did not clamp around her flesh—only the thick wool of her coat. It dove for the sea floor, meaning to drag Aylee and—by virtue of the grip she had on her friend—Shelby as well, into the depths.

Aylee took in a lungful of air just before her head went under the rollicking surf. She could only hope Shelby had done the same. She kicked out and felt her boot connect with the creature's neck, but still it held her. She struggled to free herself and managed to push Shelby up toward the surface. With the last of her strength, she wrapped her arm around the head of the creature and drove her thumb into one of the wretched black eyes. The orb was a soft jelly in the bony socket. She pushed harder. She felt the scream as much as heard it through the water. Only then did it release its grip on her.

She kicked to the surface and drug herself onto the beach as it disappeared further into the briny depths.

A sobbing and shivering Shelby lay on the shore. Water streamed from her hair and clothing. Aylee wrapped her arms around the girl and tried to offer comfort. Aylee's own limbs were trembling violently; they were likely both suffering from shock. Men's voices were calling to her, and she looked up to see both of the Cormack brothers as well as Ned Bryan and Cailean cresting the small bridge.

"M-ma-ma mean horse," Shelby stuttered out.

"Shhhh . . . sweet thing. It's gone now." Aylee's teeth chattered as she spoke.

"Aylee! Shelby! Saints. What happened?" Ned boomed.

Shelby was sobbing. "Mean horse. Mean horse."

A SIMPLE TALE OF WATER AND WEEPING

"We need to get you both inside and dry. The water's freezing, and you'll be in shock." Ian had reached the girls and wrapped his arms around them where they sat in the sand.

"We can take them to the inn. We've got plenty of warm tea and a blazing fire in the hearth. Loads of blankets and things to get you warmed up," Ned agreed.

Aylee allowed Ian to help her to stand. Cailean looked as if he wanted to hold her, but she shot him a look full of such distrust he nearly stumbled back. Instead, he helped Robbie pull Shelby to her feet and took his jacket off to wrap around the sobbing girl's shoulders.

It took only minutes to get to the inn and only a few minutes more to send Robbie off to fetch Violet. Candice Bryan cooed over both young women and fussed over Shelby in particular. She supplied tea with a good dose of brandy and warm changes of clothes.

Aylee told them she'd reached the beach just as a wave swept Shelby's feet out from under her and into the frigid surf. For reasons she didn't fully understand, she didn't mention the creature masquerading as a horse. She didn't feel guilty about her omission—despite knowing Shelby wouldn't be believed when she spoke of it. It seemed better that way. She also didn't feel guilty about letting Ian help her back to the inn and the hurt look on Cailean's face as she did so.

First the banshee and now this. She wasn't certain but believed she might have just survived a kelpie. Not only survived, but saved a helpless girl in the process.

She also knew none of these things had plagued her or the town before Cailean had washed up on shore. Despite the affection she felt for him, she couldn't ignore the events of the past weeks. She had vowed not to be blinded by her heart, and she intended to keep at least this one promise to herself. She would help him retrieve his *cotabonn* as she had promised and then she would say goodbye forever.

THIRTY

Between Mrs. Bryan's coddling and the hefty dose of liquor, Shelby had calmed considerably by the time Violet arrived to retrieve her. The two women allowed Robbie to escort them home with thank yous all around and promises from Shelby not to venture near the water unescorted again.

Cailean thought the likelihood of Violet Abbott letting Shelby out of her sight for even a moment was slim to none. The poor woman probably wouldn't sleep soundly for months, and he worried it would affect her health. He wondered what would become of Shelby when Mrs. Abbott closed her eyes permanently. Hopefully, she would have the kindness not only of Aylee but the rest of the town as well to rely on.

He knew more had transpired out at the water's edge than the limp story Aylee had given. He hovered by the door, not daring to broach the subject with so many others around. Something about Aylee's posture and the way she would look anywhere but at him spoke volumes. His suspicions were further cemented when he offered to walk her home, and she'd insisted Ian join them—giving a half-assed excuse about catching up on his success at the distillery. She was either scared of Cailean or at the very least suddenly wary to be alone with him. He meant to find out why.

The three of them left the inn as night was falling, and despite Aylee's frosty demeanor, Cailean couldn't help but be entranced by the small town. The air was fragrant with wet earth and grass, wood smoke and fresh-baked bread. The sea sang its lullaby in the hushed melody he knew by heart, and the stars twinkled overhead. Candles and lamps dotted the buildings as they passed. Since the time of the jubilee, more and more families had begun to hang evergreen branches on their doors, and strings of dried oranges and small red berries dangled from the lampposts.

He would need to have Aylee explain what all the decorations symbolized. That was if she ever deigned to talk to him again. She was doing a good job of ignoring his presence at the moment. At least she wasn't treating Ian with much more warmth than she was showing Cailean.

He was still in the dark about what had spooked her at the beach, but he was smart enough not to press. He wanted to tell her of his own brush with the sea last night but couldn't do so with Ian present. Aylee was the first to break the silence.

"Any sign of the medallion, Ian?" Her voice lacked its usual good cheer. All business and right to the point.

"Well, no. It's only been two days." Ian looked between Cailean and Aylee.

"Time is running thin. We need to know if Camden has it." Her voice held no vitriol, just a sad resignation. What the hell had happened to her?

Ian fidgeted with his hat. "I said I'd look and I'm looking."

Cailean didn't know Ian well, but he would have sworn the other man wasn't telling the truth. Or perhaps his dislike for Ian was having him jumping at shadows.

"What will you do with it if you get your hands on it anyway?" So there it was.

"He's leaving town," Aylee said a little too quickly. "You don't need to know more than that, Ian."

Cailean caught the smug smile on the other man's face just before he turned to Aylee with all innocence. "Should I bring it to you if I find it?"

"It's probably best not to. Just tell us if you see it. Yeah?" The fewer hands on the coat the better.

"And if I don't? What if this thing you're searching for is never found? What will happen then, Aylee?" Something not quite convincing lurked in his hopeful expression. Cailean decided to file it away for the moment, but he'd definitely tell Aylee to be wary around her former lover.

Aylee's voice was still small and sad when she replied. "Nothing any of us will be happy about."

Although Ian appeared to want more from the exchange, he clearly knew Aylee well enough not to expect it that night. He must have sensed her frayed nerves as well.

He left them at the corner by the bakery, and despite Aylee's insistence that Cailean not escort her past the remaining few shops, he refused to turn back to the inn just yet.

"I'm tired, Cailean. I've had a long *rough* day, and I don't feel like company just now." She looked at him and tried to smile, but the light was gone from her eyes. The small crinkle normally present between her nose and her brows when she smiled did not make an appearance. "Not even your company."

"I'll just see you to your door."

"That really isn't necessary." She quickened her steps in an effort to cut off the conversation.

Cailean grabbed her hand to slow her pace, and Aylee flinched, bringing the hand up to her chest and away from him.

Without looking at her, he quietly asked, "What happened at the shore today?"

"I told you. Shelby got swept into the water. She almost drowned." She hugged her hands around her middle. Her clothing had dried by the time they'd left the inn, but still she shivered in the crisp evening air.

"Do you remember the night I told you how expressive your face is? Well, that lovely face of yours right now is telling me volumes. Please don't lie to me, Aylee. It doesn't suit you." His voice wasn't angry. Just . . . deeply edgy.

"Doesn't suit me! I'm sorry. I guess I'm not sure what suits me anymore." She stepped back away from him again, and he swore softly under his breath.

"Maybe it's being accosted in my own town or lying to my parents or saving my friends from banshees or kelpies. Perhaps those things have started to rub away the shiny exterior and the real Aylee is finally showing. Maybe the real Aylee isn't bold and courageous enough for all of this." She spread her arms in a gesture meant to encompass not only the town and the night air, but Cailean in particular.

He ignored the gesture.

"A kelpie? Did Shelby get drug out by a kelpie?" He was mortified. He'd seen full grown men drug down into the depths by those vicious mongrels. Drug down, and then once the life was leeched from their lungs, their bodies were ripped to shreds in a frenzy of blood and gore. How had the two young women fought it off?

"I don't know as I've never actually seen one before." Her voice was still full of anger and terror. "But if they are one moment beautiful horses with the ability to hypnotize a person and the next beautiful men who offer the promise of ecstasy and then the next horrific murderous nightmare creatures . . . then I would say it's a fair bet I met a kelpie today."

"Damn it, Aylee. No wonder you're shaken. Not many are fortunate to escape when a kelpie engages with them." He could hear the panic rising in his voice. Panic because he had not been there to help her and panic because he would not be there in the future either.

"Wonders for me." She put her hands on her face and let herself cry. She must have held it in all afternoon, presumably too worried about Shelby to really think what could have happened to either of them. As the adrenaline was wearing off, the tidal wave of emotion could sweep through her.

Cailean stepped closer and wrapped his arms around her, meaning only to offer her some comfort. She stiffened as soon as she felt his touch. So different from any other time he'd casually touched her or hugged her or embraced her. He stilled, and a dagger twisted in his core at her reaction. He stepped back, keeping his hands on her upper arms but peering down into her eyes.

"You think I had something to do with this?" Of course. She'd seemed wary of him all afternoon and now he understood why.

"No. Yes. I don't know what to think." Her nose was red and tears were leaving salty tracks on her cheeks.

"Aylee . . . I . . . Actually I don't know what to say." He stopped and grappled not with the right word this time but with the idea she might be afraid of him.

"It's just a coincidence, I suppose?" She'd stopped crying and wiped the back of her hand across her nose.

He let his hands fall and tucked them into his pockets.

"What is?"

"The things happening. Here in town. These last few weeks, things have been happening. All my life I've heard silly stories about fey and magic and superstitions. They've always been just that. Stories. But now . . . well. . . ." She raised her hands in a shrug. "Since you stumbled into town, things have been happening."

"Aylee. You have to know I didn't bring these things with me." Did she though? He certainly hadn't intentionally brought them, but was it possible the magic in him somehow called to the magic in them?

"Then why is this happening? If anything had happened to her today. . ." A shudder ran through her.

He could all too well imagine. If anything had happened to either of them, Cailean would have been devastated. For Aylee, it would have been catastrophic.

"I can't tell you why these things are surfacing. I suppose I might be responsible for the banshee. She was trying to warn me, but the kelpie, Aylee. No. No, I can't fathom why it chose today to hunt."

He took a deep breath and looked up at the frosty distant stars.

"If I am somehow responsible, the danger will pass in the next day or two."

"Why the next day or two? What do you mean, Cailean?"

He told her about waking far out at sea, about his need to return to the ocean depths. He told her how he'd barely been able to fight it the first few days and saw a spark of recognition in her eyes. She'd seen him those first few mornings, sitting on the rocks and fighting the desire to simply plunge back into the murky cold. He had welcomed the feeling of having another living soul there with him on the beach, but not needing to talk or explain himself had been a blessing too.

They'd been walking and now stood outside the back door to the shop and the wooden steps Aylee would climb to find herself safely in bed after such a horrendous day. He hated himself for adding to her worries but knew he needed to tell her.

"I won't be able to fight it much longer, Aylee. Maybe another two days. Maybe three. If I don't have my *cotabonn* by then, I think it'll be too late."

He was the worst kind of bastard for telling her this. He should have just let her hate him. It would be easier for her in the end if he did. He was leaving her, and it would be a kindness to her if she loathed him when the time came. But he wasn't that brave. Wasn't that strong. He couldn't just turn around and walk away, and he hated himself for it.

"It won't come to that, Cailean. It just won't. We will find the medallion."

And there it was. Just as he knew it would be. She was a wonder really. She sounded so sure, and he loved her a little in that moment. For her conviction and her passion. Even though she was scared of him, he loved her just a little.

He nodded. "Remember the promise you made me."

He squeezed her hand and walked back to his room at

the inn.

While Aylee lay in bed that night—unable to fall asleep—another thought occurred to her. Maybe it wasn't Cailean's doing at all, this surge in unusual events. Or perhaps at least not directly all his doing. Maybe it was her.

Every time Aylee thought about naming the town, excitement seemed to follow. Cailean had told her words held power, particularly names. Was this why the town was just town? Had it once been called something else? Something that faded and flaked away as the magic dissolved as well? Were the two linked?

No answers came to her, and in the early hours of morning, she finally closed her eyes and slept.

Thankfully, she did not dream.

THIRTY-ONE

"I've come to apologize," Rupert Camden said.

Aylee, who moments before had been busy sweeping the crumbling remains of autumn's fallen sentinels from the front of the shop walkway, was briefly dumbfounded. She'd heard the motor's puttering before she turned to see the truck itself. He'd arrived in a gleaming black and green petrol-powered vehicle. She'd only ever seen a few before, and those just from a distance. To have one pull up in front of the mercantile and see Rupert Camden exit was so shocking she might have forgotten how to speak.

"She's a beauty, isn't she?" He smiled at what must have been awe on her face and looked back over his shoulder. "Times are changing, Aylee Garrow. Perhaps in more ways than one."

Interesting choice of words. It was enough to pull her from her reverie at the sight of the twin metal headlamps and the wood gated bed—just large enough for four casks of whiskey.

"Indeed." She smiled appreciatively at the gleaming piece of machinery. It was polished despite the recent rains. "I hadn't realized business was picking up so much."

"Ah well, yes, it is, but I didn't come here simply to show off my new transport. I really do want to apologize. I've been thinking over my behavior last week, and I want you to know, I never meant to be belittling or patronizing. If I came across as such, please accept my sincere regrets."

Aylee blinked a few times and brushed a loose strand of copper from her eyes. "I'm not sure how to respond."

"You don't need to respond. I just don't want things to remain so..." He paused. "*Poor* between us."

Aylee thought a moment. "Mr. Camden, might I ask you something?"

"Rupert, please. And of course you may."

Aylee smiled at the not-so-subtle correction. "Rupert. It's just, well, I was wondering... Why the proposal now and why to me? You've been a lifelong bachelor, so...?"

His face colored faintly, the blush at odds with the firm visage his greying hair and thick mustache formed. He cleared his throat. "Well, I suppose I haven't ever really set out to be a lifelong bachelor. It just happened to work out this way. I did have someone, you know. Many years ago. Someone I loved very much."

"No. I didn't know. You don't need to tell me."

A family with two small boys rushed past on the walkway and Aylee scowled as one of the boys—the smaller redheaded demon—kicked through the pile of leaves she'd just swept.

Rupert smiled as the mother chided the child and grimaced apologetically at Aylee. The expression clearly read, *you'll understand one day*.

"I don't mind, actually. Perhaps if I'd been more open before we wouldn't be where we are today."

Aylee couldn't argue with him.

"I was young and so was she. A beautiful, lovely, kind girl. Much as you are now. She meant the world to me and I to her. We had plans to marry when she came of age, and I had plans to make sure she had the best of everything. I worked day and night to save my pennies. I opened the distillery and planned to make sure it was a success before we wed. I sold my soul to that place, she told me once. At the time I felt she was just being melodramatic and told her as much. I *needed* it to be a success for her. For us. That's what I told myself. Every day I was at the distillery before the sun crested the hills, and every night I barely made it by her family's home before I'd collapse with exhaustion. She told me she didn't want or need the money, she just wanted us to marry and be together. She came of age, and still I put the wedding off. She told me she didn't want to wait and I didn't listen. I let her slip through my fingers. One day I woke to find I was ready and she was gone. Had been gone for quite a long while—not physically but in here." He tapped a finger over his heart. "I just didn't notice it happening. She grew weary of waiting, and I am still alone."

Aylee was shocked into speechlessness twice in one morning.

"She moved up the coast with one of the other lads from town not long after. I was a bit shocked. I'd never thought twice about the simple farmhand before, but I suppose that's the story, isn't it. I didn't see what was under my nose as it was too close to the grindstone."

Aylee had a flashback to the conversation she'd overheard between Rupert and Graham the night of the jubilee. She had been so focused on her own mixed-up feelings about the situation with Ian and Rupert, she had missed the point of Rupert telling Graham to be happy with what he had. To be happy with Maeve. And she had treated Rupert so poorly. She was ashamed of how much she needed to improve the way she judged those around her.

"As for your second question—why you? I should think it was obvious." A frown dropped his thick mustache further down his chin.

She had a sinking suspicion. "It had to do with Ian, didn't it?"

"Partly. Mostly." He sighed. "I understand my method was inappropriate and unfair, but I assure you my intentions were good. There is just something about Mr. Cormack I can't quite put my finger on, and I wanted to give you some time to see it. I felt I owed it to your mother. In a way."

"My mother?" She was incredulous.

"There was a time when Una and I were friends. I'll not bore you with the particulars. It's not my place. But I

A SIMPLE TALE OF WATER AND WEEPING

made other poor choices as a young man. One of those, sadly, involved my friendship with her. She needed support at a difficult time, and again I was too busy to do the right thing. In some ways, I regret it even more than my bachelorhood. Thank the saints for your father. He was there when she needed a friend the most.

"At any rate, I wanted to help her daughter. Try to right the wrongs of my past. A kind of repayment, if you will. Turns out, I don't believe you ever really needed my help. You would have come to the right decision all on your own. Of that, I am certain."

Well, that was a hefty morsel to chew on.

Aylee nodded. "Thank you. For the apology and please accept mine in return. I misjudged you, and for that, I am truly sorry."

"No need, but if it makes you feel better, I accept." He turned to go back to his shiny metal and rubber machine.

Aylee stopped him before he could go. "Rupert, do you think it odd the town doesn't have a name?"

He stilled and looked at her intently. "What name would you give it, Aylee?"

She flushed a little. Did he think her foolish for asking such an odd question?

"Well, there are lots of things which could distinguish it. Barley Meadows, Oceanside." She smiled and added in a teasing voice, "I've even entertained Camden Square."

He chuckled. "Those all fit, I suppose, but why does the town need a name?"

"I'm not convinced it does. I just feel like *perhaps* it does. Names offer distinction, power."

"You may be on to something there, Aylee. I don't claim to be the wisest man I know, but I believe you may be right, and if you are, I'm certain when the right name comes to you, you'll know. When you share that name with others, they'll know too."

She considered this and nodded.

"There is one other matter I wish to mention. It has

come to my attention your friend has lost something of rare value."

Aylee stilled. The noise from the street seemed to quiet, as if the world around her was also holding its breath.

After his previous admissions, she'd felt awkward asking him about the medallion. Was he going to simply admit to having the key to returning Cailean safely home?

"Yes. I believe Cailean has been the victim of a most devious theft." She paused, judging how much to say. "I believe he would be quite appreciative if it was returned."

"Hmm." He huffed a small laugh. "I'd wager you would be less pleased if it was returned."

"Not at all." She couldn't hide her outrage at the suggestion. "Why would you propose such a thing?"

It was Camden's turn to be surprised. "Forgive me. I was under the impression you might harbor... feelings for the young man."

"We are friendly. Any more on the subject is between him and me." She took a breath, not willing to let this conversation go wayward. "Even if I did 'harbor feelings' for him, don't you suppose I would want it safely returned? I would no sooner wish his unhappiness than my own."

"I see. But my understanding is he would then be free to... *leave*. Are you sure it's what you want?"

While the same question had been implied by Ian in the past days, it had always felt uncomfortable, as if by Cailean leaving Ian was free to assume Aylee would be his again. It was not at all the same way Rupert asked the question, as if he cared only that such a scenario might bring her unhappiness.

It was clear to Aylee then. Rupert did indeed know the power the *cotabonn* held and what it meant to Cailean. She had no reason to continue the charade. He was in possession of it, just as Graham had said. She needed to convince him to return it. It could hold no value for him unless this entire encounter was some sort of ploy on his part.

"What I want and what is right are mutually exclusive. You've been quite forthcoming with me today, Rupert. I do hope this trend continues." She stepped closer, looking up the street into the distance.

"You would like me to give you your friend's coat."

"You could give it to me, or you could give it to him. I would like either of those options equally."

"I don't believe you will ever know how truly sorry I am it has come to this."

She held her breath, waiting for the blow.

"All these weeks I've come to the mercantile, biding my time, waiting for the proper moment. I never realized how wrongly I was doing things. It's been a bit of time since I've courted. I never realized how quickly the tides could turn and in one evening the work of weeks could come smashing to an end. I got complacent and you saw all the things I did not want you to see, and I never saw all the things I should have. More the fool, me."

This conversation was not going where it should be. It was not heading to an ending which saw Cailean's medallion safely in Aylee's hands.

"Rupert, please. Don't say anything more. Just give me the coat."

He looked contemplative, as if weighing his options. "You know, the night of the jubilee, I thought he was simply some puffed up city boy, here to conquer a small town girl. Again, I was simply trying my best to protect you. I'm sure it seems humorous to you now, but at the time, I was so angry and humiliated, and I placed the blame firmly on the shoulders of Mr. Vann."

"It really isn't worth discussing further. You can just give me his *cotabonn* and we can let it all lie." She'd let the word slip out and noted the intrigued look Rupert gave at the name. Did he know what magic a *cotabonn* truly possessed?

"I couldn't understand it. Over the next few days,

things became much clearer. Once Ruthven brought me the—*cotabonn* did you say? He asked me to keep it in a safe place for him, and I began to put things together. You needed a villain, and given my behavior, I understand it was easy to peg me as one. You should know, however, I only ever wanted to be the hero in the story."

"I don't understand."

"Some of us still know the old tales. Even in the age of petrol-run vehicles, some of us know what signs to look for. Banshees crying in the night, mysterious men washed in from the sea.

"Like I said earlier, things are changing. Magic is washing in, not in great tidal waves from the sea but in the small ripples of a pebble dropped in a pond. I will never be the hero in this story, not now." He looked absently at his hands. "Before I ever really understood its power, the medallion was taken by a bigger villain than even you might hope for."

THIRTY-TWO

Deirdre Sommerson didn't ask for much in life. She was content to live in the small town of her birth, to drink a few ciders at the pub with her friends, and to one day marry and have adorable, good-tempered babies. She'd likely end up getting even plumper than she already was and would most certainly never venture farther from her home than the distance a cart and horse could take her in a day.

She was happy and content to know such would be her lot in life. What she was not content with was the idea of her dearest friend facing the same fate. Not when she so clearly wanted more. Deirdre could love Robbie Cormack, and he would treat her well and love her in return. She would, however, never love Robbie with the same fierceness and openness with which she loved Aylee. Aylee was sunshine and laughter on a breeze. She was warm woolen socks and the sweetest jam you could ever taste. She was like waking up from a nightmare to see the sunrise out your bedroom window. It had been this way since they were small girls throwing rocks into the sheep pastures on their way home from school. Deirdre would never find another soul on this planet who could compare to her best friend. Nor did she want to.

This bond of love and loyalty made Deirdre want the best for Aylee, even when the small town around them couldn't care less about Aylee's desires for independence and love on her own terms. When Ian had trampled Aylee's heart so carelessly the previous spring, Deirdre very nearly ripped his throat out with her teeth. The fact he might one day be her brother-in-law made not a damn bit of difference in her mind.

Everyone in town thought Deirdre just a happy-go-lucky dimwit because she let them believe it. Life was easier that way. Just like everyone else in town, Ian, and perhaps even Robbie, underestimated Deirdre. The one person who would never underestimate her was Aylee.

This underestimation led Ian to leave a lovely charcoal pearlescent sand dollar necklace lying on his chest of drawers. He knew Robbie invited Deirdre over regularly to share a few laughs and a few kisses. But the other evening when she'd left Robbie at the pub to join Aylee for dinner with her family, Aylee had shared a secret because she trusted her friend.

Ian, for his part, didn't anticipate or care that she would be coming over early that morning to join Robbie for a day out.

Deirdre entered their shared room in the chipper way Robbie always said reminded him of a spring chick at the sight of worms. He pulled her into a hug and, because they were in his room away from prying eyes, gave her neck a nuzzle and her backside a squeeze.

"Robbie Cormack, you behave yourself or there'll be no picnic outing for you today," Deirdre chirped.

The weather was fine. Although the air was crisp, the fog had burned off and the sun was out. It might possibly be the last clear and decent day they'd have for several months. Once winter descended full force, it wouldn't let up for some time. Any time outside and away from the warmth of the hearth would be unpleasant at best.

"I've already skipped breakfast, but I don't mind skipping lunch too if you'd rather stay here. My folks won't mind as long as you keep the noises to a minimum," he purred in her ear.

"Hands off, mister. I need my tea or I'll be a demon all day. What's this now?" She grabbed the heavy medallion from the top of the chest and flipped it over in her hand. "I assume this is for me, or else you've got a bit of explaining to do."

Deirdre did in fact know two things. One, it was not for her, and two, it wasn't Robbie's at all. How this item came to be in his room she wagered had nothing to do with her and everything to do with Ian. The complete and total arse.

Playing the ever clueless had gotten her this far however, and she didn't want to drop the ruse just yet.

"Oh, that's just some piece of junk Ian brought home the other night. No idea where he found it. Maybe he means to give it to Aylee as some kind of gift." He frowned at the shell-like piece in her hand. "Why? Do you like it?"

"I don't dislike it. Why do you say it's junk?"

"Well, look how worn the leather is and who's ever seen a sand dollar that color? You can have it if you like. I'll give Ian a few coins and tell him I gave it to you instead. Save him the trouble of embarrassing himself by having Aylee refuse it."

Ahh. . . sweet, dumb Robbie. He just had no idea. She almost felt guilty about what she was about to do.

Deirdre raised her eyebrows at him and shook her head. "Always know just the right thing to say, don't ya?"

"What? What did I say?"

No clue at all. Deirdre lifted the leather strap over her head and tucked the smooth flat medallion into her shirt. "I've got the lunch all together, but I want to stop by the Garrows' shop on the way to the cliffs."

"Yeah. Sure, Dee." Robbie gave her bottom one more quick squeeze.

The pair passed Ian on the way out the door—Deirdre blowing him a kiss as they turned up the street.

THIRTY-THREE

Aylee had gone to find Cailean shortly after Rupert left. The pair was returning to the shop when Aylee's mother stepped out onto the front walk with Mrs. Larking and little Ruby. The girl smiled up at Aylee while her mother eyed Cailean warily.

Ruby had a new ribbon flowing from one hand—a lovely moss green to match her eyes. Aylee grabbed the other tiny hand and spun the child in a series of waltzing twirls. She was rewarded with a flood of giggles. Mrs. Larking was less amused.

"Ruby, if you ruin that ribbon, you'll not be getting another."

"Yes, Momma," she replied unhappily.

Aylee gave her a guilty smile and grabbed the door handle.

"Cailean has come to help me unpack a few crates. We'll be in the back," she explained to her mother. In reality, she wanted to speak with Cailean in private, but the task did need to get done so why not put him to work helping her?

"Oh, before you get too busy, Dee popped in and made me swear on my da's grave I'd tell you she needs to speak with you." Una said this with a mixture of amusement and exasperation. "Urgently apparently. That girl! She could make a broken shoelace seem as if the world were in peril."

That seemed odd. Aylee couldn't imagine what could possibly be so important to Deirdre.

"Did the beautiful creature tell you where I could find her?"

A SIMPLE TALE OF WATER AND WEEPING

"Up to the cliffs with Robbie. They were having some sort of picnic, and she insisted I let you join them, even for only a few minutes. The crates can wait. Go have some fun." She gave Aylee a swat on her backside and smiled. "Cailean. Nice to see you this afternoon as well."

While Una had been pleasant at dinner the other night, Aylee could still sense the tension her mother felt when seeing Cailean. She wasn't sure if this greeting was for her benefit, Cailean's, or simply to show Mrs. Larking how polite people behaved. In any case, it made her heart happy.

A rosy glow surfaced on her cheeks as the breeze brought both the smell of the ocean and the sting of winter replacing autumn to her face. The air was clean and fresh in her lungs, and she inhaled deeply, thankful she'd thought to grab both mittens and a warm cap before leaving the apartment that morning. Cailean seemed completely unfazed by the temperature.

They walked up toward the cliffs in companionable silence—Pepper's black and brown form bounding up and back from them to chase the occasional bird or bit of sea thistle fluff being pushed around by the breeze. Aylee had mentioned she had information for Cailean, but selfishly she kept it to herself for the moment. Partially it was because she still felt like such a fool after her conversation with Rupert Camden and partially because she knew the time they had left together was borrowed. She wanted to savor it for just a bit longer. Once they chatted with Deirdre and Robbie and were headed home she would spill the entire conversation.

With any luck, he would be on his way home by tomorrow.

The path was smooth as it passed through the tumble of coastal grasses and horsetail ferns, still holding up valiantly in the biting cold. The rocks were coated in bright lichen, and here and there the last of the red squirrels and wild hares were foraging for small bits of food before they retreated to their burrows for the coldest of the months to come. Overhead a cry rang out, and Aylee looked up to see an osprey circling overhead.

She paused on the path, watching in quiet wonder as it tucked in its wings and dove with speed and grace in and then back out of the shallows, deftly capturing the small fish that would serve as its dinner. Absently, she scratched Pepper's shaggy ears.

"They're amazing, aren't they?" Cailean put his arm around her shoulder.

She didn't flinch back or move away this time. Her previous wariness over the magic blooming had melted away as the reality of his need to return to the sea sank in.

"They're wonderful." She smiled up at him and marveled once again at the brilliant color of his eyes. Cobalt, teal, and azure flecks perfectly mirroring the sea stretching out before them.

"I can feel it, even from this distance. The pull."

She didn't say anything, just squeezed his hand.

"It's like there's this latch. In here." He placed his fist over his abdomen, just below his breastbone. "With each wave, I feel a little tug. When the tide comes in, it gets stronger. Tug. Tug. Tug."

Aylee could feel the sting of water rising in her eyes.

"And then there is this warring tug. Here." He placed a hand over his heart and thumped his finger in time with his heartbeat. "Not quite as strong but growing stronger all the time. Tug. Tug. Tug." His voice was just a whisper above the crashing surf and the call of the seabirds.

She dropped the hand he was holding and placed it on the one over his heart.

"It's so odd. I've always loved coming on shore and spending a day or two. But always, *always*, I can't wait to get back into the freedom of the sea. Now . . . well it's not *the going* back which bothers me, it's just the *leaving*. The leaving hurts." He looked from her to the ocean and back again. "I guess that's the only way to put it. It's not the going, it's the leaving. I wish we had more time."

"I wish the same." Her voice cracked. "Where exactly will you go, *when* you go?"

"I'm not sure. I'll need to try to make it back down the coast. If I'm lucky, Declan and the others will still be in the waters near here. After I find them, I don't know. I suppose I'll still try to take my place with the guard."

"Will you ever come back? Will I get to see you again?" She couldn't hide the hope in her voice.

"Aylee, I can't ask you to wait for me. I will come back, but I can't say when. Some things may be out of my control. You need to do the things in life which will bring you joy. I don't want you sitting on the beach night after night waiting." He bent at the knees, getting face to face with Aylee's dog, and scratched her in the special spot on her back he'd found. In return, Pepper tried to lick his cheek. He moved his head back in time to avoid a face full of dog slobber.

"In other words, you don't want me to become my sister."

"I meant what I said the other day. I don't deserve you," he replied as he returned to standing. "And I can't have you waste your life waiting for something I will never be able to give."

"We could try, couldn't we?" She wasn't sure what she was asking. Have him on land one day and the sea the next? Living a half-life, never completely feeling at home in either place? Even as she said it, she knew it would never be fair. Not for either of them.

"No, I don't suppose we could," she answered for him and asked a different question. One she wanted to get his honest opinion about. "Do you think I should take him back?"

"Camden? Oh, Aylee, no!"

She laughed. "I didn't mean Rupert. I meant Ian." She desperately wanted him to answer this question correctly. Before she told him all she now knew.

A SIMPLE TALE OF WATER AND WEEPING

His expression morphed from shocked incredulity to a hard bitter mask, and although he spoke the same words, the tone in which he said them changed their meaning entirely. "No, Aylee. No, I don't think you should take him back."

They'd begun walking again, and Aylee could make out the bright red and blue check blanket further up the cliff, as well as the two people lying prone on it. She waved to Deirdre as the gorgeous thing popped up and ran toward them. Pepper barked and raced down the path to where the blanket was spread.

She felt a rush of warmth spread through her, and she smiled even though her heart felt as if it were cracking into tiny bits too small to ever be placed back together.

"Good" was all she said.

THIRTY-FOUR

Robbie grumbled as Deirdre removed herself from his wandering hands and rose up to wave at Aylee. But, because he was Robbie, the grumbling was both halfhearted and short lived. Deirdre knew he'd hoped they would picnic behind a secluded bluff somewhere far from prying eyes, and he'd nearly thrown a tantrum—also both halfhearted and short lived—when she told him Aylee would be joining them.

Convincing Mrs. Garrow it really was urgent hadn't been difficult as such, but not everyone in town took her too seriously. In truth Deirdre wasn't sure Aylee would even show. She was relieved to see her friend not only walking up the path toward them, but with Cailean in tow to boot.

As Deirdre stood, she noticed a third party sprinting up the path behind her friends. At this distance, it was difficult to make out who it was, but Deirdre's heart sank. She jogged toward Aylee in the hopes of getting to her before the sprinting figure did. Robbie, bless him, had no idea he'd likely gotten himself into a bit of trouble by agreeing to give her the treasure she wore around her neck. He remained casually spread on the sheet next to their lunch.

Aylee's dog reached the picnic long before the people did. She sniffed at the crumbs of sandwiches and lay down next to Robbie. He didn't seem to mind.

Deirdre was torn between pulling the medallion from her shirt to thrust into Cailean's hands and keeping it hidden and playing dumb. Either would be risky. Sweet as Robbie was, he wasn't the sharpest tool, and she didn't think he was likely to catch on and keep quiet. She opted to keep it tucked away under her blouse for the time being and hope Aylee would sense what she needed her to do.

Aylee, saints love her, seemed to notice the urgency in her friend's face at the same moment she heard the footsteps approaching from behind. She had her hands on Deirdre's arms, searching her worried face, but turned to look over her shoulder just as Ian called out. Deirdre thought she had seen understanding in her friend's hazel eyes. Cailean, too, seemed to sense something was amiss. Although the move was subtle, Deirdre noted how he placed himself between Ian and the two girls.

Panting, Ian placed his hands on his knees. "Aylee, thank goodness I reached you! Your mother is livid you didn't finish in the shop. I told her I'd fetch you. You'd better get back there right away."

Deirdre watched her friend closely. Aylee looked momentarily confused but said, "Oh. Thanks, Ian. I should have realized she'd want help with the pies today. You didn't tell her where I was, did you?"

She cast a look at Cailean which seemed to say *or who I was with?*

"I'd never rat you out like that, although I can't say I wouldn't understand her concern." He smiled at her. *Just a little joke between friends.* "I mentioned you might be out for a drive with Camden in his new truck."

"Thanks, Ian. You're a lifesaver." She stepped away from Cailean and hugged Deirdre briefly. "I suppose our picnic will need to wait for another day."

The cool breeze off the ocean chilled Deirdre as her heart sank. If Aylee and Cailean left, how would she get him the medallion? Ian was sure to take it at the first opportunity. She couldn't ask Cailean to stay without Aylee, could she? That would look even more suspicious.

"But. . ." Words failed her as she looked up to see the expression on Ian's face.

Gone was the warm joking Ian, and there stood

someone she felt she'd never met. Both Cailean and Aylee were facing her, so they didn't see the menace emanating from every pore. Could they feel it even though their backs were turned? What to do? She was just about to reach into her blouse to remove the medallion when her lovely dear friend saved her.

"Ian?" Aylee asked, casting a wary glance in Cailean's direction. "Would you mind walking me back to the shop?"

Cailean looked not just offended but wounded. His eyes were a winter squall, stormy and dark.

"I. . ." Ian looked at Deirdre's best friend. "You don't want Cailean to walk you back?"

"No." Aylee gave a pointed look at Cailean. "I don't."

"Well, I had meant to stay and chat with Robbie and Deirdre about a few things." Ian was clearly torn between the opportunity to be alone with her and wanting to accomplish whatever he'd come up here to do.

"Aylee, please." Cailean reached a hand up to her, but she shook her head and stepped even farther from him.

Deirdre didn't understand it. She'd noticed them stopping to talk on their way up to the cliffs. They'd looked companionable enough, but they had been too far off to really see anything. They must have had a row instead.

The seagulls crying overhead and the waves thundering on the rocks below only served to accentuate the silence between Aylee and Cailean.

"Cailean, I think it's best you let me go. You *know* how I feel." She turned to Ian again. "It's all right, Ian. I can make it back on my own. It's just—"

"Of course I'll walk with you, Love."

When she didn't object, he smirked at Cailean, a schoolboy who'd won the class prize.

Aylee let out a long breath in what Deirdre swore was relief. None of the others seemed to notice.

"Dee, don't let him get too close to the edge of the

cliffs. Come on now, Pepper."

Cailean looked at Deirdre and nodded. "I might just sit here a minute. I don't wish to ruin your picnic."

Deirdre barely heard the words. Her mind was racing. Aylee turned and walked back up the path, Ian at her side and Pepper on her heels.

She needn't have worried however. As soon as the two were out of earshot, Cailean looked at her, his face transforming from the morose face of a jilted lover to a man full of relief and expectation.

"I truly hope this bit of chicanery works. If she gets hurt, I'll never forgive myself for letting her go. Now, where have you got it?"

THIRTY-FIVE

After the incident with the kelpie and her own poor response following it, convincing Ian she didn't want to be around Cailean was no more difficult than a few well-timed frowns and gestures. It disappointed her more than anything—he clearly didn't know her at all anymore.

She hoped Deirdre had information she could share once Ian was out of earshot. She hoped the urgency meant she might lead Cailean in the right direction. She hoped she made it back to the shop without Ian riling her to the point she might vomit on his shoes. She hoped. She hoped.

She was thrilled both her oldest friend and her newest friend had played along so willingly—trusting she knew what she was doing.

And Ian. Ian. Ian. Well, he had dug his own grave with the story about her mother. Una Garrow was anything but fickle, and if she'd told Aylee to go have fun for the day, she'd meant it. No "calling her back to the shop" in a flippant change of mood for her. No. Clearly Ian had other plans. What those plans entailed, Aylee didn't know, but she intended to find out.

Hearing him call her Love had nearly undone everything. It took all of her will not to at least cringe at the word. What she really had wanted to do was to smack him in the face, but as Devon like to remind her, violence rarely solved anything.

She found it intriguing he'd mentioned Rupert's new truck. Was it just a guess she knew about it or something more nefarious? Had Ian seen her with Rupert that morning? Too many questions with too few answers for her taste.

Time to start getting some explanations.

"I really appreciate you walking with me. I know you were probably looking forward to some relaxation on your day off," she said sweetly.

As the path made its way to and from the cliff, the terrain was full of hills. One moment the cliff edge and sea were clearly visible, the next the mounds of earth and tall grass obscured them.

Aylee ran her hand along a tuft of waist-high sea grass, interspersed with small white flowers and ferns. It was one of the more breathtaking spots near town, second only to the tide pools in her opinion.

"I don't mind one bit. Being with you is all the relaxation I need."

"Kind of you to say." She smiled. "So, have you seen Rupert's new truck as well?"

"Of course. It's been up at the distillery for a few days now. He took the train to the city last week to fetch it. I'm surprised you hadn't seen it or at least heard it trundling along the past several days."

She made a noncommittal noise in response. So he had known she saw it only that morning and he just happened to know where to find her this afternoon. *Was* he following her?

"I'm surprised you found me up here. I didn't realize Dee had planned such a large party."

"Ah, well no. It was just a happy coincidence. I told them I'd join them for lunch, but when Maeve mentioned you were needed in the shop, I thought to come here first to let them know I couldn't stay and, well, here you are."

If Deirdre really had asked Aylee to meet her here for the reason she suspected, why would she also invite Ian? Maybe she was wrong. Maybe Rupert had been wrong? It was possible, but her heart told her she was right.

"Maeve? I thought you said my mother sent you."

Ian was quiet. They'd made it to the top of the bluff,

the paths leading down both sides—one back to the cliff's edge where a trio huddled together near the blue and red blanket, and one to the town's edge. Aylee turned her face to the sea, inhaling the briny air, drawing it deep into her lungs and using it to center herself. Calming herself.

"We both know my mother didn't send you to fetch me and neither did Maeve. What's this all about, Ian?"

"Why can't you just enjoy being with me, Aylee? Why does there need to be a reason for wanting to spend time together? I love you. Isn't it enough?"

She couldn't say he sounded angry, but his voice was harsher than she would have favored.

"There *doesn't* need to be a reason, but I'd prefer the truth instead of lies." *And you didn't answer my question.*

Ian raised his arm and pointed in the direction of the cliffs. "Well then, I suppose the truth is I want to get that unnatural bastard away from you, Aylee."

He must have seen the shock on her face. "Oh, come on. You don't really think I'm that daft, do you?"

"I've never thought you daft. But then again, I never thought you could be a hurtful arse either."

"I see the bastard's taught you some crude vernacular as well." He turned to look at her, and she involuntarily stepped back from the bitter look on his face. "I've played along with you well enough, haven't I? Watching as you pull me closer just to push me away again. Asking for my help and then leaving with him. I had to ask myself, why would some random bit of flotsam be so valuable? I knew it had to have more than sentimental value for you to ask me to look around for it."

Alarmed by his tone of voice, Pepper returned to Aylee's side, hackles raised. The dog issued a low warning growl. The wind carried the sound away from them along with the cry of the gulls.

"Ian, calm down." She stopped walking altogether. Arms crossed over her body, she didn't want to look at him but didn't dare turn away. She should start walking.

Should put as much distance between them and Deirdre as possible. Give her friend enough time to tell Cailean whatever it was she knew.

"I'll calm down when that *thing* stops making love-sick eyes at you. I'll calm down when we finally make this"—he gestured back and forth between them—"right between us. For saints' sake, Aylee, what more do you want from me? I screwed up. I know it. But you can't seem to forgive me no matter what I do. I know you still love me, so why can't you just admit it."

"Ian. I don't know how to say this any more plainly. I do not love you. If I ever did, I don't anymore." No wobble to her voice. No emotion. Just a statement of fact.

He took a step toward her. "*If* you ever did? What the piss is that supposed to mean?"

"It means I might have or I was starting to. I don't know. But what you did, how you did it? Whatever *was* there shriveled and died last spring. And if it hadn't, today certainly isn't helping your cause."

"Well, then. And I suppose your new acquaintance had nothing to do with it? What happened to the sweet kind forgiving girl I used to know?"

The way he said sweet and kind was akin to an insult. It held none of the adoration and warmth it did when Cailean used the same words to describe her.

"I overheard Graham and Rupert, you know. I know what he is." The clouds had parted, and a fine sheen of sweat lingered along Ian's flushed cheeks and set his sandy locks curling around his ears.

"What he *is* is decent. That is all you need to know."

The worn path was smooth, but Aylee felt as if rocks were threatening to trip her at every turn. She focused on the golden and green stalks of grass. The blue of the sky. The smell of the salt in the air. Anything to keep her mind calm. She would not cry. Would not let her voice wobble. He didn't deserve to see her upset.

"Decent. That's a filthy disgusting thing to say." He

laughed. "I'm just curious where you go to... you know... We never could find anywhere private, but I'm sure you two must have someplace special. Not that I won't appreciate whatever he may have taught you."

"That's enough, Ian," she said coldly.

Normally, Aylee would have let her dog run about as she wished, but now she signaled Pepper to stay to heel.

She didn't like the look of understanding dawning on Ian's face.

"So this was all a ruse was it? Pretending you were scared of him. You wanted me to walk you home? Why is that, Aylee? Why would you want *me* to leave *him* with Deirdre? I'm sure you don't want to share him, and even if you did, Robbie may have a bit to say on the matter, I suppose."

She wrapped her arms around her middle and turned, not giving him the satisfaction of an answer.

"Not funny?" He stepped in front of her, making her face him as his voice became serious again. "I'm guessing maybe it has more to do with what she can give him? Am I right?"

She definitely didn't like what he was implying.

When she still didn't answer, he took her chin in his hand and tilted her face up to his. Pepper barked, and he let go.

"No, really. I'd like to know. I mean, he must have been fairly entertaining, but now it's time for him to get what he wants and for me to get what I need. Don't worry. I'll make it up to you."

"What are you talking about?" She tried to keep the worry from showing in her voice.

"Oh. Aylee. You are just so nice. It's one of the things I like about you actually. You can't possible imagine it, can you?"

Again, when he described her with what should have been a compliment, it felt slimy against her skin. Ian made it sound like a fault not a strength.

"A trade. Once he's gone, we get married. We leave town to set up a new distillery—a new life—far up the coast. I get to make you happy. I also get to see the smug smiles wiped off the faces of not only Camden but that thing down there pretending to be a man."

"Rupert was right." Understanding colored her words. "You took it, didn't you? The medallion?"

"Maybe I did."

"But Rupert said it's been missing from his office for days. We only asked you to look for it recently."

"I do have a mind of my own, Love. I can make some of my own decisions."

"Why all the lies? What do you have to gain? Just give it back, for saints' sake."

"I told you I overheard Camden and Ruthven, and I figured out what that piece of junk was. I needed to make sure I had a reason for you to choose me."

"Are you really so desperate, Ian? You can find another girl, move away, do whatever it is that will make you a happier person. You don't need me for any of that. In fact, I don't understand this at all. You tossed me aside like rubbish not a year ago. Why the declarations of love now?" She studied him a moment. "Ah, because of Cailean, right? The idea of me being with Rupert was palatable for you because you knew I wouldn't ever really be happy married to him. But with Cailean, it would be so much different. He would make me happy, and you can't stand the idea of me being happy with someone else."

He sneered at her. "I thought I made it clear. I messed up, but I don't want another girl. I want you. The best part is you get what you seemed desperate for not ten months ago. And as a bonus, I won't tell everyone what a whore you are for letting that thing up your skirts."

Her reaction was swift and instantaneous. She drew back and slapped him directly across the face—her hand leaving a perfect imprint on his flushed skin.

His face was a mask of barely contained rage. He was a

stranger to her.

"I'll forgive that. Just this once." Ian grabbed her arm, ignoring the dog as she growled and barked at him.

Aylee didn't think her docile shepherd had it in her to bite the man she no longer knew, but as he dragged her back the way they had come, she desperately wished she would.

THIRTY-SIX

In the past couple of weeks in town, Cailean hadn't had much interaction with people other than the Garrows, Maeve and Graham, the Bryans, and the few bits he'd spoken with Deirdre. He had conversations with others at the jubilee and the distillery, at the inn following Aylee's harrowing encounter with the kelpie, and with a few of the shopkeepers including Jenny from the bakery. He had to admit, he liked most of them. One person he distinctly did not like was Ian Cormack. Aylee had insisted Ian's brother should not be judged too harshly on the basis of family relations, but Cailean wasn't so sure.

As far as Cailean was concerned, Robbie Cormack would remain in question until he proved otherwise. When Aylee reminded him it was Robbie who had come to her aid in the pub as well as Robbie who had shepherded the Abbotts home the previous evening, he relented a little. He supposed today would be the real test of the man's merit. In fairness, he felt Deirdre was more astute than many gave her credit for, so if she liked Robbie, he might be on the up and up.

Either way, at the moment Robbie seemed either completely unaware of the drama with his brother or completely disinterested in it. He simply lay on the blanket, eyes closed, wrapped in his warm coat and boots against the bracing air blowing in off the water.

Deirdre seemed to noticed Cailean observing him.

"Oh, don't worry about Robbie there. He's not interested in anything interesting." The words were maybe a little harsh, but the way Deirdre said them made Cailean think she was fond of him indeed.

He wasn't completely convinced but decided to trust Aylee's friend nonetheless.

"I wasn't sure if Mrs. Garrow would send Aylee out here," Deirdre said.

"Why's that?"

"Most folks think I'm a little flighty, I suppose."

"Aylee doesn't."

Deirdre raised her eyebrow at him in an expression that told him exactly how well she knew her friend and she didn't need him to inform her about what Aylee did or didn't think.

"Aylee thinks very highly of you. If you happen to be fun-loving and dramatic, it doesn't mean you can't be caring and serious as well."

Deirdre stared at him for a moment, and her face broke into a stunning smile. "I knew I liked you from the start. Naked lunatic stories and all."

Cailean laughed openly at that.

"Well, I don't just *believe* Aylee thinks highly of you as well. I know it. I also know you are going to break her heart even though it isn't what you wish to do. A broken heart is one thing. A broken heart and soul is another. And if she has to watch you suffer, it will truly break her soul. I can't and won't allow that."

Cailean was sure the pain he felt at those words was written all over his face. He took a moment to gather his thoughts and to observe his surroundings.

The pair—or Deirdre more likely—had chosen a lovely spot for an afternoon outing. Despite the bite in the air, the bluff on which they had laid out the blanket was wonderful. It rested perhaps twenty paces from the cliff edge and had a view artists would attempt to paint but never quite capture. The ocean stretched out for miles in both directions up and down the coast, the blue extending to the edge of the horizon, marred only by the smudge of a distant island.

Farther up the coast, the cliffs broke up and jagged

rocks welcomed the waves, sending them crashing into a foamy spray. But here, at this point, it appeared as though the drop was a straight shot down to a deep inlet, the waves hitting directly against the white rock face. The distance to the swirling water was far, and he wondered if this was the spot Aylee spoke of when she had told him of Shelby's father. He thought it likely this stunning view was the last thing more than one person had seen, and if it was time to welcome death, he mused, there was no lovelier place to embrace it.

"You have it, don't you?" he asked, dragging his eyes from the sea and onto the pretty young lady at his side.

Deirdre reached up to the collar of her blouse, and Cailean caught sight of the leather thong around her neck. "Yes. It's right—"

Her words were cut off by the sound of Aylee's cry followed shortly by Pepper's barking.

Cailean's blood turned as icy as the depths of the sea he'd been admiring.

Urgently he asked, "Does he know you have it?"

"Probably. I took it from his room. He has to at least suspect. I imagine it's why he tromped all the way out here."

They could just see Aylee and Ian cresting back over the path toward them—perhaps a few hundred paces away—Aylee's beloved dog frantically circling the two. From the looks of it, Ian had a hand firmly on her upper arm, half pushing, half dragging her toward them.

Cailean would break that hand.

"Keep it hidden. As best you can."

Deirdre didn't answer but tucked the *cotabonn* deep into her blouse and rearranged her hair to cover the leather strap around her neck. While Cailean normally wasn't interested in the curves and swells, he was thankful in that moment for the young lady's ample cleavage.

By this time, Robbie was rising to see what the fuss was.

"And you," Cailean said over his shoulder as he walked up the path. "No heroics on behalf of your brother. If either of these young ladies comes to harm and you play a part in it, things won't end well for you. Understand?"

Robbie nodded in a resigned way. Cailean thought Robbie was well aware of his brother's true nature and was only just then acknowledging it.

The tall golden grasses on both sides of the path were swaying in the wind. Along with the driving rhythm of the waves far below, an eerie but lovely ballad rose in the air. No one spoke as Aylee and Ian approached.

Cailean tried to remain casual but knew any pretense of civility was gone when he saw the flush on Aylee's cheek and the strain in the set of Ian's eyes. He also noted a red, roughly hand-shaped mark on Ian's left cheek and guessed Aylee's hand was currently stinging. He once again stepped in front of Deirdre, nothing casual in the movement this time. He was all guard. Ready to protect not only Aylee's friend but also the lifeline she wore around her neck. He was pleased to note Robbie—whether intentionally or not—had also placed himself between Deirdre and his brother.

THIRTY-SEVEN

How was it possible for a person to keep their true self so completely hidden? Or a better question, how could Aylee so completely have missed the signs? She had told herself earlier in the day misjudging Rupert was a terrible shame but relatively harmless in the grand story of her life. All this time, however, she had missed what a truly decent man he was, and she now knew she could think of him at the very least as a friend.

Ian, on the other hand, was not the person she felt she knew at all. She spent the moments walking back up the bluff racking her mind and memory for any sign of the man Ian had become. She had thought herself falling in love with him, but she didn't know how it could ever have been possible. Had he truly hidden all of this from her, or had his personality warped and twisted in the months when they hadn't spoken?

What if in reality she couldn't actually judge anyone's true character? She had missed Rupert's true intentions, blamed Cailean for things he could not control, been shocked by Maeve's admissions, and even balked at her parents' thoughts and actions. Perhaps Aylee herself deserved all of the blame in this terrible mess. Confusion roiled through her, but she was certain of two things—it was imperative to keep Deirdre safe and they had to get Cailean's *cotabonn* back so he could escape his otherwise terrible fate.

She was still fretting over how to accomplish those two tasks when Ian pushed her ahead of him and wrapped a possessive arm around her from behind—simultaneously using her as leverage and signaling his claim on her.

A SIMPLE TALE OF WATER AND WEEPING

"It appears Aylee wasn't needed back home just yet then."

Aylee noted the hard edge to Cailean's voice and the way he and Robbie stood shoulder to shoulder in front of Deirdre. She could just make out the wary eyes of her friend below the windswept curls peeking between the solid bodies.

"My mistake," Ian replied, his voice tight and pinched. Aylee decided she loathed that voice.

"Seems something went missing from my bureau this morning while I was out. Robbie. Deirdre. I don't suppose either of you know anything about that, do you?"

"Ah, Ian. It was all my doing. Dee took a fancy to the old shell you had, and I didn't think you'd mind her having it. I was planning on giving you some coins. Just tell me how much it's worth." Robbie looked a bit sheepish, but not altogether as good-natured as he normally did.

"I have no interest in your coins, Robbie. Deirdre, where is it?"

"I've hidden it."

"Hidden it where?"

"Somewhere secret where only Aylee or I could find it."

"Really. Why don't I believe you?"

"It doesn't matter if you believe her as it isn't yours to sell. Or to keep," Aylee hissed at him.

"Stay out of this, Aylee." He squeezed her harder against his chest. Pepper whined and danced at his heels.

"Deirdre. This is how it's going to go. You are going to give me the shell, or I am going do something I think we all might regret." He nodded to Aylee and then looked at the cliff edge.

"Remove your hands from her." Cailean was calm. So calm. No hint of the confused man who couldn't find his words. "Now."

Aylee wasn't sure how he could sound quite so menacing without raising his voice above the soft hoarse growl.

"My hands will be on her for years to come, I think."

If the wrath written across Cailean's face was any indication, Ian must have plastered the smug smile back on his own.

"Ian, what's got into you? Let Aylee go." Robbie took a step forward.

Cailean never took his eyes from Ian.

Ian ignored them both.

"We are going to make a little deal. Dee, you are going to give me the pretty little seashell. I'm sure you have it on that body of yours somewhere. I am then going to take said seashell and hold onto it for a time. If Mr. Vann here really values it so much, he will agree to my terms. He will get his bit of flotsam and he will leave town. Or he can leave town without it. I really don't care either way. Aylee stays with me. We get married and everyone lives happily ever after. I really don't care what you and Robbie do."

"We take out the middle step." Aylee's voice was firm, no cracks, no wobbles.

Cailean and Deirdre both looked at her as if she were mad.

"We take out the middle step," she said again. "If I agree to marry you, Dee just gives it to Cailean and there isn't any need for you to touch it. You get what you want, and he gets what he needs. Remember?"

It wasn't the exact phrasing he'd used, but this seemed more appropriate to her.

"Absolutely not, Aylee." Cailean had murder in his beautiful teal and cobalt eyes, but his hands were trembling. "I can't let you do that. It's too step . . . too step . . . too steep a price."

Ian snickered but said nothing.

Aylee looked at Cailean and willed him to see all the things in her eyes she could not say aloud. She wouldn't be able to live with herself if she knew his one chance to return to the sea, whole and sane, had been thrown away.

A SIMPLE TALE OF WATER AND WEEPING

If he got away now, perhaps in time he might make a journey back to the sand on a night when she might be waiting for him. This didn't need to be the end of their story. But he needed to take his *cotabonn* and go before someone really did get hurt.

She didn't know if he could read her thoughts or not, but he didn't seem inclined to budge.

Ian still hadn't spoken.

"Aylee. Please. Don't do this," Cailean said again. Gravel on glass—his voice pleading.

"I agree with Cailean. Aylee, this isn't right," Deirdre said.

"I suggest you shut your mouth, Dee," Ian spat at her.

Robbie stepped forward again, only an arm's length from his brother. His face was crimson in the cool afternoon light. "Watch it, Ian. I'll not have you talking to either of them this way."

"*Now* you want to play the hero, little brother? You didn't by chance mention it to your new friend here who it was that knocked him cold and left him for dead, did ya?" He looked at his brother and, when Robbie didn't answer, added, "No? I didn't think so."

Aylee pieced it together. The sound of Cal's voice in the pub had brought a prickling to her mind, and as Ian spoke, she could place the other voice. It was Robbie who had suggested they not carry Cailean farther up to the distillery and instead leave him where she'd found him. She wouldn't worry about it at the moment, however. In the days past, Robbie had come close to making amends.

Robbie finally seemed to find his voice. "I made a wrong choice. I'm not going to make a wrong choice again."

He looked at Cailean and gave him an apologetic shrug. Nothing more. Cailean nodded in reply and the matter was settled. At least for the time being.

Turning back to his brother, Robbie said, "You need to turn and walk away, Ian. It's done now. Whatever you thought you'd come out here to accomplish, it isn't going to happen. So just go home. Let the girls be."

"So now you're against me too? First Camden, then Aylee . . . Deirdre. And now my own brother?"

Ian let his arm fall from Aylee, and every fiber in her sighed with relief. She tried not to let it all show on the outside. She took a small step away and then another. Deirdre met her on the side of the path, closer to the cliff's edge, and hugged her fiercely.

Cailean and Ian still stood facing one another. Hate and disgust on Ian's face, calm methodical granite on Cailean's. Robbie had moved slightly, shifting toward the girls but not far enough to prevent what happened next.

Deirdre had pulled the medallion from under her neckline and was tugging it over her head when Ian moved. He threw himself at Deirdre with a cry of rage. It all happened so fast. One minute Aylee was standing next to Deirdre and the next Ian was between them, grabbing frantically at the palm-sized chunk of magic resembling a sand dollar. Deirdre stumbled back, landing hard—the air knocked from her lungs. Ian had his fingers wrapped around the leather strap and yanked. His hand came away with the *cotabonn* as well as a chunk of beautiful brunette curl. Deirdre cried out in pain and anger.

Robbie was at her side in an instant, pushing his brother away, but Aylee could only focus on the treasure in Ian's hand. He snarled—actually snarled—at Cailean as he took the medallion and held it above his head.

"This piece of sea junk? This is what you can't live without?" He raised his arm as if to throw the medallion over the cliff.

Aylee had only a moment to register what he meant to do. She tried to grab Pepper, but the dog was in motion before she could blink. Cailean's reflexes were far superior. He pushed Pepper back before she could get to the edge of the drop-off. The motion caught Ian off guard, and he lost his grip on the medallion just as Cailean's momentum took him over the edge.

Time seemed to freeze as Aylee saw the alarm and fear in Cailean's eyes the moment his foot came down, not on solid ground, but open air. He had time to blink once as his arms went wide, pinwheeling in the air, trying to right his balance.

And then he was falling. Falling over the edge and toward the sea. Falling farther than anyone could fall and survive when they hit the icy waters below. Falling away from her, from the joy he brought her, falling to his death while she watched.

She had less than a heartbeat before she too was in motion, diving on her belly and pushing the *cotabonn* off the edge—like some deranged game of pass the potato. Then she was digging her knees into the deep seagrass to slow her forward progress toward the drop.

Cailean was still falling.

His eyes found hers as she hurled the *cotabonn* with all the force in her being. She watched as the beautiful bit of magic and soul and leather streamed through the air to the beautiful man as he fell into the depths below.

THIRTY-EIGHT

Descending through air was nothing like descending through water. In water, the dive was elegant and fluid—controlled. In air, it was frantic and nauseating. One moment Cailean had his feet firmly on solid ground. The next, he felt the ground slip away and he was plunging. The water rushed up toward his back and he could see the wild terror in Aylee's eyes. He'd previously tried to memorize her precious face, those lovely hazel eyes. He never thought his last look of them would be pain and anguish rather than kindness and light.

He was falling fast—too fast for fear to unleash within him. The water was calling to his core and he was returning to it, but too fast. Too hard. He would never survive. Maybe if he had time to right himself and if he had his magic encircling him—but not like this.

A calmness fell over him. This would be the end. He regretted little of his life but Aylee. He regretted never properly kissing her. Never properly telling her how much he adored her and not seeing—if only from a distance—the long, rewarding life she so richly deserved.

He blinked away the thought as a pearly grey object hurtled toward him. It was falling faster than he was. He reached out a hand and grasped the smooth surface. His eyes flew wide. The moment the medallion made contact with his skin, he felt the surge of magic. The amazing *wholeness* of being fully himself. Fully Cailean. At his touch, the medallion warped and twisted. Hard shell was a plush soft skein of fur.

He could hear the water approaching. Sense the

violence of the impact. Not enough time. He tucked his arms in and braced his chin to his chest.

The water called. He was answering whether he liked it or not.

Inhale.

A bracing cold.

Then . . . nothing.

THIRTY-NINE

Aylee wasn't screaming. She couldn't draw breath to scream. She couldn't move or think or rage at the man she had once thought she could love. It was as if in the moment Ian had forced Cailean from the earth and into the open space above the sea, he had simultaneously forced the air from her lungs.

She lay on her stomach in the grass at the edge of the cliffs, arms outstretched toward the eddying water below. She'd hurled the *cotabonn* with every bit of her strength. Cailean had fallen with calm, but his eyes flashed with realization as he caught the powerful medallion. A brief shimmer appeared around him, a spark of relief on his face, and then he was too far away for her to read any expression. He hit the water with such force there was no possible way he could have survived, magic surrounding him or not.

He'd gone under the water and she'd held her breath, waiting for him to resurface. Waiting for his head to break through the waves. Waiting for him to calm the quivering of her heart.

Her heart was not calmed.

She scanned frantically back and forth, farther up and down the coast. Nothing. Still she did not draw air. Perhaps it was her mind's way of judging how long he could remain beneath the waves without filling his chest with air as well. Perhaps it was shock. Perhaps she just didn't care to breathe in a world without a man with eyes like the sea and wild dark hair and magic in his blood and in his words.

She sensed rather than saw Pepper curl up at her side,

the dog whining softly.

When stars danced in her eyes and the burning in her chest was equal parts fury, grief, and a dying drive for oxygen, she sucked in a deep ragged breath and slumped into the moisture of the dewy grass. She draped one arm over Pepper, who shook as much as Aylee did herself—the dog's heart perhaps breaking as well.

She was unsure how long she lay there, eyes partially focused on the sea far below. She was aware of the string of foul words spewing from both Deirdre and Robbie and directed solely at Ian. She caught the conclusion of a scuffle which ended with Ian's face bloody and bruised and Deirdre soothing Robbie and kissing his scraped and bloody knuckles.

She rose when Deirdre came to her and ever so gently helped her to sit and then stand. Her legs were wobbling and her heart hurt, physically hurt, so much she thought it would split her in two. Still she looked to the water waiting for something, *anything*, to indicate he had survived. Waiting. Waiting.

Deirdre held onto her and stroked her hair. She didn't try to say things would be all right. She didn't offer empty words or silly comments to lighten the mood. Her friend was too good to offer lies or half-truths. So Aylee watched the water and let her heart break for the friend she had lost. She let a sob escape and turned from the cliffs. Each step away was like trudging through wet sand and icy brackish water.

She looked up at Ian as she passed.

"Aylee, I'm so sorry . . . I didn't mean to . . . I don't know what came over me." She kept walking. "Aylee. Please."

She stared at him with the coldness in her soul and could tell he knew. Down in his very marrow he knew. He was dead to her. As dead as Cailean was. She would never speak his name, never remember the almost love she had once felt for him. She would pass him in the street, and if he was broken and bloody, she would not stop to offer him kindness or mercy.

Aylee had never in her life been one to hate. Today, however, if she could feel sorrow and disbelief, she would also allow herself to feel hate.

Ian fell silent and walked to the edge of the cliff. She thought for a moment he meant to jump, and she felt nothing. Let him do it. Let him be the selfish bastard he clearly had always been. She wouldn't grieve for him should he choose to end his miserable life rather than live with what he'd done. What he'd robbed the world of. *Who* he'd robbed the world of.

But Ian only looked down, perhaps hoping Cailean would surface so he could exonerate himself from the death. When no sign of the young selkie appeared, he too turned and made his way up the path leading to the bluffs and the walk back to town.

FORTY

Deirdre stayed with her the rest of the way back and sat with her as she told her parents what had transpired on the cliff top. She sat with her while Devon and Una Garrow went to speak with Ned Bryan and Rupert Camden about what could be done. The town council would need to hear the facts and decide how to proceed.

The first order was to organize a small party to search the water's edge. Men and women came together and combed the shoreline. The town's sole fishing boat trolled up and down as well, searching the churning sea for any sign. When the light finally faded, the townspeople who had braved the coastline finally returned to their homes—having found no sign of the quirky stranger who'd lived among them these past weeks.

And still Deirdre sat with Aylee, as Maeve and Graham, and then Silvie and Gertie Sommerson arrived to help with whatever needed to be done. Devon and Graham had joined the search along the rocky shore and stayed well past dark—calling for Cailean until their voices were worn. Eventually they too gave up and returned home.

Maeve remained with her sister, quietly holding Aylee's left hand as Deirdre held her right. They were in front of the small hearth upstairs when Robbie appeared—also fresh from the search—and informed them Ian had rushed home, packed a bag, and left on horseback. He hadn't said where he was going, and Robbie seemed all too happy not to have asked. Likely to the city where he would disappear for a while until things calmed down.

Everyone knew Aylee's quiet calm was not from some ridiculous strength of character but from shock and sorrow and likely denial of what had happened.

What had surely been one of the last bright days of autumn faded into a cold and bitter evening. Teas were poured and brandy added to help her sleep. Maeve sent Graham home after a time, and Una tried to get both of her daughters to sleep. Maeve refused to leave, and only when Deirdre went to Aylee's room and returned with a pile of blankets and pillows did she agree to get some rest. The women created a makeshift bed in front of the fire and huddled together. Pepper claimed a spot between Aylee's head and the small table used to hold tea things. The dog was asleep instantly.

Despite the brandy and the warmth of both the fire and her companions, Aylee would not sleep. Each time she closed her eyes she saw Cailean's handsome face shift from shock to painful calm as he fell. A tightness would begin in her chest and threaten to choke her. Her eyes would fly open, and she had to sit up to catch her breath. The cycle repeated itself over and over. Finally, she gave up on slumber. She rose and placed another log on the fire. She sat in the worn chair where only days before she'd chatted easily with Cailean. She looked over and watched both Deirdre and Maeve sleeping quietly.

She envied her sister in that moment. Maeve might be in a relatively unhappy marriage, but at least she could hold onto the hope she might one day see Declan again. He was out there in the world *somewhere*. A little hope could be at once wicked and wonderful. She wanted a little hope, but her soul refused to supply the kernel. She had seen what she'd seen and that was the end of it.

FORTY-ONE

The following days turned into weeks—all of it a garbled mess in Aylee's mind. She retained snippets of conversations and fleeting moments of emotion, but the lack of sleep and the unrelenting tightness in her heart didn't allow for much more. Despite her loved ones' every attempt to soothe her, she still barely slept and only ate because she knew she needed to.

As Cailean had been a stranger in town, no service was held in his honor. Aylee, Deirdre, and Maeve had gathered one day on the beach and said a few words, and that was all. Given the empty space in her chest where joy had once thrived, Aylee couldn't understand how it was possible, but apparently life went on.

Ian still remained unheard from, which was just fine by Aylee. She couldn't even bother to wish him ill. The hate she thought she felt while staring at him on the bluff burned out before it could turn into an uncontrolled blaze—the empty chasm of her emotion not giving it fuel to burn. She didn't want to think of him at all. He didn't deserve any emotion from her.

She tried to distract herself by being in the shop, but as ever, so many people wanted only bits of gossip, a small portion were disinterested, and even fewer still could offer genuine condolences. Devon cut folks off before they could ask her directly what had happened. She loved her da without measure in those moments. Most days, Aylee could bear the well-meant but poorly delivered words many of the town's inhabitants offered. But it gutted her to realize how few people had taken the time to get to know Cailean during his days among them.

A time or two she had simply needed to turn around and walk out the back of the shop rather than listen to what amounted, at best, to ignorant comments and, at worst, to mean and hurtful opinions about Cailean. Some folks went so far as to call Ian a hero for ridding the town of such an unwelcome influence. Thankfully this notion wasn't shared by many.

After the first week or two, people stopped asking about Cailean. The story was no longer new and interesting to others, but to her his absence was a hollow spot—an empty socket where a tooth should be. She kept touching that place, knowing something was meant to be there and finding its absence not only painful but obscene.

Aylee kept her usual schedule of clamming each morning, but instead of simply hunting for the delicious mollusks, she used the daily errand as an excuse to stare at the sea and think of all the wonders it held. She never dared hope to see alabaster skin topped with midnight and silver emerge. This particular hope had not been fed, and like many fragile things, the lack of feeding had seen it dissolve and die.

Instead, she hoped for something different. She hoped for a life which might one day see the people she cared for and the town she loved grow to accept strangers who needed aid. For those people to teach their children to be kind to other children who might not be as bright or as clever as they were. For the shopkeepers and dairy maids to accept a single woman who would rather remain single than to settle for someone who did not love her the way she deserved to be loved and accept her and her choices.

She hoped for the town to grow into a place filled with more men and women like Deirdre and Shelby. More people like Ned Bryan who'd had the good graces to befriend Cailean despite his otherness and difficulty of capturing the right words. The man was almost as torn up by the events as Aylee. On the third or fourth week after the tragedy—Aylee had lost count—Ned arrived at the shop and asked if she would take a walk with him. She agreed instantly.

They walked in silence from the mercantile toward the road leading them past the inn and the dairy. Ned's normally booming laugh and infectious smile were absent, which made him into a whole other person. He seemed more like the other men from town, not unpleasant, but plain.

The wind was blowing in from the coast, and Aylee was thankful for Ned's hulking frame. He walked as a moving windbreak for her, but still she had to wrap the woolen jacket more tightly around herself. The bitter air found its way through the collar and into her bones. She stared at the colorless scenery, not truly seeing it. Winter had a way of leeching the cheer from the land as surely as it had been leeched from her heart.

When they reached the edge of the dairy's fencing, he finally spoke.

"How're you holding up?" His words held a sad knowing kindness.

She felt the sting behind her eyes almost immediately. "Huhmmm . . . well I could be better, I suppose."

He wrapped one arm around her shoulder as they walked, gave a brief squeeze, and released her. "Did he ever tell you about the first time we met, Cailean and I?"

"No. No, he didn't." She wasn't sure she wanted to hear the story, worried it would bring a flood of emotions, but knew at the same time she needed to hear it as much as he needed to tell it.

"I thought he was a bit daffy, ya know." He made a twirling motion next to his head with an index finger.

She smiled slightly, having had the very same experience.

"He just showed up here one morning, stumbling in half dressed and talking in almost gibberish. Candice wanted to turn him out right off, but I felt this need to know what the lad was about. We brought him in, and I helped get him cleaned up, put to rights. You see, he acted as if he didn't even know how to tie his boots up. Had a bit of food on him and said he wasn't hungry, but had a nice long sleep and then we talked."

Aylee was immensely grateful for Ned's kindness. She couldn't imagine what would have happened, how things would have turned out had Ned followed his wife's advice and sent Cailean packing down the road. She wouldn't have gotten to know him, but then again he would probably still be alive.

"I got the sense right off there was more to him than met the eye," Ned mused. "I'm sure you did as well. You've always been a kind soul, Aylee. Everyone in town knows it. But I'd wager it was more than just your own kindness which drew ya to him. Am I right?"

Aylee wasn't sure what to say. She chewed on it for a minute before answering.

"I could have been nicer, I think." She brushed a tear from her cheek before proceeding. "I'm the one who told him to stop here at the inn. He was lost and confused, and I helped as much as I felt I could without causing too much trouble for myself. In retrospect, I could have done more."

He waved the words away with his hand. "Don't you dare beat yourself up that way. We both know what folks around here can be like and with you being a young woman and all. No, I reckon you did what you could. But beyond that, you were drawn to him, yeah?"

She nodded.

"And why do you suppose that is? I mean, sure, if I was a young woman, I supposed I'd find him easy on the eyes. But I believe Aylee Garrow isn't quite as shallow as all that."

Aylee smiled. She thought about it. Why had she been drawn to him—right from the first time she'd seen him shaking and confused? He was handsome for certain. He was quirky and smiled often. His voice was coarse but rarely harsh and only when provoked. She felt a deep connection when she thought of his beautiful cobalt and teal eyes. He hadn't been mean or violent. He'd never lied to her, not really. He might have kept his identity from her for days, but it was his secret to keep, and he'd had his reasons. He listened when she talked and offered helpful supporting words in return. It was difficult to say all of those things, even to Ned.

"I suppose it was because I thought he was good." It was the best she could do.

"Ahhhh." He nodded. "I agree."

He smiled then, and Aylee wasn't sure why, but it made her uneasy.

"A good lad. Maybe a different sort." He winked at her, and her uneasiness grew. "But a good lad to be sure. It's why I liked him as well.

"I'm curious, Aylee. How did your parents feel about Cailean?"

"They liked him well enough." A noncommittal answer since she didn't see why it mattered.

"And they thought he was a good match for you?"

She didn't immediately answer.

"I don't intend to be judgmental, but they don't seem to be taking his loss quite as much as I would have expected."

"It was never discussed. I . . . we . . . I mean Cailean and I. We weren't you know. . ." When Ned this time remained quiet, Aylee added, "Cailean was never going to stay, so the prospect didn't matter."

"I see, but they knew what kind of a man he was?"

"I'm sorry, Ned, but I have a feeling you're trying to go somewhere with this and I'm not following."

"I'm not suggesting you go prying into the past more than is needed, Aylee. But I will tell you this. Your mother and I, along with Rupert Camden and sweet Shelby Abbott's da, we used to be pretty close. Kind of reminds me of you and Deirdre and the Cormack boy. Robbie, not that Ian.

"At any rate, we got into a few pickles when we were young, and one of the more interesting adventures we had involved a few folks *from out of town*, you might say. Folks who reminded me an awful lot of your Cailean."

Was he implying selkies had been there before and her mother knew about them? It made some sense and went a good way to explaining Una's immediate reaction when learning Cailean was from Domanmara. Something must have happened to make Una so defensive where Cailean was involved.

"Are you telling me you know what Cailean was?" She said the words slowly, trying to judge how to proceed.

Honestly, did everyone in town but Aylee know of the fey and all just pretend not to?

"I have my suspicions, but it's not important right now. You know, one time Edwin Abbott dared me to jump from the very cliff your Cailean fell from. I was young and just as big a fool then as I am now. I took the dare and ended up with a broken arm for my trouble."

"You survived the jump? From the same spot?" How was it even possible? It was no secret several people had taken that leap to end their lives. Shelby's father had dared Ned to jump, and when the time came and he felt no other alternative existed, he'd thrown himself from the same spot and ended his existence on earth. How could Ned have done it intentionally and survived?

"Stupidest thing I've ever done, but that's also not important now. What is important is the fact that, yeah, he's a good lad." He's. He is. *Is* not *was*. "And don't you suppose a fine, strong, well-intentioned man like Cailean might be concerned about how you would fair, loving him but knowing he could never stay? Waiting for him to come back and letting your life trickle by, but not really living it because you were waiting. Not marrying or having a family of your own because you, Aylee, are not the type to love someone and settle for another. Don't you suppose a man like Cailean—a good man—might think it easier for you to presume him dead?"

The breath was knocked out so quickly from Aylee's chest she actually huffed and doubled over.

She took a deep breath of the salty air and looked at Ned Bryan. "Are you saying you think he's alive? Have you seen him?"

"No and no. I'm just saying maybe you should think on it. Isn't it better to believe he *may* be alive and out there somewhere? Even if that somewhere isn't here?"

"But. . . How could he do such a thing? I don't believe you. He wouldn't. He just wouldn't."

Ned seemed to realize he had done more harm than good.

"Of course. You're right. I don't mean to upset ya further. I just wanted you to know I miss him too. Short as he was here, he grew on me." He grimaced and shook his head. "I've kept you out long enough in this cold. Let's get ya some tea. I bet Candice even has a few extra scones lying about."

"If you don't mind, I think I'll just walk for a bit." Aylee rubbed her hands up and down her arms. "Thank you, Ned. Not just for today, but, well for taking him in and being decent when he had nowhere else to go."

"Of course, Aylee. Like I said, he's a good lad."

FORTY-TWO

Aylee did walk that evening after leaving Ned on the road near his inn. She walked and walked, until her fingers and toes tingled with numb and her nose chapped a bright merry rose. While she walked, she let her thoughts tumble and flow as they would. She knew better than to try to make sense of all she had learned and all she could speculate, for in that direction lay madness. Short of Cailean walking into her shop, she would have no clear knowledge one way or the other.

That had been over a week ago.

Grief was a fickle thing for Aylee. It was dark and sodden one day and burning white hot the next. She moved from anger to confusion to sorrow in stuttering jumps and starts. The first few weeks had blurred, but the past seven days had been sharp and clear. She felt everything. Saw everything.

She thought about the gift of her time with Cailean. It was taking on the feel of a beautiful dream. She clung to the memories, scribbling them down in a small journal she kept next to her bed, afraid if she let them go for even a moment, they would drift and evaporate like the fog on a spring morning.

Rupert Camden came in every few days, and she no longer inwardly cringed when he chatted with her. She actually enjoyed conversing with him, and the two had even gone so far as to discuss her opening a small shop at the distillery—selling not only the whiskey, which was getting a grand reputation, but also glassware, biscuits, and small gifts travelers could take home to their loved ones.

Despite the ease with which they spoke, she continued

to carry specks of shame for how she had behaved. The specks mixed with her grief, but with each passing day, both of the emotions were easier to bear. Neither would ever be gone, and for Aylee, this was as it should be. They would continue to be a part of her no matter how strong or dilute they were.

She sat behind the counter at the mercantile flipping through a favorite book, long ago beaten and battered—the pages dog-eared and the paper smoothed to near velvet finish by her repeat finger strokes over the ink. Her eyes skimmed the print, but she didn't register the words. Her mind had drifted once again to the conversation with Ned Bryan.

It was odd. It had now been longer since Cailean fell into the sea than the number of days he'd spent in town and yet . . . and yet what? She loved him more now than she did then? She felt his absence just as strongly? Neither of those felt precisely true. It nagged at her. Even more nagging was the bit about her mother and her friends having known about the selkies. She couldn't bear to ask Una directly, and she doubted Maeve would have any information. If her sister had known something, surely she would have divulged it when she lay her own truth bare.

Did it even matter? Probably not.

She went back to flipping through her book and waiting for customers to come in need of supplies.

The minutes ticked by.

Pepper nudged her foot, looking for ear scratches. She obliged.

More minutes ticked by, and she reread the same page twice more.

She wished for someone to talk to. Her parents were out, and neither Deirdre nor Maeve had been by the shop.

When it looked as if business was done for the day, she flipped the sign to closed and scribbled a quick note to her parents, letting them know she was going for a walk. It seemed unkind to drag Pepper out in the cold, so she left her sleeping by the stairs.

She walked out into another bleak and bitter day. Hoarfrost coated the grass along the walkway and crunched under her boots. The air shimmered with frigid moisture, her breath adding to the clouds as it puffed from her lips. Despite the early hour of evening, the sun had sunk below the horizon and twilight bathed the town. Lights along the homes and shops flickered through frosted windows, and smoke issued from chimneys of various sizes, perfuming the air with ice and hickory. Steel clouds obscured any sign of the moon or stars.

Aylee passed only a handful of people, most so bundled against the chill it was difficult to recognize faces. Some lifted a hand in greeting as they hurried forward in search of warmer shelter.

Her ears were numb, her fingers aching, before she made it to the end of the lane. Aylee's body was having a civil war. Her feet were subservient to her heart—marching in the direction it commanded. Her mind revolted against this treason and tried to direct them back to the warmth of her home—knowing the destination was reckless if not overtly lethal.

The closer she got to the footbridge leading to the sandy shoreline, the more biting the wind became—its every pulse urging her back the way she had come. Head down, she pushed on.

On warm summer evenings, the beach in the moonlight was a glorious thing. When the heat of the day still kissed the air and the waves beckoned in a soothing song, a person could fall in love with the ocean and all its hidden secrets. This was not one such night.

Tonight the sea sang not of love but of hunger and malice. The violence of the surf was a thing to behold. The waves crashed and tore at the sandy shore with a merciless pounding as if the earth had somehow offended the water and the waves were there to take their vengeance.

Aylee knew, as all the town's residents did, to stay far

from the surf on nights like this. The waves could sneak up and rip the feet from beneath you, sending you tumbling into the glacial waters. Her feet still did not heed her head but rather lingered at the edge of the run-up—where the waves left lines of seaweed and debris in sharp demarcation of their reach.

Water seeped through the leather of her boots and still she did not move.

Was he out there—far beyond the reaches of her imagination? Perhaps swimming through warmer waters or basking on the moonlit beach of some faraway town? Ned seemed to think it a kinder dream to hold onto, but she wasn't so sure. Maeve had been devastated by Declan's sudden disappearance. Was it truly a kindness Cailean offered her in being dead? She couldn't decide.

What she did know was the only one way forward was the way she would make for herself. No self-pity at the loss of what might have been. No wallowing in sullenness and grief. She would grieve yes. And she would be sad at the loss of such an amazing soul as Cailean, but she would be damned if she let it control her life. She had things to do and places to see. New dreams and new hopes to look forward to. Starting tonight.

Feet sodden and shaking from the cold, Aylee looked up as the first snowflakes flitted down and rested in her hair and on her eyelashes. Great lovely fat feathers of ice drifting peacefully despite the raging waters only feet away. She gazed out at the black and white seascape and smiled. A sad smile perhaps, but a smile nonetheless.

"I never said the words aloud to you, but I think you knew anyway. Cailean. I love you. I might have loved you from the moment I laid eyes on you, I'm not sure. And you may have loved me, however brief it was. I'd like to say you changed me, but I don't think that's quite right. I think you helped me to see I didn't need to change. I could continue to be me, and it would be enough. Enough for you at least. Enough for me." She wiped the snot from her nose and laughed through the tears freezing in her lashes. "I wish I'd said those things to you. Face to beautiful face." The waves crashed and roared in response.

"If you are out there, alive and well... Thank you. I thought before that it would be cruel for you to be alive and for me not to know. I don't think so now. Now, I want you to be out there somewhere. If you are, maybe one day I'll be lucky enough to gaze into those amazing eyes of yours again. That's what I am going to hold onto. Whether you like it or not."

Loud roaring crashes filled the air as more snow fell, and the wind picked up. A lone wave raced higher than the others, soaking her pants to the knees. A weight had been lifted from her shoulders and off her heart.

"Don't worry. I'll keep my promise."

She stopped one last time and said to no one in particular, "Feyport."

In so naming the town, she turned away from the sea. She wasn't merry and knew it would likely be some time before she could call herself happy, but she was content.

EPILOGUE

Gentle swells made their way toward the sand and pebble shore. The dark water broke on the shallow shelf of rocks, creating a hypnotic lullaby for those who chose to sleep with windows cracked. Fewer did these days. Magic had returned, and one never knew what might appear out of the night. The mist rising from the salty water mixed in the crisp evening air, a low blanket of fog blurring the atmosphere. As the tendrils reached above the sea, a dreamy veil blurred the full moon's light. Occasionally, a nesting sea bird would call into the gloom.

It was a typical coastal night. Briny and cool. Nothing out of the ordinary to those who lived along the edge of the sea. Perfectly beautiful and perfectly regular.

Some who lived by the sea would argue it was just as it should be; others might say nothing was as it should be. Things were changing, and the old comfort of ignorance was gone. Some might notice the sleek bodies swimming near the shore and think things were not so ordinary at all. Smooth grey and spotted white shadows spun and swirled, gliding through the murky water in a whimsical ballet. To the casual eye, they were just seals. Seals were common enough in these waters. To a more gifted eye, they might be something more. And with the full harvest moon shining down? Well, just a touch out of the ordinary for certain.

Black eyes shimmered just above the surface, inky and wet. Long lashes blinked out the salt water. One set. Then three. Eight. Thirteen. An unlucky number on a night slightly out of the ordinary.

The waves continued the gentle assault on the shore,

A SIMPLE TALE OF WATER AND WEEPING

breaking and running over the coarse pebble-strewn sand. The thirteen sets of eyes peered at the land, waiting and watching for movement. The stillness stretched out, and the waves rocked the sleek bodies slightly—the ballet at an end. Floating in the tide, they waited—and waited some more.

When all was deemed quiet and abandoned, the oldest and most knowing eyes blinked once more. The moon broke free momentarily from the fog, and silver light flashed in the obsidian eyes. Slowly, the face of a harbor seal rose from the water—tilted back as if to observe the stars. It barked and ducked beneath the waves. Water rippled as its head broke the surface seconds later. When it surfaced, it was still just the face of a harbor seal. Next to it, however, another appeared, and when this seal dove down and resurfaced, it was replaced by alabaster skin and ocean-colored eyes. One by one, the additional dozen seals barked and swam away. The exquisite creature walked rather than swam up the beach to the shore.

Silently he stepped from the frigid water onto the slightly less frigid land. He was naked and lovely. He seemed not to notice the cold but to bask in the glory of an unseen sun. Behind him, dangling from a hand with elegant long fingers and comely shaped nails, trailed a flowing skein of seal hide.

Across the beach and down the road, in the upper level of a building, in a small cozy room, a bed lay empty. Its normal occupant had slipped out in the night and stood on the beach.

The woman with copper hair and kindness in her eyes watched the lovely man appear from the water, and when he was close enough to touch, she raised up on her toes and threw her arms around his neck. Burying her face in his sea and salt skin, she laughed until she cried.

All was perfectly beautiful and perfectly unordinary.

A SIMPLE TALE OF WATER AND WEEPING

ACKNOWLEDGMENTS

Authors often say how it takes a team of people to get a novel written and I never really appreciated how true a statement that could be. When I first began writing, it was merely an exercise I used to help take my mind off the stress in my life seeing patients. I'd sneak a few pages in at lunchtime or when I needed to unwind after a particularly intense day. Not many people around me even knew it was something I did. A couple of years ago, a few friends really started to encourage me to follow my dream of finishing a novel. I am so thankful I listened and have truly loved this entire process.

First and foremost, I need to thank my amazing editor, Karen Robinson. Your attention to detail and mastery of language are truly something to behold and your talent helped make this book what it is.

To my beautiful Lily, thank you for your guidance and honesty, when I didn't know how to tie things together or if the whole thing was just trash. Your brilliance knows no bounds and you will always be my favorite test audience.

To my lovely Addie, thank you for being the sunshine I need on cloudy days and for gracing me with your sweet smile. Mostly though, thanks for showing me it is possible to be kind and accepting of everyone and everything all the time.

None of this would have been possible without the love and support of my parents Sharon and Ralph and my siblings Jen and Ralph. My family is kind of amazing and I couldn't ask for more.

More than anyone, I need to thank my wonderful

husband Brian. I don't know how I would have gotten through life if I hadn't met you. You have always been there to lift me up and push me forward. I can't thank you enough. Also, I really appreciate the countless hours of design help and Photoshop guidance. You are one of a kind.

And while this is the part where I get to say how thankful I am this book has been completed, I am also thankful for so much else in my life. The last couple of years have been insane. As a medical professional, I never thought I would see something like this pandemic. It has been tough on so many. Writing this book has helped distract from the dark news I, like so many others, face every morning heading to work. So as I close, I have just one request—the real world is a tough and brutal one—please be kind to one another. It's the least we can do.

ABOUT THE AUTHOR

Kami King Larsen is a native of the desert southwest and studied biology before attending medical school. Although she is a practicing pediatrician by training, she is a bibliophile and lover great stories by birth. Kami lives in Nevada with her husband, two daughters, and two dogs. This is her first, but hopefully not her last, published novel.

Made in the USA
Las Vegas, NV
02 October 2021